# WIFE
# SHAPED
# BODIES

# WIFE SHAPED BODIES

A NOVEL

LAURA CRANEHILL

LONDON NEW YORK TORONTO
AMSTERDAM/ANTWERP NEW DELHI SYDNEY/MELBOURNE

1230 AVENUE OF THE AMERICAS, NEW YORK, NEW YORK 10020



First Saga Press trade paperback edition April 2026

SAGA PRESS and colophon are trademarks of Simon & Schuster, LLC



Interior design by Erika R. Genova

Manufactured in the United States of America

3 5 7 9 10 8 6 4 2

Library of Congress Control Number: 2025940170

ISBN 978-1-6680-9810-3
ISBN 978-1-6680-9818-9 (ebook)

*This is for my enemies*

# CHAPTER ONE

The night before my wedding, my mom shaves off my growths. I climb into our cooking tub and undress. An expression somewhere between pride and fear passes over my mom's face as she stands beside the tub, razor in hand. Then she leans over and begins.

It takes hours. She starts at the creamy-orange shrubbery of my shin. Works her way up the woody folds coating my knees. Slices into the overlapping tangles at my thighs. My hip growths are moist enough that they splatter when they hit the porcelain at my feet.

She skips over the complicated masses at my torso. She'll do those last. I extend my neck so she can get the razor into the doughy polyps at my nape. I lean back and expose my throat so she can slice away the leathery kernels at my jugular, the fingerlike nubs cresting over my sternum, and the beads along my jawline, like an extra row of teeth that sharpens to incisors at my chin.

"It won't take so long next time," my mom says in a soothing voice.

I'm silent as all of this comes off me, as I am cut down to the size and shape of a wife. I watch my clippings roll into the drain in slippery trails, gathering streaks of ash.

As I lose more of my body, I lose track of time. I close my eyes and steel my jaw each time the razor cuts in. It doesn't hurt, not exactly. But it's something like pain.

"I don't feel good." I put my hand on the edge of the tub to steady myself. My body revolts. I want to throw up.

"I'm almost done, and then you can lie down." Mom pats her gloved hand between my shoulder blades, on my spine, which she has just cleaned of its downy spurs. She whispers, "It's okay. You'll get used to it." That's the last thing I hear her say clearly.

She helps me out of the tub and dresses me gingerly. I am too aware of my new, raw body. I am ungainly as she puts me to bed.

I lie motionless and stare at the ceiling and spin and spin. I fall into a tunnel of blackness from a great height, no room to remember before I hit the bottom.

# CHAPTER TWO

On the morning of my wedding, I wake to the sound of a woman weeping.

At first, I think it must be an effect of the shaving. That from now on, I will always wake to this sound. But even after I blink away my more persistent dreams, I keep hearing it coming from inside the house. Coming from my mom's bedroom.

I roll out of bed and open my bedroom door and walk down the hall. My heart pounds, disturbing the rashy stubble on my chest. With less of me, the blood is confused. I hear the whoosh of it in my ears. As my pulse quickens, more of my skin flushes with itch and pain. I totter, can't find my balance. My breath hisses fast through my teeth. A heaviness builds in my chest as I get closer to the keening. Part of me wants to hurry. Part of me wants to shut myself up in the closet and go back to sleep and never see what's waiting for me. I stop between the sawed-off braids hanging on the wall. I stare at their ragged ends as I catch my breath.

I push open my mom's door. The usual smell of mildew hits me. Then another, like the ointment Mom gives me to put on my lips when they're dry. It's so strong that I can taste it, bitter and flaky.

Wearing just a sheer nightgown, Mom lies on her bed, her hair fanned out around her. Luminescence spreads over her pillow and the top of her blankets. My throat aches as I swallow. Every day of my life, I wake up knowing that this is a possibility. And here, it's finally come.

Except for my mother, the room is dark. A gash of sunlight perforates the drawn curtains, slicing the room in half. Mom's eyes are closed, her breathing is labored and fragmented.

I'm surprised to see my older sister, Maggie. She sits cross-legged on the floor, beside the mattress. She lifts her face, misshapen and swollen from crying. "Look who finally decided to grace us with her presence." Her eyes may be dull with grief, but her mouth is as acidic as ever.

Her daughter, Eloise, sits sobbing beside her, just out of reach.

"Mom?" I step into the room, cross the slice of sunlight. I reach out, ready to fall onto the mattress beside her.

Maggie grabs the neck of my shirt and yanks me back. "Don't touch her, you idiot."

"I'm wearing gloves." I snatch my shirt out of her hands. She's right, though; it's dangerous. Gloves fall apart too easily at the seams. My mom doesn't move, doesn't acknowledge that I'm in the room. "What does this mean?" My voice sounds high and childlike.

Maggie says, "Shut the door, Nicole."

My first instinct is to balk at any of Maggie's commands, but I close the door quietly. The longer Reese doesn't know, the better.

Several flies, fat and clumsy and pregnant, circle around the room, bumping into walls and faces. They won't settle. They are hot and confused and too heavy with young to cling to the lace curtains, and there's nothing else in the room but the mattress, a dresser, and a single, mildew-warped picture of Reese and his first wife on the wall.

I sit next to Eloise. I can't remember how old my niece is. I've seen her out in the street, but she's never been inside the house before. She's tall enough to reach my chest when she stands, but right now, hunched over her folded legs, she looks smaller than that. Her eyes are wet and needy. I'm always shy around her. When she comes to the window, she never talks, but always looks like she expects something from me, and I never know what to do. Not knowing what I should do to help, and unable to swallow down the tightness in my throat, I look away.

Heat collects like a wet rope around my neck. The humidity is awful in this shut-up room. This side of the house faces the sun, and the day is gathering strength. I wipe my forehead with the heel of my glove. It comes away slippery with mucous, leftovers from the egg-shaped lumps that used to grow there.

"What happened?" I ask.

Mom blinks slowly. I sit up higher, ready to go to her. Did she hear me?

Mom keeps silent. I force myself to slouch back down. She'll say something when she's ready.

Maggie says, "What does it look like? Fell on a lantern. I found her like this."

"You came over?" I frown. My mind is whirring. "In the morning, while Reese is here?"

"I had a dream. A feeling things weren't right." Her eyes slide over to me in condemnation. I slept in. I wasn't in tune enough with Mom to know that she was in trouble, even while living in the same house. She looks away. "Also, I brought your outfit."

"Outfit?"

"Your bridal outfit. From your husband's house. He picked them out." She gestures to a T-shirt and a pair of jeans sloppily thrown at the foot of my mom's bed.

I close my eyes. I'm going to lose my mom. I was prepared to lose her today, but not like this. I open my eyes and try to soak her in. The landscape of her fungus, grown overnight, pokes into the threadbare fabric of her nightgown. Caps and puffballs and branches bulge and swell against the holes in the lace. Through the sheer fabric, I can see dim streaks against her glowing flesh, like someone has dragged their fingertips against her thin body. Abrasions discolor her chest and obscure her new glow, as always happens with lantern fungus. The touch of it bruises women from the inside, chews away at their ribs and bones until they break.

"Where's the lantern?" I stand up halfway. My voice rises in panic. "We aren't sitting in it, are we?"

Mom gasps, and her eyes open. Our heads jerk toward her.

"Mom?" we say in unison.

It's more of a choking gurgle than words, but I can just make out, "Get him."

She's not looking at me, not looking at Maggie. Just at the ceiling.

"No, Mom, no," says Maggie. Her voice breaks under the strain of trying to sound firm.

Each of my mom's words is deformed, altered as if she's speaking around knots in her throat, but she manages to say, "I lived under him, I'll die under him. He's my fate."

"No," says Maggie. "I won't do it." Her hand darts out and pins Eloise's knee down. "Eloise, stay."

Eloise shows no intention of obeying her grandma, whom she barely knows. She grips the carpet with her fists, her body tense, like she's about to bolt out the door.

Mom's eyes widen, and she makes a pathetic, muffled sound. "Get him," she pleads again.

Her weak panic tugs at my heart. She's afraid and in pain. I stare at her, willing her to stand up, to ask for tea, for a wet washcloth, to tell me to get dressed. My need unfocuses my eyes. She becomes a swarm of bees, a tangled rat's nest, a field of dried grass. I blink. She becomes my mother again, suffering. I stand up. An obedient daughter to the bitter end, I guess.

As I go, Maggie cries, "Nicole, come back here."

I whirl around. "Do you want Mom to beg on her deathbed?" Maggie's eyes are sickles, cleaving into mine. Before she can let out whatever evil is in her mind, I turn away. "You can't control everything, Maggie."

When I walk down the hall, I expect her fist to take me from behind. Expect, and a little bit hope. She doesn't chase me, though. As I peek into each of the rooms, I consider how to break the news to Reese gently. I dredge through words, trying to pick the ones that would be least likely to direct the blame toward me. I knock on his door and swallow hard. Silence. Only the belief that he's not in there gives me the courage to open it.

He's sitting on his bed, face drawn, and I see that he already knows.

"She's ready," I say quietly.

His eyes are rimmed with sleeplessness. I wonder how long he's been awake.

A luciferin lantern lies at his feet, smashed. Strewn across the carpet lie shards of glass and sticks and the bioluminescent fungus that makes the lantern glow. It was in Reese's room where Mom fell on the lantern, touching the fungus, meeting the inevitable.

Reese's hands lie open in his lap as if they've been sitting like that for a long time. "It's not my fault."

I don't look at him. I don't do anything he can interpret as accusing.

He gets up from the bed. I stand aside and bow my head. He lumbers through the doorway, his head lowered as if his top half is too heavy to hold upright, as if he's about to tilt forward and walk on all fours like a beast.

I follow him at a distance down the hall, but I don't enter my mom's bedroom. Through the open door, I can see the dresser and the window, but not the mattress where my mom lies. Reese passes through the slash of light, then out of sight.

"Come on, Eloise," I call out. I don't want her to see.

She runs out of the room like she'd been waiting for

someone to give her permission. She darts past me, stops at the end of the hall, and turns to stare. Far enough from this soldier of Death, but not too far from me or her mom. Maggie lingers in the room, eyeing Reese like she's going to push him out with her speckled, meaty hands. Of course, she won't. You can't just shove a man around, even to save your mother.

"I have to collect Mom's things," she says.

It's not clear who Maggie's talking to, but she walks to the dresser in the corner and rifles through the drawers, pointedly not looking at Reese or the bed. I can't believe she has the audacity to be in there right now. She goes through Mom's personal items, taking out a couple of stones and a dried flower, a daisy chain I made for her a week ago. She stacks the fairy-tale book on top of the one with the Greek myths, the only two books I grew up with. But Maggie can't take them, and I can't. We have to leave behind anything that will be useful to Reese's next wife, a girl named Rebecca with the same strong jaw and gap between her two front teeth as my mom. She's been living in a house three doors down with her mother and younger sister, waiting her whole life for Mom to die.

Maggie is stalling, but there's no point. Reese might as well be a storm. Weather doesn't listen to reason, or people.

Eloise is watching me, her long sleeves pulled up over her mouth, her eyelashes just cresting over her arms. She watches me while I watch Maggie. Mom murmurs something to Reese I don't catch. Reese doesn't answer. There's a whine and an awful choking noise. The sound of too much weight on a mattress, floorboards straining. Toward the end, Maggie looks up. I see on her face when Mom is gone, and Eloise sees it on mine. In this way, Mom's death passes through us, a chain of grief, the shadow of a crow passing overhead.

Eloise whimpers like a baby animal, and finally, it occurs to me what she needs. I run into my room and grab a pair of jeans off the floor. I emerge back into the hall and throw them over Eloise's shoulder so I can drape my arms over her, my curtain of hair closing around us.

I often see the women outside holding each other when the men aren't around. I watched girls my age with envy: Esha, Tyra, Teaghan, especially Teaghan, grabbing each other any chance they got. Specters that slipped out of sight just as easily as they entered. They might have been my age, but their lives were so different from mine, grabbing hands and laughing, tossing aside the danger of contamination.

Rarely, tensely, and with discretion, my mom and I would touch each other with gloved hands. It was nerve-wracking. Every night, while Reese prayed before dinner, alongside his litany of asks from God, he'd pray that my mom and I had not touched each other because he didn't want to have to kill us. "Amen," all three of us would say.

My heart thuds to hold Eloise now. To hold and be held like this is terrifying. She's not as careful as I am. She grips my shirt and my gloves, pats at my hair, crying, as if she's *trying* to find a way to my skin. She doesn't know the danger we're in, like this, with Reese around.

When Reese comes out of my mom's bedroom, I feel his leaden shadow trudge behind me. In the doorway of his bedroom, he turns and looks at the two of us holding each other but says nothing. In his hand is a mass of something furry, like a flayed animal skin. My mom's hair, which he's shorn from her scalp. I lock eyes with him. A dare I'd usually regret. But today is my wedding day. Someone is waiting for me. He can't kill me without having to answer for it. He takes the hair into his room and closes the door behind him.

The first thing Reese is going to have Rebecca do when she arrives is braid my mother's hair and pin it up in the hallway with the others.

Eloise trails behind me when I walk back into the bedroom. A blanket covers my mom. Maggie is putting on a pair of garden gloves she found in the bedside drawer.

"What are you doing?" I ask.

Maggie says gruffly, "We have to get her in the ground now, or we'll have to wait an entire week before we bury her. Lucky it happened on a Saturday."

I look at the blanket, the lump under it. "Lucky?"

"A whole week of watching over her body, making sure no one's curious kid sneaks into her room and touches her? No thanks." She's right. Saturdays are the only day the women are left to their own devices, because the men have their own gathering then. Maggie puts on a pair of leather gloves over the gardening gloves. "You have so many goddamn gloves in this house."

"We're careful." I look pointedly at Maggie's bare arms, her bare legs that poke out from under her shorts. I pick up another pair of gloves and tug them over the polyester pair I'm already wearing.

She snorts. "There's no reason to be crazy about it. I mean, really? You have to sleep in them?"

I shake my head. She lived with Reese too. She knows his rules.

Maggie pulls the blanket off my mom. We strip her of the nightgown and peel the underwear from her body. We can't bury her in them. They belong to Rebecca now. After all, what would the next wife wear, if we all lost our clothes to the dead? We slide her carefully into the blanket and roll it up, making sure none of her luminescent skin brushes against us. Someone will have to bring back the blanket later.

When Eloise tries to help, Maggie barks at her to get out of the way.

Lifting my mom's body is otherworldly. Like something other than myself is buoying her forward when we carry her through the house.

I stop at the front door, knowing that I'm supposed to open it.

"Wait." I stare at the doorknob.

"Wait for what?"

To Maggie, it's just another door to walk through. To me, it's the door I've stared at my entire life, waiting for the day I get to leave. Maggie sets her jaw. "Open the door, Nicole."

"I said wait."

I want to make Maggie leave by herself. I want to go back into the bedroom with my mom and shut the door. Climb into bed with her. I'd put a blanket between us, and then around us, and it would be okay.

"Nicole," Maggie hisses. I want the darkness.

Her voice rises with fury, "We're already late."

I want to sleep forever. "I just need to think."

"There's no time." She pushes the body forward, forcing me to back up. I have to open the door and go through it, or my mom's body will crash into me.

Just like that, I'm out of the house. I feel the enclosure of the walls fall away.

After I fumble my way onto the porch, I say, "I could have dropped her." I stare at Maggie. "Or died."

"You didn't, though, did you?"

I turn away, thinking of my mother. Our mother. I should be angry. Mostly, I'm tired. The blood still thuds heavily against my sore skin. I register the breeze on my face and the openness around me with a numbness. I look down the street and see the houses lined up, then turn to look down the other side and see more houses. I thought leaving the house would be freeing. Instead, the sky looms heavily overhead, wheezing a soggy breath on my scalp and neck. It's too big, and the clouds too close, the grayness thick and unyielding. I breathe heavily and feel my legs weaken. I shake my head. I'll handle it later. I'll return to normal, get used to my new body later. Not now, with my dead mother in my hands. My hands, which do not feel, or look, like my hands.

When I pause and try to manage my way over the steps, Maggie huffs impatiently. "This way." Again, she tugs on our dead mother to rush me.

I can't believe her callousness, her lack of reverence. "You'll have to excuse me," I mean to say it vehemently, but it sounds oddly flat and disembodied. "I don't know where the old golf course is, exactly."

Maggie turns to me, her brow furrowed, as if just noticing that I'm beside her, though she's been yelling at me this whole time.

"The graveyard," she corrects. "Reese isn't here to make you use his words. So don't. It's annoying."

No men are in the street. They must have already left to go drinking in the work yard. It must be later than I realized. As long as I've been alive, Reese has never been late for that.

Two women stand together in the neighbor's yard. Sara and Adelaide. I know their names because my mom used to point at them through the window and tell me her memories of them from when she was young. When the women see us, they stop talking and stare. Their eyes dart to the blanket bundle between us. Realization unfolds on their faces. They look at each other, then rush forward to help. They don't ask questions, just murmur sympathetically to Maggie and glance curiously at me.

We trudge past the houses I've always been able to see, and we begin to see new houses I haven't. Each with their own irretrievable past, shedding off layers to the ground. One house is so smashed, its pieces flung so far and wide, its scraps bleed into other yards and the ruins of another house. The trees are all leveled to stumps. Yard ornaments, benches, buckets, and misshapen lumps I don't recognize, their uses gone and forgotten, all embedded in the shivering green landscape. We see the beige house that's been turned into the granary, and the gray house that's been turned into a shared tool shed. The house with the stone statue of a man that is half-man, half-goat, and fully naked. The house with not one, but two broken-roofed cars parked in the driveway, their paint now a luster of speckled rust, gathering pockets of dust and dirt in the seats and growing weeds. These are the places my mom described to me all my life.

We shuffle past the lab. No one says anything, but I know it's the lab because it's larger than any two-story house, surrounded by a large fence, and made up of windows so black and glossy I can't see in past the sun's reflection. When my mom had drawn the lab to show me what it looked like, she was never satisfied with the product. She'd eye her work, turn her head one way, then another, shrug, and say, "The windows look black, but they shine like mirrors. If you stand on something to look over the fence to try to see inside, you can't. All you can see is yourself." She was right. The square thing she'd drawn in the dirt really didn't do justice to this ominous building with the ominous things growing inside.

I can't look up at anything after that. I don't want to. It isn't supposed to be like this. My mom is supposed to be here to guide me, joke with me, laugh with me, show me our world. Reese promised we could both leave the house on my wedding day. It was the one reason we'd been looking forward to it, even though it meant we'd be living separately from then on. I can't look at the houses, and I can't look at the women, so I look down. I can feel my mom's heels through the blanket. I walk alongside the other women in silence. I won't talk to anyone. If I don't talk, I don't have to find any words to say. I don't have to think.

Jess, a woman who was old when my mom was a child, is standing in the middle of the street, looking at something, or nothing. Like any wife, she's shaven this morning. But pink, warty growths persist in her eye ducts and inside the rim of her eyelashes, dangerous places to shave too much away. They give her a knobby eye shape and a forlorn, myopic look. When she sees us, she joins. "Oh, poor dear. And today, of all days. Not many of us make it to a second daughter's wedding." Her voice is soft and sweet as she squeezes my elbow in sympathy.

I go rigid at her touch but I don't say anything.

Maggie spits. "She didn't make it to her first daughter's, either. She had to stay in the house for mine."

"Or Easter! It was her favorite holiday." Jess sweeps her eyes skyward and speaks dreamily, as if she's been talking about my mom in the past tense for a while, has already grieved and moved on.

"Back when she was allowed to go," says Maggie.

Jess ignores her and faces me. "Well, it happens all the time, dear. Women tend to get emotional on their daughter's wedding day." She pats my arm. "Especially their second."

"It was a lantern accident," I say dully. "It didn't have anything to do with emotions."

She eyes me for a long time, then squeezes my elbow again. "Yes, I can see that."

Between the five of us, it's easier to carry our burden. I stumble a bit and keep stepping on Sara's shoes, who's in front of me and pretends not to notice. Eloise trails behind us, her hands worrying themselves in front of her. She cringes with every sound, every stray rock grinding beneath her feet, as if she's afraid the world is about to burst into fire. I want to smile at her, say something reassuring, but I don't have control over my face anymore. If I smiled, my face would break. Something would definitely break, if not my face. I'll do something nice for Eloise later. It can't be easy, with a mom like Maggie. I'm lucky. Was lucky. My face burns thinking about how Maggie used that word earlier.

I can feel the other women staring at me.

"Hello," says Adelaide.

I glance up at her. Her eyes are dark, her lashes long and beautiful, though the other parts of her face seem mismatched, like they belong to someone else, someone not so pretty. I open my mouth, but the word doesn't come out at first, like hitting two stones together and waiting for sparks. I close my mouth, open it, and try again. "Hello."

"I'm Sara," says the short woman in front of me.

"I know."

They look at me. They want more from me. But all I can think is, *I'm holding my dead mother in my hands, which are not my hands.*

The wind picks up as the houses drop away.

"Not much longer now, the graveyard's just over the hill here." Jess speaks in a singsong voice, obviously for my benefit.

Maggie hefts our mother up, grunting, the strain getting the better of all of us.

A pathway slices the hill in two. We climb up the path. I can feel them before we crest the hill. We get to the top, and the graveyard opens in front of me. Dusty and sun-scorched, nothing grows in this dry and scaly field. This is the largest space I have ever seen. It's big, bigger than I imagined. Our yard could have fit into it two dozen times. There's a chain-link fence surrounding most of the graveyard, though it's twisted and broken and bowing toward the earth. Ancient, misshapen trash has gathered against the fence and cemented into discolored mounds. The men haven't bothered to collect it while wearing their expired hazmat suits, aren't worried about its toxic exposure leaking into our houses from all the way out here.

And in the middle of the field stand all the women and children in our community, about fifty all together, humming and waiting. The graveyard is a vast, empty space, but the women are concentrated in the center, jostling among themselves. They are a hot, bullish swarm, each vying for the others' attention. With their hum in my confused skin, I can't think, can't move, their murmuring vibrates in me, trying to wake something, but all I want to do is stay numb. I'm holding my dead mother in my hands, which are not—

"Your mother is our only death this week," says Sara.

"The poor dear," says Jess.

I face away from the women, trying to get a hold of myself.

This is a mistake. I was prepared on some level to be here. To feel the women as they vibrate together. But standing on this hill and looking over the enormity of the compound and seeing all of it, all at once, is too much. The houses sprawl out in a confusing, crisscrossing whirl of streets and yards. I can see how the center road, where we all live, has been comparatively well maintained, despite the sodden weariness. The other houses, without their patched roofs and stabilizing poles, are collapsing under the weight of greenery past their seeding. The imploded windows and doors and smashed walls are dark and yawning and black as earth. Their skin sloughs off, their broken backbones poking through their splintered shoulders. A great leveling is happening. The undergrowth swells over the earth to flatten the machinery of civilization, subsume its lifeless limbs into its own verdant, seething corpulence.

At least the orchards and crops and fields are planted in manicured rows and squares. But even they go on for too long, until they're stopped by the black wall that surrounds our compound.

On the other side of it, the poisoned woods. I can see only the edge of the forest, before the slope of the mountain curves down, bringing the forest with it. But that edge is still too much to take in. The trees are jumbled together, rippling in the wind, surging and straining against the wall that is supposed to be holding them back.

The houses sway, heroic and sorrowful in their struggle to keep buoyed against the melt of time and nature. The plant-covered ground rustles and shimmies, as if the earth is preparing its throat for a big swallow.

Then, everything blurs. I'm crying. No. Not crying, my eyes are watering from the wind. I blink, try to slide the world back into place. I grip my hands and feel my mom's bony ankles. With a sickening lurch, I realize I've never touched this part of my mom before, wouldn't have dared, even through a blanket, when she was alive. My knees buckle. I grip harder.

Maggie hisses, “Goddammit, she’s going to drop her.”

Someone grabs my shirt at the shoulder and lifts me up sloppily until I get my legs straight again.

“I’m sorry,” I say, though no one hears because I don’t put enough force behind my words, and Maggie is still swearing loudly and commanding me to get a grip. I want to say that I’m not usually like this. When I am whole, I am strong and stubborn.

The women in the bald field notice us. They stop chattering and rise from the muddy puddles and surge forward like a squall eager to engulf.

“Let us take it from here,” says one woman. A wife, shaven down.

“You rest now, hon,” says another. She’s not a wife. Grainy, purplish knobs wreath her nostrils and spread over her cheeks.

“Yes, let us take her,” repeats another woman who is not yet a wife. The black gills of the gray, pitted caps on her forehead are dissolving into a black liquid in the heat, dripping down the contours of her face and streaking her cheekbones before falling off her chin in shivery, inky tears.

I clamp down on the blanket. When they take her from me, the blanket slips, and I catch a glimpse of my mom’s glowing face. Her open eyes, her agape mouth.

“Careful, we don’t want anyone else to get contaminated!” Jess chides me gently. She pries the blanket out of my fingers and carefully rewraps my mother.

“Come with us, sweetie,” says Sara.

“I’m Teaghan,” a voice whispers in my ear.

I jerk my head toward the noise and am nose-to-nose with a face framed by a dark braid like a thick rope slung over one shoulder. New nubs of pink, funnel-shaped growths flush up her neck and the side of her jaw, overtaking her ear so that the cartilage barely peeks out. We are so close, we are sharing breath. I gasp, and breathe in more of her smell. Splotches of black soak into my eyes, and I can't think. My mouth speaks for me. What comes out is, "I know who you are."

*My best friend.* Of course, I don't say it aloud. I am embarrassed to even think it. You can't be best friends with someone who has only ever seen the edge of your silhouette. My throat clenches, like the knuckles of growths inside me are swelling it shut. I can't duck away from the pressure of her staring at me. She peels with laughter and sinks back into the crowd, and I lose sight of her again. The other women also laugh and clap, delighted, like I've made a joke. I'm a celebrity. Someone new who isn't a newborn. They've been waiting for this day too. Like a holiday. They pass my mother through the crowd. Maggie scuffles behind, grumbling. Hands push me along as well, ungloved hands, dangerous hands, guiding me after my mother.

"Right here." Amy nods to Sara.

Four shovels appear. Four women start to dig. The ground is soft from last night's rain, but the earth is thick with a web of white string, and the shovels rend through the tangled mesh, filling the air with ripping noises.

"Connor is here," someone says.

"Where?" someone else asks.

"In the back."

"What's he doing here? This is our place," Sara complains.

Adelaide looks at me. "He must be afraid of her."

All the women eye me with a measure of newfound respect.

"I guess now we'll have to pull out the Bible and read a verse," Sara mumbles.

Jacinta, the only woman left on the compound who can read, picks out a tiny pocket Bible from the front of her overalls. She opens it somewhere in the middle. The others resume their digging.

"Don't mention anything with blood," Jess whispers. "It's not appropriate for a burial."

"I know, I know," Jacinta hisses from the side of her mouth, as if the man could hear them from where he is standing.

Jess ignores the annoyance in her tone and adds, "No blood, birth, violence, or foreskins."

"What are foreskins?" Abigail peeks over Jacinta's shoulder, looking at the Bible as if there might be pictures.

"No one knows." Jess shrugs. "But it sounds gruesome."

Jacinta clears her throat. She lifts one hand, deepens her voice, and projects to the crowd, "'And Esau said to Jacob, "Let me eat some of that red stew, for I am exhausted!"'"

The women around her nod solemnly, and Jacinta looks pleased with herself.

The grave is finished. It's time to put Mom inside. I have to do it, because I'm the one holding my dead mother in my—

But I'm not. I look down at my hands. I've already let her go. I've already given her up.

Other women get on their knees and lower her into the grave. Maggie reaches in and unravels her, yanks the blanket out of the earth. I can't see my mom. I'm standing too far away. But I can't force myself forward. Maggie's the one next to the grave, holding the empty blanket, looking down with a grimace.

A wail crawls up inside me and I can't stop it. I hear the despair in my voice, but I don't feel it. It's startling and frightening. I think of the way my mom used to describe Demeter when her daughter gets dragged into the ground by the tapered hands of a cruel, subterranean god: an ocean at high tide, unable to contain herself.

All those stories from far away that my mom explained with sea metaphors, a place neither of us will ever see, though Mom always said she wanted to, but knew she'd never, and I know I'll never—

The women start singing along to the sound of that disconnected despair. Maggie stares at me jealously, angry that I should be the first to scream and not her, the firstborn. But then her face crumples, and she stares down at the ground and joins the singing. A gruff noise, at first, but then the act of it soothes her and she starts to join in for real. She has a nice voice, actually. I think of her singing Eloise to sleep, when she was just an infant curled in that intimate space between Maggie's chin and sternum. The singing tugs at me. Another wail burbles in my chest, but it is partially dissolved in the women's song. Another rises after it but comes out as a small sob. The tide inside me lowers, the dark stain on the sand receding. Another line from the same story. They sing, and something closes inside me. A sleeping animal finds the cavity at my center and drifts into a staggered, aching sleep, but a sleep nonetheless. And then I'm singing too.

I know by heart Reese's church hymns, "Again Another Fleeting Year" and "Ah Lord How Apt I Am to Stray," and the songs the men sing after they overflow from the work yard onto the street on Saturday nights, with their drunken folk ballads of "Just a Small Town Girl," "Load Up On Guns," "Blame It All On My Roots," and, the one I like the most, "Ice Ice Baby." But women's singing is not like men's singing. Our songs aren't predetermined or learned by rote like theirs. We don't sing in words. We feed the notes to each other, sense the harmony before it happens. Rising as one, falling as one, holding one note concurrently.

In this way, the women absorb my emotions into their own. The stabbing grief slides away, the center of me sliding with it. I'm crying; we're all crying. I gaze around the edges of the crowd. I don't see any men. Connor must have left.

The men don't like our singing voice.

The women drop leaves and sticks onto my mom's body.

"To feed the decomposition," Jess says. "This far into the year, most of the flowers have died and rotted. All except these ones. We're lucky they're so hardy. It means we still get to cover May in flowers." She shows me a basket of big yellow flowers and small blue ones next to a bundle of sticks. This is the second time I've been told today that the timing of my mother's death is lucky. But Jess's voice is so gentle, so loving, and I'm worn out. There's nothing left in me to fight. She twirls one of the yellow flowers between her fingers. "These we call graveyard marigolds, because a few summers ago they showed up in the graveyard. Of course, they don't grow here anymore. Nothing grows here for long. They pop up around the rest of the compound, though. And when someone, I can't remember who, asked her husband what it was, he answered, 'Some kind of marigold, I guess.' The name just stuck." She drops the flower and picks up a blue one next and continues, "We call these false daisies. We used to call them daisies, but one of the husbands said, 'Those aren't daisies!' So now we call them false daisies." She picks up a branch filled with small, beady red berries that look like drops of blood. "We call these Mary's eyes." She scrunches up her face. "I don't remember why."

Maggie dumps the basket into the grave, over Mom. She does it hastily, with a defeated expression. I notice a yellow flower on the ground, unceremoniously knocked to the side. I step forward and pick it up. It lays like a crumpled sun in my palm. I look into the grave and see my mom's naked body. It's jarring to see her like this. She looks too thin. Her elbows and joints are knobby and weak. How did those skinny limbs ever hold her up? How did they ever propel her forward? Eyes wide, mouth unhinged. Her shorn hair shows bald spots now, where Reese cut too close to the scalp.

Death is already changing her. All her holes are opening wider, pockets of darkness blooming across her face. She doesn't look calm or restful. She looks like a sloppily placed corpse. No one wants to reach in and rearrange her body. The fungus in her would touch the fungus in us, and we would light up as she lit up. Then our men would kill us, too, to protect the other women before we could contaminate them.

I think of the way she smelled last night, leaning over me with her gloves and razor. The deadened plop on the ashy porcelain of the bathtub. The dizziness that came after.

To feed her decomposition. I don't really know what that means, but it sounds important. I drop the flower, and it lands on her bruised rib cage.

I'm tired. My body is sore. I can't imagine doing anything except standing here until I die.

Something round is thrown on top of my head. I jump, almost into the grave. My hand darts out and I thoughtlessly grab the wrist near my temple.

Teaghan stares at me, grinning, her pupils wet and swollen with the cloudy sky. "What? Did you forget it's your wedding day?"

Bewildered, I touch the crown on my head. Flowers. I take away a petal and inspect it. Graveyard marigolds.

The other women's waterlogged eyes crowd around me. They smell of salt and earth and wet things, their faces briny-raw with crying. Their hands pat me and push me as they sing another song. A livelier song, more cheerful and also faster. I step forward to catch myself as they push me along, around them, around the cemetery, around and around. The women push harder if I stall. I stop drifting ahead on my own and am whipped around by the force of them. They twirl me, twist me so the graveyard goes by in a stormy blur. Sky, mud, puddles, the crisscross of broken fence. I am still part of their song, still feel the rise and lift and drop of it, but when they push me, I am jolted and confused. Their song hypnotizes me into peace, but their abuse shocks me out of it. They queue ahead of me, two lines facing each other, arms extending overhead where they join hands. They become a tunnel of women. Blow by blow, they thrust me through. The women's song turns into one like a man's, with words. I've heard it before, chanted by the girls in the street as they played a clapping game.

*Baby's been born and when Mama's done drying*
*Baby's getting married and Mama's still crying.*

The women across from each other clap a rhythm before and behind me, over their chests and their knees, reaching through the gap in the tunnel to slap each other's hands. They're laughing, but in my disorientation, it sounds like echoed cackling.

*First comes marriage, then comes a baby,*
*Then comes love, and a sister maybe.*
*Then comes Death in a carriage and all,*
*Hubby so happy He's at last come to call.*

When I pass Sara, she leans in close so I can hear her over the song, "Sneak into the house." She pushes me ahead.

Emma, her ponytails hitting my shoulder, offers, "Run when you first get there. Hide." I jolt away.

Victoria is next. Sweet Victoria, who just got married and never smiles, even when the men are gone, because she can't seem to get rid of the black mold that carpets her gums and makes her teeth very small as it curtains down throughout the day. She bares her dark mouth to me now and hisses, "Don't look him in the face."

Shyla commands, "Don't be in the same room with him."

Lottie grabs me hard by the biceps. "You disgust him." She spins me hard.

Someone catches me. I think it's Allison. "Stay in your room. Make your room wet. He'll learn to leave you alone there."

I don't know who is who now. A blur of blonde hair approaches. I can't hear what she says, just the last word: "—pregnant."

I'm alarmed. I should have heard that. What if it's important? I plummet forward, and the beginning of my next advice also gets lost. All I hear is a rasp against my neck and, "—baby gone."

Sky, mud, fence. Eyes, fingers, mouth, fungus. No one is saying words anymore, just laughing. Cackling. Coughing out malformed birdcalls. Tweets, whistles, caws. Just as I think there's no exit to this tunnel, the bodies around me collapse. My stomach reels and tilts. My legs stagger under me. I can't find the ground, and then all I see is the ground. The rest of me falls, my feet unable to keep up. I lie in the dirt, look up at the sky, and watch the world spin.

"Congratulations!" they yell, and then it's over.

# CHAPTER THREE

A wife. I'm a wife now.

I find Maggie afterward. I had felt a finger of grief and anger in the women's burial song, and had immediately known it was Maggie. I understood her, deeply, while I was singing, but now it feels vaguely dreamed.

We were never close. I barely remember when Maggie still lived in our home. I don't remember her wedding day, when she left the house for good and was not allowed back. Mom gave in and talked to her every once in a while when Reese wasn't home, through the window at the back of the house. Occasionally, Maggie would weasel her way inside, especially once Eloise was born, though she made Eloise stay in the yard. I didn't like Maggie's visits. For days after, Mom always cried too readily over nothing at all.

I find her standing over the fresh grave, head bowed. Our mother has been covered, erased to a bare spot of earth.

"Maggie?" My throat is fragile, my voice charred.

"What do you want?" She sounds tired.

"I wanted to know . . . " I stop and furrow my brow. What did I want, exactly? I want her to explain herself to me. I want to understand her again. I try, "Are you okay?"

She scoffs and turns to glower at me. "Yeah, fine."

"I meant—"

"He did it on purpose."

"What?"

"Reese threw a lantern at her on purpose. He killed her so that you'd have no reason to come back, no longer have anyone to see and no one who wants to see you." She holds her hands out and looks around the graveyard, like there's evidence around us that will help her case. She looks back at Mom, her face going still again. "You're not going to survive for long in the outskirts by yourself."

The stunted fungus nubs at the back of my neck, where the skull meets the spine, fill with lightning. I swallow and calm myself. There's no way this is true. Maggie didn't see the look on Reese's face this morning. He felt real grief. Besides, I take up little space in Reese's thoughts. I could never be a reason he does anything, let alone be a reason to end his wife's life. Maggie is irrational. She blames me because I'm the easiest person to blame. Someone who has even less control than she does. If I was a better person, I'd remember the understanding we shared and give her a kind word. I'm not, though. I spend some seconds trying to come up with something cruel to say back, then turn away and look for Eloise. I find her with Jess and a few others, their arms entangled. I eye their naked flesh and sigh. My niece seems taken care of, at least, by women who know her better than I do.

A few women, not Maggie, offer to walk me to my new house. I decline. I want to be alone now. Talking to strangers is too draining. They give me contradictory instructions on how to get there, but I already know where it is. I start my way up the road feeling raw and wounded and motherless.

The surge of feral freedom I expected to feel today doesn't come. A few times, noises or movement in my periphery make me wonder if someone is following me. I imagine Reese coming to tell me that I'm not going anywhere, that there's been a change of plans and I have to go back home and marry him. I quicken my steps. When I check over my shoulder, I'm all alone, but this only quells my misgiving for a few moments.

The leftover rainwater is a glossy rind that makes the empty houses brighter and sharper. They carry the silence and solemnity of old tombs. A few of them have been boarded up by optimistic homeowners of the past, as if a few bits of wood could shut out the future. I wonder if they boarded up the houses before they left or boarded themselves in. Farther down the road, the houses get bigger, and so do the yards. An overflow of thistles and thorns has swept in and spilled over. Roots and tendrils atrophy brick and cement. The snake and waxy tentacle of vines, bushes, flowers, and thick grasses, lush and crawling, all uncontained, spill over pots, into broken windows, and crack open houses. The smell of leaves and woody fiber and rot, and the post-spring smell of wasted pollen and sex detritus, collects in a spent layer of wet, matted lacquer.

Reese, the ogre. Reese, the foul braggart, the old wretch, the malicious whisker-cleaner, the piebald devil who deserved nothing more than to have boots thrown at his head. Reese had a lot of names for me, but I didn't like to use them. I got mine from the fairy-tale book. But now, I'm free of him. And so is Mom. I don't have to think about him anymore. Maybe that was Maggie's true intention, her true cruelty, to make me think of Reese even as I shed him like a dead skin.

My bridal crown of flowers unbraids as I walk across the split asphalt. I try to take it off and toss it into one of the yards as I pass by, but it's too enmeshed in my hair. I only manage to ruin it more. I take off my gloves. The peel of them off my new, raw flesh makes me shudder. I throw them as far as I can, which turns out is not far. They lie some small distance away, crumpled and discolored. For a second, I think maybe I should pick them up. I'm going somewhere where there aren't women, but it's wasteful to leave them on the ground. You can't just throw away clothes. I should go get them. Before I can give in, I walk away.

When I was young and curious, my mom drew a map of the community. So I know my husband's house is down this road. All the women who gave me instructions could at least agree on that. I also know this road is an oval circling the compound, three miles long. I don't know how long a mile is. When I asked, my mom's only answer was, "Longer than you can imagine." I can imagine how long now, after seeing it from the graveyard hill.

When I was young and had boundless energy, I'd run laps around the yard without reason or goal. As I've grown, I've paced restlessly through the hallways of Reese's home, or walked back and forth along the fence, stopping every once in a while to stand on my tiptoes and peek over it. The two houses on either side of us were empty, but I always hoped I'd see someone in another yard farther away. Teaghan, maybe, with one of her friends. She tended to pop up in places where she didn't belong.

I had gotten to see her at the wedding. Most of all, she had seen me. I close my eyes to remember her smell better, a bit like burning leaves, a bit like rain-softened wood.

It's hot and muggy. The heat is baking the road, making the air chalky and full of degrading asphalt. The growths trying to push out of my pores lather with mildew and stick to my clothes. The bottoms of my pants are getting muddy. My armpits are raw with blunted stems. They chafe and ache. I pause in front of a damaged pink bird sticking out of a yard, one of its legs folded in. It must have had a mate at one time, because there's far too many shreds of pink plastic piled beneath it to account for the missing pieces of one smashed abdomen.

My heart sinks. I never put on my bridal outfit. My first task as a wife, and I already messed it up. I wonder why Silas chose it. Were they the clothes his first wife wore when he met her? The ones she gave birth in? The ones she died in? I can't predict what meaning they have to him, or how angry he will be that I didn't obey this first duty. Mom said women make the most mistakes when they are newlyweds. That the first year is the most fatal. I shut my eyes and remember my plan.

Silas lives in the outskirts. He has never had a wife since his first died. We don't know why. We can't. None of the women know anything about him. My mom always felt inadequate that she couldn't fulfill her motherly duty to teach me how to make him happy, and how to keep myself alive.

So I have to hide. Leave him alone and learn as much as I can from afar, especially about his first wife, whose qualities I must accentuate in myself. When I get pregnant, he'll become attached to me. Learn to accept my faults along with my virtues. It would be easier if Mom were here. If I could ask her questions. Grief threatens to sweep me to the ground. I don't let it. I open my eyes. I do not know what the future will hold for me. I do know, with certainty, that I have left the control of a tyrant. I never have to set foot in Reese's house again. Things might get better.

Ahead, in the distance, sits the mauve house with stone lions in the yard. Silas's house. My house.

I take a deep breath and keep walking down the road.

# CHAPTER FOUR

The house rears three stories high. The roof was originally black but has been repaired with so much mismatched material that it looks like a patchwork quilt. The mauve paint is chipping, and much of the siding is missing, like a raw, unfinished house is breaking apart the polished facade from the inside. With such a big house, it will be easy to be alone here, to find a nook of my own to keep. My new husband and I won't even bump into each other. Not until one of us plans it.

I walk up the mangled stone steps, weeds growing through the spreading cracks. Beside the porch, an old garden gnome leans against the house, buried up to his knees in mud. His face is caved in to show the hollow porcelain of his insides. His arms encircle a lamb with broken ears, a chain of violets around its neck, its mouth just a smear of pink paint on the tip of its snout.

I lift my hand to the doorknob, then hesitate. I live here now. But it doesn't feel right to barge into a place I've never stepped foot in. I don't want to bother Silas by asking him to answer the door. And didn't someone say that I should sneak into the house? I stand on the ripped welcome mat feeling stupid, like a deer caught in headlights, as Reese says. Though, like most things Reese says, the words themselves are meaningless. I don't know what headlights are. I assume there aren't any left in the world. I've also never seen a deer, though I know what they look like from my fairy-tale book. There might not be any deer left in the world, either. Or maybe there are, but they've changed into something unrecognizable.

Then I remember it's Saturday. Silas is off drinking with the other men. I sigh with relief knowing he's gone. Maybe I don't have to meet him at all today. I could push it off for a week, even.

The door in front of me whips open. I take an involuntary step back and almost fall off the porch.

I've never seen the man. As far as I know, he's never walked by Reese's window. But when I see his face, even obscured by the screen door between us, I know by the heaviness in my heart that this is my husband, Silas.

He is a giant. It takes my breath away until I remember he is on a step above me. Still, he's bigger than me, of course. Taller than Reese, even, though gaunter and more skeletal. The mycelial roots in my skin have been itchy and restless with a desire to expand, but a wave of cold goes through my body, as if the stunted growths are second-guessing their desire to grow. He smiles at me apprehensively, like he's been standing on the other side of the door waiting for me, also unsure whether to open it. Through the mesh, I see his large brown eyes, his immense and gnarled beard, reddish, with two long streaks of white hair that start at the corners of his mouth, like teeth.

"Hello." His voice is deep but not unfriendly. Still, I know all men have their own language of intimidation. I'm sure I'm about to find out his. I move away from the edge of the porch and find a more stable place to stand.

"Hi."

He opens the screen door. Rusted mechanisms in the doorknob stutter, click, and snap. I cross my arms over my chest and shift my weight from side to side. I wish I had a bag or sweater, or one of my mom's books, something of my own to block my body. I'd feel safer if he couldn't see all of me.

The season of wet is almost finished, but the house still has an aura of chill that envelopes me as I step over the threshold. The air is dense and dewy, the wooden framework is swollen with trapped water, and the carpet flourishes with mold. It's nice, actually, to have some relief from the heat.

The first room is vast. It's framed by a staircase that wraps up and around before disappearing into a half-shadowed hallway upstairs. All the rugs, wood, and furniture are dark. An enormous chandelier hovers above me. I wonder how long it has before it crashes to earth. Hopefully not in my lifetime. I don't want to deal with picking up all that glass. Nor do I want to be skewered on its way down.

The screen door slams and startles me.

"Sorry," says Silas. "The spring is wound too tight. Been meaning to fix it."

I take a deep breath to slow my heart. "No problem."

I expect him to excuse himself, or maybe just whirl around and disappear into his room without a word.

Instead, he stands and looks at me. It feels odd to have someone's eyes on me, someone I don't know. Is he mad that I'm not wearing my bridal outfit? I can't tell.

"I'm sorry I didn't go to the wedding," he says. "I, uh . . . " He clears his throat. "The women don't like it when men show up to the wedding, and I try to respect that."

I blink at him. His apology puts me off-balance, like he's in the middle of clearing space at a table I don't want to eat at. "It's fine."

"How was it?"

I think of the pushing, the shrieking. I think of falling. "Nice." I glance at him. He wears jeans with grass stains on the knees and a T-shirt with something hard in the shirt pocket. I know he's not one of the farmers. He works in the lab, like Reese does. Reese always wears shirts with buttons and tattered collars and acts like it's some virtue that he does so.

I feel a vague sense that I've seen him before. A vague flicker has haunted me in the background for as long as I've known, one that's almost the shape of his face. My mom said the past follows us, but maybe I was seeing the future. Sometimes I have dreams that are so odd and out of place that I think, maybe these aren't my dreams, but someone else's memories. There's no way to tell. In the daylight, all dreams seem born from another person's imagination.

"Should we . . . sit on the couch?" he asks.

I bite my lip and try to smother my rising irritation. "Sure."

I follow him through a room with a fireplace against the wall, then another room with another fireplace, this one in the middle of the room, surrounded by ornate grates. We go through a dining room with a long table topped with a threadbare tablecloth with red ribbons. I don't see a couch, though there's plenty of overstuffed, uncomfortable-looking chairs. We walk past a kitchen with two sinks and too many cupboards. How many people lived in this enormous house? The next room isn't quite a hallway, but it's much smaller than the others, like an afterthought of the kitchen. Its main purpose seems to be to connect the two larger rooms beside it. There's a single couch facing a large window and a tiny dresser. Mounted on the other wall hangs a TV that no one's removed. I don't know why he picks this claustrophobic room over the grander ones we just passed.

We sit down. He sits all the way at one end of the couch. I press myself against the other, practically draping myself over the arm. I look out the window instead of at him, and I can feel him doing the same. In front of the window, a sprawling bush overcomes a table and garden chair, so that they're half submerged in a wall of greenery. No one bothered to dislodge them. I spot a bowl upturned in the mud that no one's picked up. Beyond, a lake reflects the passing clouds. The reflections of the other houses across the lake jut toward the center of the water. No house is as big as this one, none have this large of a yard.

"Nice yard," I say.

"I like the lake," he agrees. "Though most of the year it's barely a puddle." He chuckles. "I like to call it the lake-lake. You know, because this whole place used to be called Mountain Falls Lake."

I nod as if I already know this.

"Back in the day, places like this were named using a string of random nature words. The retirement community of Mountain Falls Lake! So, this lake would be called Mountain Falls Lake lake. Right? That's why I call it the lake-lake."

He wants me to laugh with him. I can't exactly muster it, though, so instead I ask, "Retirement community?"

He tilts his head to the side. "It's like, a community where people would live when they were done working. I think you had to be at least fifty-five years old, or something like that."

"Aren't all of you are at least fifty-five?"

He chuckles again. I tilt my head so it's at the same angle as his. He seems nice, I allow myself to think cautiously. Reese was not a man who laughed much, in any form. When he did, it was bad, it meant he was in a dangerous mood.

"Most of us are, it's true! But it's hard for me to think of retiring. That's certainly not in the cards for me." He taps his foot nervously. "Or being someone who was like the people who used to live here. It was only for rich people." He holds his hands out and gestures to the house all around him. "As you can see."

I don't see what he means. More importantly, I'm not sure what kind of test this conversation is, or how long he'll make me sit on this couch before he lets me escape. I should smile, but I know it won't come across the way I want it to. An off-putting smile is worse than none at all. I politely say, "Very pretty."

He's appeased enough by this offering. Men don't like to explain things about their past, until they do, then they love it. But it's a hard balance to predict. He taps his knee to some rhythm in his head, then notices and stills his hand. "There's a few differences, living out here instead of on the center road. But not a lot. I can show you how the rain barrels work tomorrow."

We sit in silence for too long. He stinks like a man. I don't know what's wrong with men, their smell is always so strong and unnatural, like leather treated with cleaner, or musk from a sick animal that should have fur to keep all its rankness in, but somehow has found itself bald in most spots, meat exposed, illness leaking. Silas is so hairy, like an animal. I want to wrinkle my nose but stifle the urge. He's watching me as I study him.

"I probably smell like isopropyl alcohol. We use it in the growing labs."

"I didn't notice," I lie.

"Well, I suppose Reese smells like it too. You're probably used to it by now."

I don't like the mention of Reese, but I feel like it's safer to nod agreeably again. He reaches for the dresser next to the couch. The house is so quiet that when the drawer squeaks open, it's so loud that I imagine a hole has ripped open underneath us. I jump and my hand darts out onto the couch cushion between us as if to catch myself. I think of Persephone again, and how her husband opened the earth when he came to claim her, how the earth swallowed her. A bare spot, consumed.

He titters awkwardly. "Everything echoes in this house."

I shift uncomfortably and scratch at my neck, feeling the newborn pelt of fuzzy fungus ooze and burn under my nails. I sit on my hands and remind myself not to scratch anymore. He watches me with mournful, hesitant eyes. I don't understand the emotion there at all and it shocks me into wide-eyed stillness, and I can't move until he looks away. He frowns and closes the drawer, deciding not to retrieve whatever he was looking for.

A brown bird, small as my palm, lands on a branch near the window and cleans its toxin-stuffed feathers with its beak, squeezing poisonous dust into its mouth.

I hiss, "Is your gun nearby?"

"Do you know how to shoot one?"

"No," I say guiltily. It's a woman's job to rid the compound of any creature that might bring forest toxins into the home. At the center road, the sighting of a rodent or bird would drive any nearby woman out of her house and into the street, rifle raised. My childhood was punctuated by gunshots. "Our yard wasn't big enough to learn how to shoot in."

The bird flits and preens its wings. It peeks its head over the edge of the branch, searching.

Silas's mouth twitches. "I know the compound is cleaner without animals. But . . . I don't like killing them. It feels cruel."

I gape at him. "You don't . . . " I can't find the words, so I foolishly repeat, "*like* it?"

He shrugs. "Not really."

I'm disappointed that I won't learn to shoot a gun after all. It seems fun, gleefully squeezing the trigger and yelling, "Got one!"

But now I will get to go outside. Even if I don't get to shoot, I will have more freedom. I squint my eyes at Silas again, search past his hairiness. I'm not so stupid I can't see the advantage in having a husband that chooses gentleness, even with small, poisonous creatures. Especially with small, poisonous creatures.

His eyebrows rise and he slaps his knees with both hands. "Can I show you the rest of the house?"

He shows me the rest of the house.

Silas takes a luciferin lantern with us. I can tell which places he uses the most, because clusters of lanterns glow only in a few rooms. If I slow down and put distance between him and myself, while we are in the unlit innards of the house, all I can see ahead is a bobbing light and Silas's hand, the outline of his hulking body.

He calls over his shoulder, "The lanterns aren't very bright. But at least you don't need to relight them, right?"

I blink at him. I'd never thought of a lantern needing to be brighter. Nor had I ever thought of relighting them. Occasionally the fungus inside them dies, and the men have to replenish it from the lab supply.

He shows me a two-story library with something called

a Juliet balcony. There's not many books inside it. Mostly, the shelves are lined with a sprawling collection of farm animal trinkets dressed in baby clothes. There's a room with only giant windows for walls and a single bathtub that could fit six people. No ashy residue stains the porcelain. No one has ever cooked in it. Maybe it's too dangerous, since the cook would have to climb inside while the fire was burning just to reach it. Or maybe it's because there are nine other bathrooms. Three bars, a couple of side kitchens. A room with a single pool table, olive-green walls, and a few hanging photographs of boats and docks. Next to it, a room housing something called a ping-pong table.

"The ping-pong balls are all lost now," says Silas.

Dust rises in his wake as he walks down the hall, lacing the air behind him with a squirming sheen and a stale taste. Every upstairs room has its own balcony, every downstairs room has a sliding door that opens to a porch. I lose count of the bedrooms. Everything has the stifled, ammonia scent of trapped spaces.

I didn't expect the house to be so full. Compared to this, the house I grew up in was empty, with only a few utilitarian pieces of furniture. A chair and table, a mattress. A dresser for storage. I don't know who decided to empty it. Must have been Reese, or maybe one of the two wives he briefly had before my mom. It could have even been my mother, though I doubt it. The state of that house had been set long before my mom made her way into this world.

Is he showing me the house to lay his claim to it? So I know none of it is mine? I keep thinking he will tell me that I am not allowed in certain rooms as we pass them. But he doesn't. He shows me everything. Opens every door, every closet. Sometimes he seems surprised by what's inside, like he's forgotten. He shows me the basement.

"It's pretty boring," he says at the top of the stairs.

But I go down anyway and take a look, just to see if he'll stop me. He doesn't, and he's right. It is boring. Unpainted concrete walls and a cement floor crowded with stacks of ruined antiquities tucked away in ruined boxes.

There is a bedroom on the ground floor that's closest to the front door. It is the biggest and the grandest. He doesn't sleep there. He sleeps in a different bedroom, upstairs. I don't know why. Perhaps it's too close to the door. I've heard some men can be paranoid about their front doors. I try to learn what I can about Silas from the house, but none of its furnishings are his. The only thing I can discern from these rooms is that he's the type of man who moves into a house and leaves all the dead occupants' belongings where they are.

His own bedroom is as bleak as the mouth of a carnivore. I glance into the doorway to see a dark bed with pillars, a place where a canopy should have been but was long torn down. I don't step inside. I can feel Silas wanting me to step inside, closer to the bed, and it makes me especially not want to. I plant my feet and smile pleasantly. We walk on.

He says, "And this is the nursery."

Humanesque forms litter the rooms. I hadn't known what they were until Silas told me. Dolls. In here, there are mountains of them. They sit at miniature tea tables, in miniature rocking chairs, laying glassy and stiff-armed in miniature strollers. I don't like the look of them and their immobile eyes. Fading scenes of fairy tales wrap around the bedroom's walls. Little Red Riding Hood, Rapunzel, skinny Hansel and Gretel holding hands, cheeks rosy, eyes wide and rimmed with starvation, looking for candy. All the figures are eerie and gaunt, peeling and succumbing to time.

Silas wags his eyebrows and says in a jokey voice, "You'll be spending a lot of time in here." I must not respond in the way he wants, because his face collapses into something crestfallen, then serious. He clears his voice and taps the doorknob nervously. He's not used to speaking to people. Certainly not to women. Certainly not to a wife. Silas's eyes roam the walls. "I don't come in here much. Sometimes the dolls laugh or talk, and it freaks me out." He picks up a curly-haired doll in a polka-dot dress, then flips it around to look under its skirt, taps a hidden compartment in there. "I mean, it's a miracle that the batteries have lasted this long. By now, though, they must be corroding. I don't know. I don't really get electronic stuff."

He sets the doll back down. Painted in the corner, there's a sly wolf placidly licking his lips, the shadow of a hunter with an ax sneaking up behind him. Silas puts his hands in his pocket, turns to me and smiles. He's too close to me. The intensity of his face is unnerving. I edge toward the wall.

"Where's my room?"

"Well," he says, then trails off. "Well . . . "

He doesn't want me to sleep in a bed. In the house at all. I clear my throat. "The garage will be fine."

"No, no," he says waving his hands in the air like he's scared I'm going to jump past him. "I mean, I was just thinking that if you want, you can sleep in my bed. Our bed." He hesitates again. "If you want."

I want my own room. I want a place where I can curl up or stretch out and be myself, a woman without a man. I think of the dark room with its dark bed, the dark wooden pillars holding up nothing. I almost insist on the garage. The basement, the yard, anywhere else. But this is the test. I can see it now. He led me up to this point, and now here we are. Nonchalantly, I tug my ear and say, "If that's what you want."

He smiles and sighs in relief. "Sure. Let's try it out for a little while. What do you think?"

I make a move to go back into the hall, until the thought of him behind me, unseen, stops me. I pause so that he'll go first. But he doesn't walk ahead. He nods and makes a gesture, smiles as if he's being polite. I clear my throat again and a smile flickers across my face. I step ahead of him and my smile drops. As we walk down the hallway, I watch his shadow as it jumps ahead or falls behind, depending on the bounce of the lantern behind me and the positions of the lanterns in the hall.

When we are in the blank, unlit space between two doorways, his hand raises above my head, like the hunter with the ax. He touches my shoulder. My hand flies to the back of my neck, the other covers my scalp. I scream. He jumps back, the lantern swinging dangerously. When I turn around, his hands are out, palms facing me in supplication.

"Sorry!" he says. "Sorry."

"Sorry," I also say weakly. I'm breathing fast.

"I just, ah, I just—" He lowers his hands. "I just wanted you to know—I just wanted to say, that it's been difficult. I haven't had a wife in a long time. I know you must know that already. But . . . " His fingers twitch by his side. He pauses for a second, then his hand darts out and grabs mine. His face is tender and terrible and breakable. "I'm so happy you've finally come. I hope you'll like it here."

In the hallway, with his fingers over my hands and his eyes searching mine, I am hit with the sense of his loneliness. It lies empty and inert in the casing of the house, but in his body, the loneliness is heavy and oppressive and boiling. I can't understand this ancient man who has lived through a thousand starvations and awful lifetimes, so many lifetimes. No wonder men are so deranged. He lives the life of a ghost but is made of meat, so the pain stays in him instead of sliding through. He puts my hand to his cheek, closes his eyes, and lays his face against my palm. He is sweaty.

"I don't know you," he whispers. "But I feel like I do."

I nod. I know what he means. My entire life, his name has hovered over me. The way promises and threats do. I have always felt like a shell for him to crack open. Like my life was to begin at the start of my marriage, and my childhood was guiding me toward that becoming. I don't want to be cracked open, though. I've seen Reese break so many things. Angrily, carelessly. Silas has always been an unknowable exit from Reese's house. A promise, and a threat.

I say, "You've been my destination my whole life."

He sniffles and his hand trembles in mine. He lowers his head so that we are seeing each other at eye level. It's the first time that a man has really searched my face, and it stops my heart. This is what a rabbit must feel when seeing the flash of a predator's reflective eyes between the trees. I didn't mean it as a compliment. I don't mean it at all how he obviously takes it, but I don't know how to correct or take back what I said without disturbing some equilibrium.

He tugs me along. "Come to bed. I won't touch you, I promise."

What a thing to say while he's touching me that very moment. But for some reason I believe him, and I let him drag me along.

"Now?" From the hallway, I can't see out any windows, but I know it's not even close to dark yet. "I'm . . . so hungry." I haven't eaten all day.

"I have food waiting for you in the bedroom. Our bedroom."

He leads me into his reeking cavern. He clutches my hand until I walk through the doorway, then he lets go. I think of running through the empty house, alone, but don't, because the next image that follows is him chasing me down the dark hallway, overcoming me, dragging me back to the bed by my hair with a troll lurch, chanting, "Our bedroom, our bedroom, our—"

This whole room smells like man. It's the only place in the house where his odor overpowers the smell of decaying heirlooms. Clearly, he spends most of his time here, sleeping, filling the area with his heat and sweat and feral musk.

He digs into a dresser drawer and pulls out a pickle jar of preserved veggies. Peppers, it looks like. Waterlogged, they push against the side of the glass, congealing at the edges.

I sit at the foot of the bed, and he sits against the headboard. I open the jar and offer him some.

He shakes his head. "It's all yours."

His eyes stay fastened on me. I turn my back and do my best to block him out of my mind. I hunch over the jar, using my fingers to fish out the peppers, since he's given me no silverware. They are cold and soggy and glutinous, but I'm so, so hungry. I swallow them down and drink the last of the crystallized broth at the bottom. When I set the jar down on the floor, next to the bed, I don't turn around yet. I sit very still and stare out across the room. Unsure of what to do with my hands, I keep them in my lap and try not to fiddle. I think of running into the hall again, but imagine him dragging me back. I can feel him as he takes off his shoes and lies down in bed. It groans and creaks beneath him. I peek over my shoulder and see him facing the wall, still clothed. He doesn't coax or pressure me. And yet, the air is tense with his waiting. Eventually, I lie down too. I don't want to face him, but I don't want to sleep with my back to him, either. The bed strains toward his weight, and I'm just a pebble in his mountainous gravity. I stare at the ceiling.

The room shifts. His breathing elongates. He must be asleep.

I've never listened to a man fall asleep before. Is it normal for it to happen so quickly? His rich grease on the threadbare blankets and pilling, wine-colored sheets is overwhelming. If I drag my finger over the pillow, I bet it would come away buttery. After an hour, I toss and turn, and then I can't stop thrashing. I'm nervous at first that it will wake him, but my legs are painful with restless tingling. I can't tell if it's my own restlessness, or the growths muscling out of my skin. Soon, it becomes clear Silas isn't going to wake up. It's also clear I'm not going to get any sleep.

The door is open, a wide rupture exposing the intestinal darkness of the hall.

I've already broken the convention of avoiding being in the same room with a new husband until pregnancy, but what am I supposed to do? Where else would I go? If he found me curled up in another bed, how angry would he be? Would it be enough for him to kill me and wait for another wife who was willing to lie next to him and tolerate his intolerable heat? I feel lost. His snoring is awful. But after an hour, or two, or three, he moans in his sleep. A deep whimper that draws on some molten sadness I can't comprehend. I stare at the ceiling and listen. He whimpers again, one more time. For some reason, this pathetic mewling is what finally lulls me into semiconsciousness.

During the moments in the night when I wake up, I sense his fever-beast presence in the room. He's standing beside the bed, against my side, and I feel him as he eases himself over me.

He slides his fingers into my mouth. I flail my arms. I wail, the germ of the sound is primal and savage, but it comes out half-suppressed by sleep. The bleat of a pounced-on, half-dead rat. Whatever vision lowered itself onto my body dissolves into the blackness of the room again.

It takes me a long time to go back to sleep. Each time, I stagger into my halting dreams like a drunk, or a child running from her own shadow.

# CHAPTER FIVE

The next morning, I feel a tug like I should be doing something. It's a ploy, a trick. All my effort goes toward staying asleep.

Dead women in the ground, searching for me. Skeletal hands tangled together in the compressed, fossilized earth, finger bones wriggling like larva as they search, reaching up through the ground to pull me under. I dream of Hades's red teeth. Yellow flowers and dirt falling over rocks like a waterfall, clumps and petals bursting apart on impact. Girls lie curled on the ground like young beans. They convulse, then push and push until a sprout bulges out of their shared intestine, sweet leafed and bunching.

I feel one more tug. Insistent, intrusive, like a needle going into my ear canal, and I open my eyes, still sludgy from the dreams now slipping out of my skull as rapidly as water through a sieve. I remember where I am. A large bed, a gloomy home. Light slivering in through the bay window. The uncomfortable pressure of the mattress makes me too aware of my unfamiliar shape. A fungal patch on my midriff glistens, matching a silvery wet blotch on the sheets. A crust dries on my arm, and red jelly burgeons on the back of my hand. New growths have sprung up while I slept, some of them large enough to have budding caps. I run my hands gently over my skin until it becomes too painful. I don't know myself. My body is nowhere near what it was two days ago, when I still had the unfettered armor it had taken all my life to grow.

Silas is gone. Why didn't he wake me? I think of him regaining consciousness and moving around the room while I slept, and I shiver. I squeeze my temples and groan. It's too much work handling a man. I don't know how my mom did it, how any of the women do it. I try to swallow, but I can't. I'm so, so thirsty. My mouth is a raw, aching pit. My tongue has swollen into a thick wad. I see a full glass of water next to me on the dresser. I snatch it and suck it down as fast as I can, watching the bottom of the glass near and knowing it's not enough.

I realize Silas must have left it there for me. His hands touched where my hands are touching, where my lips are on the rim of the glass. My stomach churns. My mom kept a pitcher of water next to her bed. Every morning she woke up incredibly thirsty. I always thought of it as a quirky trait of hers, but it must have been because the growths need moisture to labor to life again.

I am being taken over by my own body. It should feel good, regaining myself, but it doesn't. It feels like an attack. Will it always be like this? I am sensitive, hurting, and sore. The sun is too loud, colors too bright. And the aching dryness and the electricity of sudden growth is hot and painful on my skin. No wonder my mom was so slow in the morning, so slow to return to equilibrium. She had always said that she was not a morning person. I wonder why she didn't warn me what made her that way. Why didn't she think it was important to prepare me for this? No, no. Don't think of Mom.

I'm a wife. From now on, my mornings will be spent shaving. A jagged spike of nausea slides into my gut at the idea of returning to the suppressive fog I spent all of yesterday in. Some of that was also from losing my mom. But judging from how incapacitated I was the night before, when my mom was still alive, not all of it was.

The grief is a seed inside my chest, threatening to sprout at any thought of my mom. I want to go back to the graveyard, where the women's song soothed me, allowed me to share my grief with a larger body. The memory catapults through me, too vivid. The start of a keen rises, uncalled. I hunch over to tamp down that voice. Rock my body back into silence. Don't think of her, don't think of her.

Eventually, the silence comes again.

I heave myself out of bed and leave the bedroom, seeking water and a room with more darkness and less color.

Silas is in the hallway. I notice him right away, standing in one of the doorways to another room. The light from behind him illuminates his dark shape. He is standing so still, a mug steaming in his hand. How long has he been awake that he's been able to build a fire and boil water?

I decide to pretend he's not there. When I'm in front of him, he jerks like he's just noticed me. I rush to get past him, but he reaches toward my brow, squinting in concentration. I halt in my tracks and steel myself for his touch. He disentangles something embedded in my hair.

"You've still got flowers." The head of a graveyard marigold plops to the ground, only a few petals left. My hair releases the smell of withering. A smell I prefer, to be honest, than when the flowers were fresh, though I know men like their flowers best when they're first picked. He chuckles as he shows me the tip of his finger, a browning petal still clinging to his skin. "Well, I saved one, at least. I haven't slept that well in a long time." We stand there facing each other. He is backlit so I can't see his face properly, but when he speaks, his voice is striped with disappointment. "You don't . . . look happy."

I scoff. Does he expect me to be happy? I study the geography of his face. The air heats around us. Murky dreams finger the spongey part of my brain, hovering, menacing, tugging at my memories. Some warning that dissolves before I can catch hold of it.

"I have something for you." He steps aside, revealing a water-damaged cardboard box. He opens it.

I peek inside. "Clothes."

He smiles, proud of himself. "Your clothes." He speaks with such ceremony and gravity, even though this is something he's supposed to do. "They're less worn than the ones the other women wear. Practically in mint condition."

I pick up a yellow-and-white dress.

"Pamela often wore that to church."

Reese talks about church a lot. Apparently, they used to try it with the women every week, but it never took. Sometimes, when they get drunk, they do church in the street on their way home, which from what I can tell is mostly kneeling in the gutter and praying and crying and worrying whether God still loves you.

"There's jewelry down there too."

"Jewelry?" I feel something hard beneath the clothes. I pick it up and it dangles, flashing in my hand.

"That was once her grandma's necklace." Seeing my confusion, he adds, "You wear it around your neck. For decoration."

A chain around my neck? For decoration? I narrow my eyes at him to see if he's joking.

"The other men don't give their wives jewelry. They think they'll lose or break it. You'll be the only one." I look up at his face, startled, wondering what I did wrong. Then I see that he means this as a compliment, or a privilege. *The only one.* He watches me closely with his hands in his pockets. His eyes are glassy from the sun coming in through the window. "You'll be the envy of every other woman."

"Oh," I say. Why does he think the other women would care what I wore? They have their own clothes.

I drop the dress back in the box. "Sure. Thanks."

Now that I've been given this gift, I am tasked with the responsibility of returning to the bedroom to sort it all into the dressers. I do so, dutifully and regretfully. Now, the man smell in this room will seep into my clothes. I will walk around all day, marked by Silas, chased by his stink. I put the shirts, underwear, and socks into the drawers, trying to only take up a few, though now I certainly have more clothes than Silas, who only takes up one drawer.

I peel off the clothes I've been wearing for too long. Silas has a pile of dirty clothes building in the corner, so I toss them there. I pick out a shirt and shorts and change into them. It's an immediate relief to no longer be covered in this heat. Curiously, I poke at the jewelry. I pick up the grandma necklace. It takes me a moment to understand the hook at one end is supposed to go through the hoop at the other. I put it on and look at myself in the mirror. The sudden weight is draining. I have a patch of growth at my sternum trying to resprout, and the necklace stones, hard and glinting like a set of eyes, are too much of a burden. The necklace bears down heavier and heavier onto my chest the longer I stand there staring at myself. I scramble to take it off and accidentally yank it against my throat in the process. I throw all the jewelry in one drawer and close it with a click of finality.

When I'm done, I don't want to go out into the hall again and allow Silas to give me another gift. I wait in the bedroom. Four dressers, three mirrors, two tables, a wardrobe. Paintings nailed so high on the wall that I couldn't reach them even if I stood on my toes. Girls on swings, women with umbrellas, a glimpse of a skirt through a pathway that disappears into the trees. None of the people in the paintings have faces, they're all seen from behind.

I look at the bed and feel an uneasiness rise. I go to the window and look out at the distance of green, the houses rimmed around the glassy lake. The lake-lake. The wind picks up and rolls over the house and slams into the window so hard, it shakes the frame. A wave of loneliness sweeps through me. All my life, I've never been allowed to talk to the people on the street. But I've at least been able to watch them, to listen to them interact with each other. Here, there's no one. I am more isolated than ever.

Past the houses, I can see the wall. Ominous and unyielding, a line drawn thick around the compound, as tall as a two-story house. Branches and vines catapult over the sides, eager to get over and into this small pocket of land that a small pocket of humanity is trying to keep for themselves. The plants carry forest toxins, soaked up from their roots. The animals bring them, too, and carry them over the wall and into our homes. The mushrooms are most dangerous because they spread the toxins in the air. I don't understand the curse that came over the woods, over the country, over the world. I know that women changed because of it, that everything living changed. I know that it will last thousands of years.

Our compound is safe. The men do their best to keep it that way. They remove the mushrooms that grow in our homes and on the center road. We do our part by getting rid of the animals that make it over the wall and not touching each other. We may have developed an immunity to our own mushrooms, but not to each other's. *Like snakes and venom*, Reese says.

Something catches my eye. As if summoned by my melancholy, a fleeting smear of white dashes in the distance. I squint. It takes a few minutes for the phantasm to appear again. When it does, I know immediately who it is.

My heart beats faster, a squirming pulsation as my chest growths engorge. I whisper beneath my breath, urging her closer. And, by some miracle, she does creep closer. She disappears behind the sparse houses pockmarking the land, and in a few moments, she's at the edge of Silas's yard, my yard, crouching behind a fence post, looking up at the house.

She scans the windows, and at this moment, I can't think of what for. She sees me, I think. Her face is pointed in my direction. She lifts her hand hesitantly, and waves. Before I wave back, she points to the side of the house. To herself, to me, then to the side of the house again. I shake my head, no, no, not so much denying her but denying the possibility that this could be real. She nods, yes, yes, and then she takes off running toward the side of the house.

I glide through the hallway, down the stairs, keeping close to the wall and softening my footfalls as best I can. No sign of Silas, as if his absence is part of this dream I'm still conjuring out of the depths of my loneliness. There's a door at the side of the house. I wonder how she knows about it, if she's been scouting this house. Though there are doors everywhere. It could've been a lucky guess.

I open the door and she's there. I can smell the muted decay of the lake-lake, and I can smell the tender pollen-reek of her, breathy and prickly in the heat. It never felt possible that we could stand in front of each other like this. We lived in two different worlds. Still, I had imagined many different things to say to her, if we ever did. As a child, *Will you play with me?* Later, *Will you take me with you the next time you disappear?* But they all seem naïve and embarrassing.

Now that she is standing in front of me, she feels like the only thing that's real in this house. The only thing that connects me back to the world I know.

"I'm Teaghan."

"Yeah, I know."

"I know you know," she says, putting her hand on her hip. "I'm the one who put the bridal crown on your head."

I furrow my brow. "You grew up right across the street from me. I saw you every day."

Teaghan tilts her head, smiles in a way that makes me think of the cat in the fairy-tale book when he lies to his mouse-friend about the pot of fat he licked up. *Top-off, Half-Gone.* She flicks her hair back, pleased and self-satisfied that she's been watched this whole time and didn't know it. "Every day I was home, you mean." *All-Gone.*

"Yes," I say. She'd run away often. Her exasperated mother would go out into the street after the men left for work and call her name like a widowed goose until her daughter returned, or until the men did, and she had to be quiet again. Teaghan turns and a splatter of carmine droplets on her shoulders glisten in the sun. She's wearing a thin, gauzy blouse with exaggerated bell sleeves. Now she reminds me of the picture I used to moon over as a kid, of Rapunzel, draped over a windowsill, hair dripping down the stony tower alongside oblong tears and arms outstretched, the whole length of her elongated, stretched nearly to the ground in her longing. "What are you doing here?"

She reaches out, like it's nothing, and slides her fingers into mine, her white bell sleeve engulfing my naked hand into its wide opening, hiding our two enmeshed hands. Instinctively, I jerk my arm toward myself, but she clamps down tighter with a widening grin. An iciness, silver and alien and beautiful, like I imagine a fish feels, slides into my skin. Something transient and night-like. The chill slides through my fingers, into my palm, up my arm and across my chest, swimming circles in the greedy water of my body until it finds my belly and rests inside, pulsing. I gasp. A few more seconds pass by, slow and blind, before I rest my hand on the doorway and brace myself, mustering the strength to dislodge my hand from hers. But before I can apply force, she lets me go easily, with a twitch of a smile.

I find my breath. "You have to go. I don't know where Silas is. He could round the corner at any moment."

She rises on her tiptoes and peers past me into the house. "What will he do?"

"I don't know." I swallow, suppress a ragged breath. "I've just met him."

She raises her eyebrows. "Something bad, though."

"Something bad," I agree.

"I'll leave. But tonight, sneak out and meet me at my house." I breathe harder, pressing my forehead against my hand, which leans against the doorframe. I still feel her, coldly brilliant, inside me. She bends closer as she whispers, "Don't you want to be with us? No one likes to be alone."

I can't look up and watch her go until I am sure she is far enough away that I can handle the sight of her. When I do, she is a tiny speck on the cusp of a faraway hill. Then, like the green flash of the sun after it drops below the horizon, she's gone, and I can't be certain she was ever really there at all.

I find Silas in the library. He is too busy to look up and see me.

I think of all the stories I've been told about how dangerous it is for women to touch each other. I could be poisoned now. Teaghan could have unknowingly touched an infected mushroom on her walk over. Her touch would have transferred the sickness to me. I think of my mom, lying on the bed, illuminated in light and bruises.

I also think of all the fungus the men work with, all that dangerous potential. Reese told stories at the dinner table of fungal apparitions that grew overnight, poking out of the bones of houses. Of women and girls who accidentally touched these sneaky mushrooms, and the atrocities that followed when their bodies couldn't handle the poison. Blights that discolor a woman's flesh before boils spread. Fungus that liquefies the mushroom parts in a woman, and rashes that inflame the human parts before it peels away their skin layer by layer. Before my mom was born, there was a woman who walked away from her skeleton. Took five steps until she collapsed into a pile of exposed meat next to a heap of bones. All from a mushroom she glanced against the night before. Two other women followed the next day, and another the day after that. They had touched each other the night before.

I asked my mom why the women touched each other if it was so dangerous. *Because it's still worth it. For them, but not for us,* she said. I think of this and the way my mom would stare at her hands sometimes, touching one to the other, as women passed by. How, if Reese wasn't home, she'd call out in a quiet, unanswered hum.

Silas putters around, muttering to himself and dragging his feet along the carpet. Dust jumps around his toes like fleas in the sunlight, drifting like dandruff. Sometimes he raises his voice loud enough, as if he's talking to another person. His conversation sounds mostly good-humored, though I can't understand what he's saying.

I close my eyes, and the memory of Teaghan washes over me. Even the thought is an exhilaration, exuberant and wild. *Don't you want to be with us?* she had said. I don't know who she means by "us," but, with a line of puerile growths on my spine shivering, I can't help but interpret it as *Don't you want to be with me?*

Tonight, if she does it again, I will clamp down on her hand, cling to her naked fingers until there are no gaps between us. I will make her hand mine, and my hand hers, inseverable.

# CHAPTER SIX

I have nothing to do, and I am miserable with restlessness. I wander the house, keeping to the rooms with lanterns so I don't have to carry one myself. Meanwhile, the air outside turns golden, the shadow of the old, broken greenhouse spreads and lengthens toward the house.

Listlessly, I end up in the fairy-tale bedroom. On the walls, the wolf's red tongue slips out of his pink lips. The starving children clutch hands and gawp at the forest. The child with a red, pointed hat crawls up a beanstalk as the top of it disappears into the clouds. Seated around the room, dolls slouch in rocking chairs and tea tables. They peek out of pink-stitched pillows in the reading nook of the bay window. They lie in mini baskets, stand with their backs against the wall, grins frozen, hands stretched out, like they're waiting for an invitation to dance. One of them laughs. I jump, my heart pounding. The doll's laugh continues, distorts, then twists away at the end.

My eyes dart around the room, trying to find which one is the culprit, but the dolls remain motionless. I am alone, but the memory of the laugh prickles. I used to hear laughter erupting from the edges of the road and think nothing of it. I close my eyes and conjure Teaghan's touch. This time, an ache dislodges from the pit of me. It slowly bubbles up my stomach, up my sternum, and comes out as a soft dribble of a moan.

I want to give her a gift.

I search through the closet and find a small backpack covered in stars, with a white kitten on its front pocket. I find shirts in the closet. They're too small, but she can give them to girls she knows. I flip through a few books. I don't recognize any of these stories, so I pick out a few with the prettiest pictures. I leave the dolls. I don't know what you're supposed to do with them.

Teaghan didn't specify a time. But surely, she meant after the men go to sleep. I'm too scared to leave the house until Silas is unconscious.

Teaghan. I squeeze the backpack to my chest hungrily. *Please*, I beg. *Please. Please make her love me.*

"Make who love you?" Silas's voice booms into the empty, doll-filled room. I startle and slacken and drop the backpack. I hadn't known that I spoke those words out loud, had only felt them deep inside. And, of course, I hadn't known Silas was there.

He is staring at the backpack, zipper open, shirts and books hanging out. "What are you doing?"

My mind races for an excuse, but my brain is filled with a white buzzing.

"Are you going somewhere?" His voice is slow and

dangerous. The back of my neck tingles with a warning. "Were you . . . ?" Sadness and anger compete in his oversized body, tensing, tightening. "Were you running away?"

I can't answer. I'm too afraid. With Reese, I knew the basic edge of his limits. With Silas, I know nothing. He begins his prowl around the room.

"Who are you running back to? Your sister? Reese?"

Reese! Even while in danger, I almost laugh. I thought there would be no way to trick someone so old, so wise, who must know everything I'm about to do before I even think it. But he thinks I'm running back to *Reese*? Silas's anger peels off him. I saw this often in Reese, a silhouette ballooning from his body, a mass of heat large enough to fill the room. Silas's anger body unfolds from him, shimmers and shifts, fracturing everything behind it. So hot it gives the illusion of water.

"Who is it?" he hisses. Then, this time anciently sad and pathetic, "*Who?*"

I can't tell him that I'm not running away, because then I'd have to explain I was escaping only for the night, that I only want to see Teaghan. But some instinct tells me this is a worse admission. I stay silent. His body is too giant; he's coming too close. I take a step back. This sets him off. The air is laced with his fury. Tangible as smoke, he fills the room, thickens the air to an unbreathable viscosity.

He says, "You don't get it."

A mechanical laugh erupts at our side. My eyes graze over the dolls to make sure they're still motionless. That they're not part of some army that answers to him. "I can't even begin to explain—" He puts his hand up to his temple and groans. "So much pressure, from all sides."

He reaches out. My muscles stiffen, my bones lock too tight in their sockets. I am luminous with dread.

He touches my cheek. He takes his hand and brushes it, once, through my hair.

His jaw shudders. A long, straining sigh, like he is relieving his body of the building pressure. He brings his hands to his face and covers himself. Is he crying? He pulls away.

"I'm sorry."

He's quickly gone from the room, but his anger still hangs in the place he stood, looming and man shaped. I step forward, away from the awkward line of dolls, and am submerged in his leftover heat. It surrounds me, taking up more space than I ever could. I listen as he stumbles down the hall. I listen as he leaves the house, slamming the door.

He didn't ask if I was escaping to see my mother. He already knows she's dead.

I kneel where Silas stood when he touched me. I can still feel the pressure of where his weight had been. I imagine it burning a hole in the carpet. Over the years, the hole will become a spreading crack that takes over, splits the floor and the walls, forces apart the roof, and with a puff of wind, the house will all fall down.

# CHAPTER SEVEN

Men cry all the time. Not as often as they get angry, but enough that I am used to it.

What I'm more concerned about is how he'll feel afterward. Will he be angry enough to come home and kill me?

I try to prepare myself. I try to come to terms with it. I wander the rooms, deciding which one I want to die in. This one, with the stripes and lace and mirrors? This melancholy one, with the birds and the violin? This one with the marble women, their sad eyes rolled to the sky, lined all in a row?

Silas is gone for a long time. I don't really think he'll come home and kill me. Still, I don't know. It's unbearable, having to wait. It occurs to me to try to find Teaghan. But that's the stupidest thought in the world. If I get caught, Teaghan will be punished too. I pace the entranceway. The chandelier catches the last of the day's light in its crystalline body. Then the whole room gets dark, then darker.

Eventually I see a faraway lantern out the window. My pulse surges, clenches my throat, and enrages a few patches of growth. I could run and hide. But I've been waiting long enough. I throw open the door. A few desiccated leaves sweep over my feet and into the house.

The light crosses into the yard. Silas. His lantern sails in such a fluid line, like a boat gliding through a river. He becomes brighter as he approaches, his face larger in the light.

"Hi," he says guardedly as he walks up the porch. "Can I come in?"

I hesitate at the gentleness in his voice. I move aside. The moon comes in through the window, casting the room in a metallic, liquid movement of light that squirms over vases with their bulging heads of plastic flowers and big-cheeked buds, faded and dull. It streams over the blanched photographs in their ornate frames, the old glass bottles, and a gilded hairbrush set on top of a side end table. Silas closes the door, and the chandelier beads click together, pearls tinkling until it barely breathes. He sets his lantern on the floor. He wipes his forehead with the back of his hand.

"It's hotter than it looks out there." A sour nervousness clings to him. He clears his throat. "Listen. I want to—" He looks up suddenly, his eyes wide with surprise, like I've yelled at him, though I've been standing a few feet away in silence. He blinks hard, gets his bearings again. He covers his eyes. "The way it used to be, it's—" He grunts in frustration. "This is so awkward." He's wobbly, tilted to the side. Even from where I stand, I can tell he's squeezing his face too hard.

Uneasiness spreads in my stomach, but I give him some time to recuperate. He sounds so pitiful. His pupils swallow his irises, like a drunk's. But there's no booze on his breath. When Reese came home on Saturday nights, his fermented, sickened reek wafted across the house. It clung to him all through Sunday, a maudlin smell that wept out of his pores and became a sticky glue on his hairy parts. Silas doesn't smell like that at all. But something in his brain circuitry is slowing him down. It makes me ashamed, though I couldn't say why.

He sighs deeply. "I have been lonely for so long. I couldn't bear the thought that you'd just leave before even taking the time to get to know me. I'm sorry. For getting angry." He gesticulates to the side, like he's arguing with someone standing over there. "I don't believe in that stoic masculinity bullshit. I'm a man with strong feelings, and I'm easily hurt. I suppose that's going to be part of you getting to know me. But I'd never hurt you, never touch you. It looked like . . . you thought I would."

It's the same promise he made to me last night, that he wouldn't touch me. I believe him less now. He must see this hesitancy, because he adds, "At least, I wouldn't touch you in anger. Can I show you something?"

His eyes are wide and swollen and wet, like a rabbit's.

He waits for me to say, "Sure," which is nice of him, I guess, then leads me through the house again, the same way he took me when we first met. When we are at the couch, we sit down again, each on our separate sides. Silas opens the drawer, and the creak echoes through the house. He pulls out a photo album, places it on his lap, and takes a deep breath. My chest flips as he flips to the first page.

"This was taken in Wyoming."

I steel myself and lean over. In the photo, a woman stands in front of a vehicle, her hands on her hips. She's skinny, except for a bulging stomach. She has to lean back to keep her balance.

"This is Pamela. My first wife. She's eight months pregnant here."

She looks exactly like me. Brown hair, curly and wild. Small eyes with hardly any eyelashes. Mouth long and broody. She even looks about the same age as I am now, though I know she's not. She's old. Any foremother is impossibly old. I touch my cheek, feel the fissures and ripples and bumps where there should be stems. She looks *almost* exactly like me, anyway. Silas politely pretends not to notice me touching myself. He taps the picture.

"This was right after she delivered Nola's baby." He itches his nose and smiles to himself. "A midwife's work is never done, even when she herself is ready to burst."

As he speaks, his breath creeps through the air toward me, wafting off that fat, blood-filled tongue inside him. It smells hot and terrible, like jagged metal left to rust in the sun. Not like a woman's breath, cool and moon filled. In my head, I correct his grammar. A midwife's work *was* never done, even when she herself *was* ready to burst.

He looks at me. "Do you know what that means? A 'midwife'?"

"No."

He smiles tenderly. Clearly, giving explanations is where he finds himself most comfortable. "A midwife was someone who helped women give birth. Back then, it wasn't always men."

I try to imagine and can't. I can't imagine birth at all. I know it happens in the bedroom, but when I think of it, the only image I can see is a closed door.

Silas smiles down at the picture again. "A lot of us knew each other before the war. We used to drive around together to teach people about sustainable mushroom farming. To most of them, we were a bunch of hippies, never mind that we all had master's degrees. Not me, I was still in college, but still, I was planning on it. The day that picture was taken, half the people at Isaac's lecture came outside to watch the birth instead. A doctor from the university clinic came over to help, but Nola wouldn't let him near her. She—" He laughs, genuinely. I look at him in surprise. He shakes his head. "She didn't trust any of them as much as she trusted Pamela. Pamela grew up in a commune and had delivered a hundred babies by the time she was eighteen." He straightens his back proudly.

Sitting here, concentrating on the photo album, Silas enters a state of peace I haven't seen in him yet. Some of his drunkenness clears away.

I ask, "What happened to Nola? Does her husband live in the compound?"

"No. She only traveled with us for a little bit, then left when her husband got sent off to fight. He was a good mechanic." Silas puts his finger on the second photo. "This is Arkansas. This is our wedding."

I don't know where these places are, Wyoming and Arkansas. "Why's her face covered?"

"It's a veil. Brides used to wear them back then." Silas chuckles. "During the ceremony, our van got broken into. We didn't have much to steal. All they took was a cooler and the birthing stool. No idea what they wanted with the stool, probably didn't even know what it was. Probably thought it was a toilet."

He turns the pages, telling me the names of more places. In one of the pictures, he's standing with Pamela, his arm around her shoulders. He looks much younger and a lot thicker than he is now. Without the beard, he looks naked and strange. I look up at him.

"Silas?" The name is dry in my mouth.

He lifts his eyebrows.

"How old are you?"

"Sixty-six," he answers.

"Wow," I say. "You've lived thirty-three times as long as I have."

"Yes, I know." He returns to the album.

I should be embarrassed, I suppose. I sound naïve. Of course he knows I'm two. That's the age women are when they get married. And he would have known when I was born. I stare at him while he politely pretends that I didn't just say something idiotic, and a flare of hope sparks within me.

"Silas?"

"Yes?"

"Do all these places still look the same?"

"Um, no. A lot got destroyed." He worries at the plastic coming loose at the corner of the album. Eventually, he adds, "You probably don't know much about the years before we settled here."

The haunting years. He's right, I don't know much. Reese doesn't talk about it, and none of the women lived through it.

"All I know is the curse killed all the women who came before us," I say.

"Right. And . . . " He pauses. It doesn't seem like he wants to go on.

I prod him, as gently as I can, "Why do we live here, away from everyone else?"

"Well, there's not much left of everyone else, to be honest. Countries attacked other countries. Those who had bombs used them. Everyone was scared. And when people get scared, some of them, not all of them, but enough of them, get violent. People blamed other people and hurt them. But that's why we're here, you know? In our community. Trying to make it right again in our small pocket of earth. Make it livable again." He speeds up with enthusiasm. "What I mean is, we're mycoremediating the ground so that it's farmable again. One day it won't just be scientists and farm laborers here, but regular people too. I mean, that was the plan, anyway. It's proving more difficult than we thought. It doesn't help that before the radiation there were a lot of chemicals and microplastics everywhere, poisons. We were destroying the earth long before the plague. Luckily mushrooms have been saving the earth for a long time, taking the poisons out of the dirt. Now we're trying to work together with them. Most people don't go to the really bad radiation areas, but we're here because of our expertise." He smiles. "Our mushroom expertise."

I look at the buildings in the photos, so shiny and new, and imagine them crumbling or leveled entirely like the houses around us. "So that's why we can't cross the wall? Because of radiation?" I ask finally.

"Yes. Radiation has a tendency to . . . change a person's body and make them sick. We've taken measures to make sure the compound is safe. Mostly." He points to a picture of Pamela with mountains in the background. "This was taken in Colorado. It might still look the same there. Most of the trees have burned down there, I bet."

I stare at the picture, though I'm not really looking at it. I've craved something like this my whole life, but after what Silas told me, it's hard to focus. I think he is telling me something the other women don't know. Surely, my mom didn't. "And I'll get radiation on me if I touch another woman's mushrooms?"

"No, no, you're conflating two things. The radiation in the woods is man-made. The reason you can't touch other mushrooms is that they're highly competitive. They'll try to invade you even if it kills you in the process."

I try not to look at the place where Teaghan touched me, or think of the woman who walked away from her skeleton. I try not to remember how good it felt to be invaded.

Silas taps a photo. "Look at this one! I love this look on Pamela's face here. Ah, what I wouldn't give for a Mountain Dew."

About three-fourths of the way through the album, Pamela isn't pregnant anymore. The pictures become more sporadic. The seasons in the background cycle through faster. At the last page, he stalls, holding the album close so I can't see it. When he sets it down on his lap, I see that the last photo is of Pamela and a small child. Her child, I realize. I lean closer. The child has short hair the color of Pamela's and is missing a few front teeth. I can see the wet bulge of tongue pushed up against the gap.

Silas is staring at me intently. He's waiting for something specific, but I don't know what he wants from me. He drops his gaze. "There's something else you should know about me. It's about Pamela too. Pamela was pregnant many times. Six, to be exact. We lost all of them except the last." He sighs. "It's very hard to talk of those times. The war is a tragedy I share with all the men here, but this is a tragedy I share with no one else." He shakes his head, still staring at the ground. "The losing, the gaining, the losing, the gaining. After a while, it all feels like losing. Whenever she got pregnant, going to the doctors felt useless. Building up hope felt like self-sabotage, since it was always followed by the next time she filled the toilet, the bathtub, everything, with blood. Neither of us believed that we would be parents. But the chance for it, you know? We couldn't just . . . not take the chance. But the anxiety of making another baby, of waiting for its life to end, even though I wanted to be a dad so bad, it was almost a relief when the baby was gone, because I no longer had to wait for it to happen. Does that make sense? Probably not." He looks up, finally, and

I see in his eyes that he means probably not *to you.* "And then we got Joseph. He was our miracle. The whole thing changed Pamela, and it was painful, but we got Joseph out of it." He holds out his hand. I am meant to lean over and take hold of it. When I don't, he scratches his beard. "I'm glad you're asking questions. If you ever have any more, even if they're about the years before we came here . . . " He pauses. "Especially if they're about those years, don't be afraid to ask. I'll answer as well as I can."

"I wouldn't know where to start."

"That's okay. I just mean in the future." He closes the album and touches the pink roses swirling over the cover. He can't seem to keep his hands off it. "I'm sure it's odd. To live with people who have gone through things you can't wrap your head around. It's hard for us to talk about, but also unhealthy to never mention. You know?" He taps the photo album. "There's something else." His voice is nervous, but pushing, pushing, like a boat nudging onto a beach, almost to its destination. "I think it's time to get you pregnant."

"Oh." It's less a comment and more of a release of noise. I breathe but can't get enough air. "Oh."

Of course. These are the steps of marriage. He won't murder me for trying to escape, and we'll progress to the next stage.

"Don't you think?" he prods gently.

I nod. Anyway, pregnancy is supposed to be when a man and woman get close. It's stupid to be around each other before then. A man is dangerous before pregnancy forms a bond between him and his wife. Silas is more ungainly in this new marriage than I am. It shouldn't be a shock that he wants this done now. Though that is what I'd call it, this numb, electric fog accumulating at the back of my neck. Shock.

"Love begins now." He puts his hand on mine. "Soon," he corrects himself. He touches my face. Runs his fingers down my neck. My skin protests with achy jolts. I swallow, trying to fight against the pleading, insectile hope crawling into his eyes. "I've chosen a face for our child."

I look at him. The women have a system. It depends on a lot of factors: who's getting old, who's died last, who's already had two children, who has a volatile husband. It's not perfect, but it's designed to make sure that there aren't too many daughters waiting around and no husband goes unwed. An unwed husband is dangerous and chaotic.

"Who have you chosen?"

"A face you've lost." He smiles. "Who better to love in the future, than someone you've loved so deeply in the past?"

I look down at his hand trapping mine. It dawns on me that he thinks this is another gift. Silas has defied convention for me. He has chosen our daughter to look like my mother to make me happy. What it means, though, is that when she is grown, I will have to give her up to Reese. She will live her life isolated in a prison of a home until she enters Reese's prison of a home, and Reese will lumber into her room and press her into the mattress and saw off her hair. I should be grateful. I am grateful that Silas didn't kill me after my transgression. He didn't even show much anger. But he's returned home with a different kind of death. One that extends into the next generation. I disentangle from Silas and step away from the couch and turn toward the clarity of the darkness so I can catch my breath again.

Behind me, Silas says, "It will get better after this. Easier too. I promise. Love makes life worth living."

# CHAPTER EIGHT

Silas tries sex for the first time that night. He gets something out of it, and I do not. He pulls me under him and props himself up so that his weight isn't all on me, but it's still enough weight to make me want to squirm away.

Sex is fine. Not horrible. It's uncomfortable. Not physically; his body fits into mine after a brief adjustment. It's uncomfortable like being bored is uncomfortable, and unsettling and gross because a man is straining so close to my face, soaked in his own miasma, which is soaking me. He tries to kiss me, but stops when my face sours. He buries his head in my shoulder. This is much better. I don't want to look at him.

I wonder how many times Teaghan has had to do this with her husband, or if she ever has at all. My mom said sometimes sex is a normal part of what a man wants, but not always. No one knew if Silas was one of those men. Now I know he is. I am learning, at least.

Silas pulls something out from under his pillow. I try to prop myself up to see it better, but he's still on top of me, blocking my view. It's a purple velvet pouch with gold tassels. A plastic bag inside is poking out of the top.

"What is that?" I ask.

"It's . . . " He clears his throat but doesn't answer.

"What's it say?"

"Crown Royal. It's . . . not important." It's unusual that he doesn't want to talk. Like he's rushing to get somewhere. His jeans are crumpled next to us on the bed. He fishes around in them for his pocketknife, flicks it open, and dips it into the pouch's plastic bag. When he pulls it out again, the blade has a dainty mound of powder on it. He extends the blade out to me. "Here."

I lift my eyes to meet his. He nudges the knife so its point pricks my lips. "Open your mouth."

There's a heavy command in his voice. Not gentle, not sweet. I open my mouth.

"Look at me." His eyes are intense. Too wide, like he's looking at something awful. I maintain eye contact with him as he slides the knife into my mouth. He holds it very still. I don't know what to do. I'm scared he's going to cut me. "You have to eat it."

I flick the tip of the knife gingerly with my tongue. He slides the knife out again, slowly against my lip, wiping it clean against the corner of my mouth. It clicks against my teeth.

"Swallow." His voice is so unlike how he's spoken before. My saliva is thick and dry and clotted when I try to swallow. The powdery substance sticks together. My throat muscles work at it, wedge it down. My next breath is a gasp, cut short.

When I pull away from the knife, there's still streaks of black residue on its edge. "Lick it clean."

I don't want to lick it clean. I don't want my tongue on the blade anymore. My eyes flicker to him again as I squeeze the blade with my fingers. He says nothing. His eyes stay glued to my mouth. As I lick my fingertips, a few clumps fall onto my hand. So I lick my palm, lick up all of it, like he said to do, and he watches. I don't see the apology he said to me earlier in the day, before night fell, and now it seems to me that his earlier contrition was a mask, and now the mask is sliding off and his true face glows with predatory power and a desire for humiliation. I look away, squeeze my eyes shut, and brace myself as Silas starts sex again. My legs get restless. I stay very still, though, until he's done.

When I open my eyes, he looks embarrassed. Even more embarrassed than I am. My shame was sudden and strange and fleeting, a source of temporary confusion, but he looks like he has encountered a sin he has committed before, one he has never truly been able to root out of himself. Reese looked like that, sometimes, after he was violent. Not always, but when he did wear that face, I knew he'd be nicer for a few days. I avoided him even more then, resentful that I had to stick around to let him pay off his debts, one almost-kind word at a time.

I gag a little. A small cough. I can taste the loaminess of it in my nostrils. Silas looks away. I do my best to recover. If I act nonchalant, maybe I will feel more nonchalant later. He dresses with his back to me and leaves the room.

The swamp-funk of him is all over my side of the bed. Now

my side smells like his too. Mammalian glands and oily follicles, pore excretions. Ugh.

That night, when we are both in bed, I am certain I know what the powder is. My mom said Reese fed her hers during dinner. It sounded more polite and solemn than what happened to me, but she told me to be prepared because some men have their own way of doing things.

Through the rumble of Silas's agitated snoring, a memory surfaces of a woman in front of the neighbor's house, scooping dirt into her mouth. My mom told me when a woman is trying to get pregnant, eating dirt helps. I hadn't thought to ask who it helps. The man? The baby? The woman?

I don't feel like I'm allowed to leave the bed when Silas is in it. He's never said anything, but it's implied. I reach out and touch Silas while he is sleeping. Once, twice. I feel his heat on the tips of my fingers. He's ruthlessly, deliriously hot, like touching the outside of a bathtub while a fire rages inside.

I roll off the bed and land on the floor as quietly as I can. I tiptoe out of the bedroom. In the backyard, I can feel the cold grass through the round holes in the bottom of my slippers. I glance back at the house to see if Silas is there. He could be watching from any of the dark, gaping windows.

He wouldn't be. He's sleeping. My heart is beating too hard, and my growths buzz uncomfortably. It is not worth getting caught outside. I can't let Silas think I'm running away again. I don't know what he will do to me, but it won't be good.

I promise myself, after this, I won't go outside again. Not without Silas telling me I can first.

I crouch down and grab a stick and stab at the hard earth. When a piece comes loose, I shove it into my mouth. I expect it to taste like spring and rain and happiness. Life and earth and fertility and moisture. Of coming home and being born and the mothers who lie in the ground and bloom in the darkness. Of composition and decomposition and feeding. Flooding and clouds, movement and water. After-life and life-before.

It doesn't taste like any of that. It tastes like grit and sticks to my teeth the rest of the night.

When I next wake, Silas is standing at the side of the bed, leaning over me. A hiccup of panic lodges in my throat, but I can't move. He grabs the back of my neck and wrenches my head back. He slides his fingers into my mouth. Spreads them and pries my jaw open. It widens more than I thought possible. He inserts something else along my tongue, something long and thin, cold and metal. He slides it back farther. He slides it back too far. He stabs my throat until it ruptures.

When I startle awake, Silas is still sleeping next to me. It was just a dream. Still, my throat is sore.

The next day, my stomach hurts. I'm a little shaky. I find walking helps a little. So I walk through the house. When I reach a dead end, I turn and walk some more.

When Silas comes home, I tell him that I feel weird. "I think I'm pregnant."

"No, no." He rubs the back of his neck. "It's too early for that. But . . . " He pauses shyly. "I'm glad you're excited."

It's not excitement. I just feel weird. He insists it's completely normal.

After dinner, I sit next to him the rest of the night in misery, stifling the urge to keep walking.

The next night, after dinner, Silas stays downstairs, but I am drawn upstairs. He likes me to stay with him all evening, after he returns from work. I think he will call me down, be angry at me for not staying with him. But he doesn't. Or he does, and I don't hear him.

It feels good to walk. I wander and wander, circle through the dark parts of the house, the unchanging parts where the air doesn't move much and the sun never leaks in. I churn. That is what it feels like. I am churning the gut of the house, like I am something bad it ate, like I am an upset to its digestive system. It soothes me. Over and over, the churning.

Sometimes, when I look up or move from a place of darkness into a pocket of light, I see a flash of shadow ahead. I squint, though the figure disappears if I look at it too hard. I blink, rapidly, and it dawns on me that this whole time I've been walking, I've been following someone else.

# CHAPTER NINE

Days and then more days pass as I watch out the windows for Teaghan. She never visits. At least, not while I'm looking for her.

One late morning, I see Maggie crossing the neighbor's lawn toward the house. I could pretend not to see her. Pretend to be sleeping, or dead, but there's no point. And anyway, I'm glad to see someone who isn't Silas. Even if it's Maggie.

I wait outside the front door, in the shade of the porch. She totters into the yard, her curls slipping out of her baseball hat and bouncing around her shoulders. She's holding a clay pitcher of water, which sloshes out of the spout and stains her shirt. Her apron is tied across her round middle, squeezing her waist. Instead of slimming her down to the size of her husband's first wife, which is the reason she wears it, she just looks uncomfortable.

She grips the bill of her hat, like the whole thing will blow away if she doesn't hold it tight in her fist. She clutches hold of everything with that intensity. The pitcher in the crevice of her arm, the hat, the apron in her other fist, lifted out of the reach of the weeds. When she cuts through the yard, she stomps over the grass with exaggerated steps, as if walking over the unpaved ground is too much for her. As if, out of her regular environment, she's barely able to keep herself contained. She looks up only when she's directly in front of me, her brow furrowed like I've only appeared to bother her.

I cross my arms. "Hello, Maggie. Didn't bring Eloise with you?"

She sweeps some of her loose strands of hair behind her ear. "She's over at a friend's house." She doesn't mention which friend, pointedly assuming that I wouldn't know who she was talking about anyway. She brushes past me, grunting in irritation, and elbows her way inside the house. "I'm exhausted! Terrible, you living out here in the middle of nowhere. I'd go crazy if I lived so far from everyone else." She waves her hands out in front of her, warding off the idea like a swarm of mosquitoes. "Though I guess you're used to that sort of thing." She stands in the entranceway, blocking the doorway, so I'm stuck outside in the heat, and glares at the chandelier, the staircase, and the rugs. "Your house is too big. There's too much to clean."

"I don't mind." I don't tell her that I don't clean it, though it might be clear to her already.

"Oh well. I suppose the lake is nice." She points the ends of her mouth down to make it obvious that she doesn't actually think it is. She turns to me. "Well. I'm glad to see you alive." She doesn't look glad.

"Oh yeah?"

"I figured you'd be dead by now."

I narrow my eyes at her. "I don't think you're allowed in here." I'm not sure if this is true, but it feels true.

"Oh I know I'm not allowed in here. But the men are working, so who's going to know?" She was like this with Mom too. Mom didn't like to let her into the house too often because she was scared of getting caught by Reese. But Maggie got her way plenty, by bullying Mom and chipping at her guilt. "I brought you a pitcher of water, since you don't come to the stream. But I damn near spilled most of it coming here."

"Silas keeps rain barrels."

"Rain barrels, pah! You need stream water. Nice and filtered and moving, none of that stale taste." She puts the pitcher of water on the floor. I guess she's refusing to carry it any farther. "I'm going to need that back, by the way." She takes off her baseball hat and hangs it on the end of the banister of the staircase, fluffing up her hair with her other hand. "I hate hat hair, but the mugginess is messing with my curls."

It's too bad for Maggie that her foremother didn't wear fancier clothes. Maggie would have been better suited for sundresses and wide-brimmed hats. Instead, Maggie inherited T-shirts and ratty jeans. The only feminine thing she owns is her apron, which has a discreet lace trim on the bottom. Maybe that's another reason why Maggie wears it so religiously. She assesses the house, already deciding what she's going to tell the other women.

"You should really open some windows in here. It's stuffy." I can see the stub of a mealy orange growth cluster on the back of her neck, irritated from the apron string rubbing against it. She probably has a hard time shaving it herself. Maybe Eloise helps. Though I imagine she insists on doing it alone, even if she hurts herself. "Your husband will get sick. Women like the dark, but husbands like the sunlight."

"As you said, my husband isn't home."

"They can tell when they return to a house that's been shut up all day." She shakes her head and lowers her voice as if talking to herself. "It's like you have no self-preservation at all. Honestly, it's a miracle you're still alive. I mean, look at you. You have to shave these off!" She waves her hands in front of my face. "Don't you have a file? A razor? Even a steak knife will do, though it chafes more."

I touch my cheek defensively. "Teaghan doesn't shave."

She lets out a guffaw. "Yeah, exactly. That girl's asking for it. If you know what's good for you, you'll stay away from her." I glare at her and say nothing. Maggie smooths back her hair, and a little smirk emerges on her face. "Well?"

"Well what?"

"Are you pregnant yet?"

I narrow my eyes. "No."

"What's wrong with you?"

"Nothing! It's only been two weeks."

She shrugs. "Well, you're lucky if you can escape the whole pregnancy ordeal, the whole mom thing, without your husband punishing you for it."

"That's a mean thing to say about Eloise."

"It has nothing to do with her. Having a baby breaks you. Breaks your body almost clean apart. And your mind is never the same, either. It's tough."

My tongue is ready to lash out, but the look on her face stalls me. She looks so vulnerable, some deep-rooted memory running through her. My eyes scan a wrinkled patch that spreads over her chin and down her neck, cradled by her cleavage. A section where her growths are trying to germ. The denuded skin exudes a silty, scarlet discharge that weeps against her shirt. Poor Maggie. It must be exhausting trying to rid her body of its fungal excess.

"Well, all right then." Maggie looks behind her, trying to find an excuse to excavate deeper into the house. "The women wanted me to remind you to have a baby as soon as possible. I did that. They'll be relieved." She roughly sweeps past me again, though she has plenty of room, and heads out the door.

She stops in the doorway and tips her head outside to inspect the porch, like she's suspicious of it. "I wonder if Eloise has driven Becca crazy."

"You left her with Rebecca? At Reese's house?"

"Yeah, what's wrong with that?"

I stare at her. "What if Reese comes home and finds someone besides his wife in the house?"

She laughs, too long and too hard. She presses her hand to her chest, appalled and surprised and delighted. "Wait, you don't know?" She laughs even harder. Her uproarious derision echoes through the chambers of the house so that its many empty spaces laugh in unison. I feel the heat rising around my mouth as I blush angrily. "Until you came along, I was a regular kid. Mom was a regular mom. Reese was a normal man. We all went in and out of that house like regular people. And now, Becca does the same."

I feel a dizzying pressure. "What do you mean?"

Her smile is like an egg cracking, and I wonder what's going to hatch out of her mouth. "It wasn't Reese who made you stay inside the house, who married me off early, who took Mom away. It was Silas."

I take a step back. "Silas?"

"Silas gave Reese specific instructions to never let you or Mom out of the house. He wanted you to grow up that way. Reese even said it was a lot of trouble for one girl. I doubt he would have even listened if Silas wasn't some big shot in the lab." I put out my hand to make her stop talking. She doesn't. "It ruined Mom's life. And then Reese killed her for it. That's what they do. Mark us with lanterns so no one questions anything. Most of the women don't think it's true, but it's awfully coincidental when women start glowing. The bruises are always the same size as the husband's hand. I guess I should have seen it coming, but I didn't." She shakes her head. "You should see Reese now. He's pathetic with grief." She drops her hands to her hips. "Bet you wouldn't have gotten Reese so quickly that morning if you had an inkling what death meant. What being motherless meant."

"Maggie—"

"But it wasn't a big deal for you to lose her. You were going to lose her anyway. Out here, you'd barely ever see her again. I was supposed to get her back that day."

I shake my head. I don't understand. I clutch my head, then my stomach. A familiar rusty dread congeals in my chest. "I have to go lie down."

"You should." She cocks her head. "You look terrible."

# CHAPTER TEN

Silas is the reason I was isolated all my life. There is nothing I can do with this anger.

I am a glutton for the house when Silas isn't in it. It comes alive when he is gone. I've never had so much room to roam, so much to look at. Some rooms with windows are transient, filling with sun that softens, goldens, and recedes at the close of day. Others are steeped in permanent night, permanent stillness.

A fear takes root in me, alongside nausea. An unnamable, insatiable anxiety. It is connected to the powder I ingested, somehow, I am certain of it. The desire to get up, to move, to scream. It resurfaces, like my body has some need I don't understand yet, something beyond hunger for food or sleep. I need movement. The feeling is small, a kernel, then it grows. When it's too much for me, I like the stagnant, inner rooms, the rooms of solid darkness.

Each night, before we sleep, Silas takes out the Crown Royal pouch and feeds me a spoonful of dust. I tell him on the third night that I can do it myself, that he needn't bother, but he says the whole point is for us to do it together. I don't agree with that. The whole point is I eat the dust, and I'd rather hold the knife myself and eat it without anyone staring at me. Well, truthfully, I'd rather not eat it at all, and maybe he knows this. Each day, my stomach hurts a little more. I walk to soothe myself.

"The dust makes me sick," I tell him one night as he puts the knife to my mouth.

"No, no. It doesn't make you sick. It's just nerves."

I open my mouth to say something more, but he slides the knife in, a little crooked. If I move my mouth I will bite the blade. I am startled and forget what I was going to say. I swallow what's in my mouth.

I wonder where Teaghan is. If she is mad at me, if she's given up on me after I abandoned her.

I can't walk around on most nights. Silas expects that his wife stick near him. The foremothers must have been more similar to the men than to us, the way he remembers them and expects me to act. The other men have been trained out of these expectations, but not Silas. I have to be gentle in my training. It has been so many years since he had a wife, I can't change his mind in one night, it would break him. And then what would become of me?

Nine days after Maggie visits, while Silas is at work, while I'm circling the house, I wander into a room of glass. It holds a dozen mahogany cases, all with glass doors and insides lined with mirrors. Half the cases are filled with crystal glasses, the others with glass women. I stay in there for a while, watching how the light folds inside these objects and turns vibrant, how the sun reflects off the mirrors and suspends the room and me in a bubble of white iridescent light. I am still suspended when Teaghan taps at the window.

It surprises me, but only for a moment. I open the window, which takes me an inordinate amount of time because of how lodged it is in its swollen frame. At least, once it's open, I have a reason for panting and my hammering heart. She sweeps aside a few withered insect husks, leans in, and puts her arms over the sill and lies her head on her arms and looks up at me, the stained curtains fluttering around her. I don't know how to interpret the way she's looking at me. No one has looked at me like this before. Her eyes are like sunlit metal. Something deep twists at the bottom of my stomach. It's as brilliant as fear. A pulling, a tugging, a plunging forward.

"You haven't shaved since your wedding."

"Neither have you."

A smile grows on her face, then on mine. I decide right then that I will never shave again. I had been putting it off, trying to avoid the subject, glad Silas hasn't mentioned it. Even if he does, now I am sure I will refuse. He will have to pin me down himself, and I'll scream and scratch. I don't ever want to feel that brain fog, that horrible aching confusion in my skin. And I want to always be able to draw looks like this from the wild, tangled woman in front of me with a viscous, vermillion rind around her mouth and caps growing up the side of her face like a pastel staircase.

"You didn't come the night I asked you to meet me," Teaghan says.

"No. Silas caught me. Now he's trying to get me pregnant."

"I wouldn't do that if I were you. It's harder to sneak out with a baby strapped to your chest."

"I'm sure those are his thoughts exactly." I bite my lip. "I don't have a choice. None of us do."

She tilts her head. "Just don't swallow his dust. Pocket it in your cheek and spit it out later."

"Does that work?"

"Not as well as not putting it in your mouth at all, but it's better than swallowing it. It's kept me clean so far." Her tank top's blue strap divides her bare skin from the rubbery canker sores on her shoulder. The strap pushes on the growths, forcing them to cave in, and I wonder if it hurts. I have an urge to reach out and move the strap, to relieve her pressure. To gently thumb the ripening growths. I try to goad my hand forward, but in the end I can't. She grins. "Anyway, I came over because I found something."

I smell her dewy effluvium, her hard and chitinous crust. I lean closer. "What did you find?"

She pulls a set of keys out of her shorts pocket. Reese had one. A single one with which he used to lock his bedroom door at night.

"Someone got too drunk and lost them last night in the street." She dangles them off the end of her finger, shakes them to make them tinkle. She sees the shock on my face and her teeth, white and pale, bloom inside the moon of her face. "Don't worry. No one will suspect the likes of me. Why would one of us want to go into the lab, anyways? Wouldn't we all die?"

"Well, wouldn't we?"

She looks at me. "Do you believe we will?"

I pause. "I don't know."

"I don't believe anything they say." She takes a few steps back and beckons me to follow. "Will you come with me?"

Once she asks, I have no choice. Of course I'll go with her. If she's going somewhere, anywhere, I'll go with her.

"We can't go now. All the men are working."

"It's Sunday."

"Sunday?" I turn to look behind me, into the room of suspended light. "But Silas is at work."

She shakes her head. "He's not. I've been watching the lab all morning."

"Where is he?"

"How should I know?"

I look behind me, into the house. Is he here without my knowing? I've been circling the house, around and around with abandon, thinking he wasn't home. I haven't run into him. I suppose he could be on the third floor, or the second. Have I gone upstairs lately? I turn back to Teaghan. "You're sure?"

She nods, and I give her my hand. She grabs my wrist. Her violet-dark chill floods into me. I grab on to the windowsill to support myself. She yanks me hard, through the window, and it is all I can do not to tumble out, laughing.

In the yard, I stumble. The sky and the ground swim around

me. All I can concentrate on are the sticky curls on her fingertips. The fleshy knots that dot her knuckles. A pulse rises out of her and sinks into me, and my growths thrum deep into my bones. She pauses to let me stabilize. I concentrate on my breath, and it's easier to find my way through the overwhelm than it was the last time she touched me. I've been waiting for this.

I look up. Teaghan takes it as a signal to pull me forward, across the lawn. We dash down the street. She runs like someone younger than she is. My chest bumps with excitement as I follow behind, trying not to step on her feet. She throws a smile at me every few steps and laughs. I forget about how ungainly I am and find myself laughing too.

I shout at the back of her head, "Why are we running?"

All she does is laugh harder and kick up her heels higher as she runs and spins me through more yards, dodging between houses. The mulberry fungus growing from the small of her back rides her shirt up, pushing out from the top of her shorts like fresh plums. They slide and ripple with the movement of her hips and something inside me tightens and tightens.

When we reach the lab, the gate is locked. She slides the biggest key into the keyhole. It takes her a bit of jiggling and maneuvering, but eventually she turns it, and we hear the click of metal as it unlocks. The men must have built this fence after they arrived. Now that I'm closer, I can see it's made from the bits of other houses. Most of the paint has faded or been sanded off, but some of it is still left.

I run my fingers over the words carved into the door. "What does it say?"

"Who knows?" She rolls her eyes. "Probably just a Bible verse. Help me open it, it's heavy."

I heave the door with her. I groan, "Why's it so stuck?"

The door yanks open and throws us both off-balance. We each give a yelp of alarm. I look around to see if anyone is looking. It's daytime. I shouldn't even be out of the house, let alone this close to the center road. I promised myself I'd never leave the house, and I did it so readily, so thoughtlessly.

She grabs my arm and yanks me into the yard. "Shh! Someone just came out of their house."

I duck, even though we are inside the fence already, and whisper, "Who?"

"One of the men. Help me close the door."

It's much easier to close than it was to open. Teaghan locks it again. We both turn around, hearts pounding. I look around me at the work yard. It's enormous. There has to be a hundred greenhouses fading into the distance behind the lab. Many of their windows are ill-fitted, the gaps covered by plastic tarps that bang and warp in the wind. Their roofs rise and fall against each other, cresting toward the blackness, then falling away. It is like a sea of glass, a sea of trapped sunlight.

We walk down the sidewalk path. Logs line it, all in a row, like the beginning of a nursery rhyme. Fungus warps the silhouettes of the logs into monstrous shapes, like many fingers, many bony toes. Reaching up, searching for something. The men have been tending mushrooms right next to us. They demanded that we stay away from the mushrooms that grow in old houses and keep our distance from each other, but this whole time, spores have been swirling into the homes where we cook our food and raise our children.

When we get to the building, Teaghan uses another key, and it goes much more smoothly than the gate. I see myself in the mirrored windows and then look away. Before we step over the threshold, I cover my mouth. I can't help it.

Teaghan says, "You don't have to do that. I came in and out just fine. Nothing got me."

"I thought you just got the key last night?"

"I meant, last *Saturday* night." I give her a look, and she shrugs, cat-satisfied. The inside is dark and cool. I can hear a rumble and purr. So strange, like odd animals lying in wait. "Grab a lantern."

They are lined up against the wall. Teaghan picks one up. The sticks jostle inside the glass. I jerk back and hold my hands out to protect myself. The thought of the lamp smashing against me is enough to make my forehead sweat. I think of my mom, glowing on her bed, and the grief comes out of nowhere, a throbbing cramp in my stomach.

Hoarsely I say, "No thanks."

She shrugs and brings the lantern back to herself, the green glow lighting her face from below, flooding the folds of gills protruding from her cheeks. At the sight of them, my stomach squeezes and twinges below my belly button.

The lab begins as a long hallway. Rooms branch to the sides, and from their open doors, I spy the strange machinery of science: bizarre jars filled halfway with peculiar liquids, the odd tools of measurement, the odd tools of containment. Folding tables and hard chairs. It smells sharp. But despite the acrid bleach pungency, there is also a smell of earth and decomposition.

I look into a room and catch a tang of deep-seated rust. Bins of dirt lie beneath a few lanterns.

"What are all these things?"

"Microscopes, petri dishes, agar fluid. Things like that."

"How do you know their names?"

"My husband."

I stop walking. "He told you about them? He . . . talks to you like that?"

"No. I know from touching him."

I don't know who her husband is, I realize. I've only seen her on her own. "You know things from touching your husband?"

"Yeah. Don't you? Haven't you changed since you moved in with your husband?"

"No. Or—" I realize she's leaving me behind, and I start walking again. "I don't know. Maybe I have."

"You will, with time. It's a lot harder with men than it is with other women."

I catch a glimpse of her face in the lantern light, and it hits me how strange this is, how like a dream, that I am here with Teaghan, in the lab. I have always wanted to go with her, whenever she wandered off from the center road, and here I am, in the last place I thought we'd go. I wonder if I would have joined her before I left Reese's house. As much as I wanted to, I don't think I would have. I would have worried about the consequences for my mom. Reese would've hurt her.

Teaghan's right. It's hard to sneak out after you have a baby, not just because of having one strapped to your chest, but because you'll always worry about the consequences for those you love. I will spit out the dust. I won't get pregnant.

She pauses when she reaches the next room. Her lantern hovers over a sign with four letters. The two in the middle are circles. They look like empty eyes staring back at us. Teaghan shoves open the door. We're in the largest room yet, larger than any of the rooms in Silas's house, even.

"Careful," she says. "There's a big pit in the center. Don't fall in, you'll get really hurt."

"What was this place?"

"I don't know. I don't know what they possibly could have done in here."

We step in. The smell of old cement and ensnared moisture hangs in the air, and another smell, like how I imagine the sea to be: a rich rot and the density of salt and creature. There are a few windows on the ceiling. Long pillars of light drape down but lose strength quickly and barely enter the room's depths. The dust in the air swirls and flashes white in the pillars that divide the darkness.

I peer harder into the void, trying to find the shape of what I'm seeing. My mouth fills with musty, fermented chill. Teaghan walks forward, swinging her lantern haphazardly. She pauses, and I can see by the dim light of her lantern that she's paused in front of a bed. On top of the bed is a lump covered by a blanket. She pauses, looks meaningfully at me, and leans down. For a second, I think she's about to crawl into the bed herself. She touches the top of the lump, her hand outspread. My breath hitches in my throat in confusion. A violent shiver threatens to topple me over. The smell of this place is really getting to me.

I look again at the bed, at the lump, and gasp, "Let me . . . let me see her."

"You knew right away too?"

I don't know what it is, not really. I said *her* because it felt right. If I try to grasp concrete thoughts, they disperse before I can catch them. Something giddy and glowing is unfolding inside me. Something like sorrow, something like fear or a burst of pleasure.

My brow wrinkles, I want to cover my face. I inhale, then repeat, "Let me see her."

I can barely see the top of the bed. But when Teaghan lifts the blanket, the salty, muscular, animal smell balloons out and hits me with a heady funk. Teaghan moves her lantern closer. The light falls over her in a green veneer. The woman is barely contained by the small bed, a child's bed. Her stomach is distended. The slits of her eyes are like two even incisions chiseled on a white pebble. The gray mushrooms between her lips force her jaw so agape that the corners of her mouth are split open, her lips shiny with gelatinous scum. Her dark hair is streaked with gray, though she doesn't look very old. Her eyes stare unblinking at the ceiling, bulging in permanent surprise.

"A foremother?" I put my hand on my chest. She is an ancient, mythical being. She is a tender, broken thing.

"Yeah." Teaghan turns behind her, swinging her lantern away. "They're all here."

"All of them?" I look out into the large room. For a moment, I'm unmoored, floating among the distant lights. The foremothers have been here this entire time, and I didn't even know. I want to kiss the foremother's temple, her forehead, and put my hand softly against her neck. I want to cry into this ancestor's mouth. I want to push my palm against her throat and see if she is alive enough to swallow down my moisture and salt. I want to tell her that everything will be okay, and for it to be true, and I want to hear her whimper in relief. "I thought they were all gone. I thought we were the only women left on earth."

The foremother stares up at the ceiling. I want to hold her close. Is she in pain? I have a deep urge to pull her off the bed and bring her to my chest and pat down her hair. I am close enough to do it. Her gums are fuzzy with spores, and her teeth so blackened she looks like she's missing most of them. The mushrooms that extend out of her mouth are wet and glossy, like exposed organs. She reminds me of the moon, with all its nights of illuminated swelling and all its nights of airy decay.

"Whose foremother is she?"

"Can't you tell?"

I shake my head no.

"She's yours."

I look again and I do see my face in hers. Of course, I have never seen my own face wearing this swollen expression, seen such growths explode out of my own mouth. Pamela's face is warped so badly that her jaw has shifted out of place, must have severed its connection to the skull. Our hair, though, is the same. Her shirt is bunched up, showing off her lumpy, distended stomach. I try to pull her shirt down, but it's too small to fit over her rippled girth. I remember her picture in the photo album. "Is she pregnant?"

Teaghan shakes her head. "No. They're all like that. I think it's the fungus."

"That's all fungus in there?"

"Yeah. I think it crammed itself into all the empty spaces it could."

Teaghan shifts, and so does the glow. I can't see Pamela anymore, only the bottom of Teaghan's face. She asks, "You want to see the rest?"

I follow her. There are more women lined up, sleeping in beds, stomachs bulging. I stop at one woman's bedside since it has a lantern resting on it and peer closer. Her profile is hidden by a lace cloth over her face. Like Pamela's bridal veil. Her long neck is bared to show a thin necklace with a heart pendant. She's grim and serious, her hair pinned back, her mouth yawning open to make room for the dark swarm in her mouth. I bend over, so close I can smell her strange breath. Close enough that if I leaned in more, I'd be kissing her.

"They're so pretty."

I touch the rim of one of the mushrooms at her mouth, then pull my finger away. Dust, wet, and grimy. Pregnancy dust. One of the pustules on the roof of her mouth gives a soft burp. The intestinal mist rises from her mouth and fogs my face. She smells like she's been pickled. Parts of her skin are living, parts of her are dried and hardened. I have the urge to lick my finger, but I restrain myself.

"Women were always trying to change the color of their mouths and eyes. Make themselves look more beautiful, I guess? Nowadays, no one tries to look beautiful. We just try to look like them," Teaghan says.

"Them?" I ask.

"The foremothers. Beauty isn't what gives women power anymore. It's nostalgia." She flicks the toes of the woman in front of her. "The men like to pretend that it's before the haunting years. Before the war."

The lace covering the foremother smooths her so she's just an outline, the specter of a woman. She wears thin slippers with pearls sewn into them. The nodules of her toes strain against the fabric, threatening to pop through, her overgrown nails pushing so that the top of the slipper is no longer round but jagged and clawlike. I reach out to adjust one, but fail to get it placed better on her feet.

"Why are they all wearing veils?"

"They're not veils, they're shrouds. Her husband probably died, so there's no reason to make her descendants. See how skinny and shriveled she is? I think they do something to preserve the ones they want to keep."

I frown. "How many do you think there are in here?"

"A hundred, at least. I haven't actually counted. I don't like to stay down here too long. It makes me angry."

"Angry?"

"When I think about them like this, all isolated in their own beds where they can't talk to each other, with the men digging into them to get their dust, it makes me sad. But the anger?" She lifts the foremother's shroud and leans down. For a second, I think she's going to kiss her. She stares into the foremother's bulging eyes. "That's from them. They're the ones that are angry."

"Why would they be angry?"

"They want to change."

"Change? Into what? How do you know how they feel?"

Teaghan shrugs. She drops the shroud and keeps walking. I touch the foremother and close my eyes. I swear I can't feel anything.

"Look." Teaghan calls from a few beds away. "Here's your mom's foremother."

My heart beats faster as I move closer. She's not wearing a shroud. She's lying on the table, and there is a circular metal tool in her mouth. The corners of her lips are sliced and her jaw is pried open too wide.

"What's inside her?"

"It was like that last week too. Augustina is getting pregnant." She nods toward the foremother. With my mother dead, and Reese remarried, a new baby who will grow up to look like his current wife, Rebecca, needs to be raised as a replacement. No one knows that I'm trying to do this as well. I should tell Teaghan, but I don't. It won't matter if I keep spitting out the dust anyway. Mushrooms grow inside the foremother's cheeks and gums, stretching her lips as they balloon outward like the petals of a blooming flower. The circular tool leaves space in the center so I can see into the cavern of her mouth. Blanched pustules the size of knuckles grow on the lining of her throat, like another row of teeth. And then another row, pale and bald, some darkened with spots of tar, spiral farther down the cave of her esophagus. Some of the pustules have been sliced open, dust streaking the skin, like it's been scraped out.

I wanted to see my mom's face one last time, but not like this. I shouldn't be here. Whenever I dream of my mother now, she'll be sliced wide and scraped hollow.

"Do you want to see my foremother?" Teaghan asks gently.

"Yes." I step back, grateful for the offer.

She's not far away. Teaghan lifts up her foremother's shroud, but the woman's black hair snags on the intricate design. Teaghan yanks unceremoniously, and the woman's hair flings back like a mass of spiders skittering over her face. The foremother's face is hollower than Teaghan's. I don't know if it's because her foremother was so skinny in her last living days, or if it's an effect of lying in here for so long. Her eyelids are half-open, and I can see how enlarged and black her pupils are. Something preserved and sweet, something from the underworld, suspended between ghost and woman.

"She's pretty," I say. "Extra pretty."

"Mm-hmm."

On the underside of the shroud, where it once hovered over the foremother's mouth, a black cloud clings to the cloth, as if her last breath stained the lace. The dark dust of the spores speckles her cracked-dry lips. A streak reaches from her mouth toward her eye, like a spreading vein. The mushroom caps crowd against one another, squeeze to find the air and breathe spores out of the open hole of her body. Her lips outspread, her mouth swollen as wet fruit. The feeling comes over me again. I want to comfort her. Kiss the corner of her eye, kiss her temple, kiss the corner of her split lip. Take my fingertip and circle it around one of these ripe mushroom caps protruding in the dark.

I suddenly realize how close Teaghan is standing next to me. She takes a lock of my hair and gently places it behind my ear. My hair isn't straight and silky like hers, it just springs back into place as soon as she lets go.

"Teaghan—"

"You can call me Teacup. That's what my mom called me." Her interruption startles me, and I don't know how to retrieve the sentence I was about to say. "She's dead."

"Oh, I'm sorry."

"It wasn't your fault." Teaghan coolly drops the shroud.

Here, in the dark, Teaghan's girlishness falls away, leaving behind something authentic and raw and unpolluted.

"My mom is dead too," I say.

"I know. I was at her burial. Remember? Why didn't you come to the funeral?"

"Funeral?"

Subtly, at first, then overwhelmingly, I can smell Teaghan. She has an odor like the unfinished basement of my childhood home, where organic debris collected, getting wetter and wetter throughout the rainy season. As a child, I used to peel layers off when I was alone and inhale. The closer I got to the decaying core, the stronger the ripe aroma. Something about the smell excited me then, and it excites me now. I lick my lips nervously. Teaghan leans toward a foremother and pats down the lace.

"I asked someone else to come here with me. She was too scared." She looks up. "But you aren't."

She puts the lantern on the bed. The light spills over the foremother's body and heightens the shadows against Teaghan's mirrored face. Teaghan's skin beads with moisture, shines, becomes more translucent. The surge and rush of her circulatory system, part fluid-rich mycelium, part blood-pumping veins, seethes inside her. Her smell is stronger now, like I'm getting close to her center.

"Coo," she says in a lilting voice. I furrow my brow. "Coo," she says again with her rain-gutter mouth.

Inexplicably, an answer burbles out of me, drawing from the core of my stomach rather than my lungs. "Coo."

Confusion and embarrassment rush up my body. My face burns. I wonder how deeply she can see inside me, how transparent I am to her.

Teaghan says, "Do you ever wonder what we could make on our own?"

I start to shake my head no, but stop. I want to say yes, I want to please her. I want to say the right thing, to make her feel like I'm the one she's been searching for. Make her gasp in surprise and delight. But I have no idea what she's saying. I start shaking my head no again. Her eyes are black and dilated and beautiful. Swollen and glossy.

"Coo," she says again. The spit in the corners of her mouth collects in tiny, delicate bubbles, the smell that blows off her is fermented and yeasty.

She touches my bicep. Her touch is sticky, her fingers daubed with mucus. Belatedly, I think of jerking away, but I can't. I'm frozen, unable to get away, unable to move closer. Her silvery-violet lips are wet with a lustrous sheen of drool. So wet, and so enlarged that they warp her face. I watch them balloon and darken right in front of me, like an eye after it's been punched. I open my mouth in response, then find myself leaning in. My skin feels tight on my cheeks. Stretched taut. My lips spread of their own volition. Her mouth is so close to mine, but not yet touching. Her lush, bready breath envelops me.

Something rises in my throat. At first, I think it must be my tongue unraveling from its base. I don't know where my tongue starts, I realize with alarm. I don't know how deep into my body it goes. I think it must have detached from the top of my pubic bone, and now it's sliding out of me, the whole thick muscle wad of it. My throat separates, yields to it as it rises. It almost feels like vomit, red and ichorous, surging upward. The weirdness and awkwardness of this sensation panics me. I don't want Teaghan to see my tongue fall out of me like that.

Before her mouth touches mine, I gasp, "Stop." I turn my head away, breathless, and gawk at the shrouded woman prone in front of me. I think of all the women around us whose insides swell with growths. I think of Pamela, who needs someone close to her. I think of my mother's foremother, that tool in her mouth. I think of Silas digging into her to find dust for me to swallow, and I go cold. I hold my hand up. "No more."

I step away. When she takes her fingers away from my arm, there's a slick residual thread connecting her to me. The gelatinous string strains as it lengthens, tenses, finally snaps apart with a liquid pop. Teaghan doesn't look right. She's out of proportion, lopsided. Her eyes gleam black and greedy out of her misshapen body. I step back again, breathing hard.

"I have to go. Silas might be looking for me."

She grins. Her lips pull over her face so wide that she exposes all her teeth and her shining gums. I can see the chute of her throat past her wet tongue. "I don't hear him calling." Her voice is low, wooden, like someone trying to speak into a hollow log.

I turn and run in the direction we came from. I don't bother to grab a lantern and end up slamming into a few of the beds, the rattle of stiff bodies against blankets and metal emptying into the dark.

As I scramble against the wall to find the exit, Teaghan shouts after me, "When will I see you again?"

My throat is constricted. Still, I'm able to call out, "Soon. I want to see you soon."

She answers with a swaying yell of laughter.

The outside light is blinding. I run away from the lab, away from Teaghan's changing shape.

Returning home takes forever. When I do get back, I shut

the front door, but I can't shut out the enormity of what happened. I'm scared Silas will come home, or is already home, and will round the corner and see me like this: panting and quivery with inexplicable shame.

I'm so moist. There's so much drool leaking out of my mouth. When I wipe my chin, I see my spit is tinged with blood.

In bed, as Silas sleeps, my fingers extend. Tip by tip, hyphae stretch and form knots. My fingers grow long and search, search, search. They root through the shell of the house, and wind into the earth. Then, in some moist spot, I find someone else's finger. Small and tiny, this other finger digs inside me, burrowing, insistent.

When I wake, my arm is numb. I've slept on it wrong. I straighten it and wait for the slow seep of sensation to return. I pinch the skin, but I can't feel anything. It's like pinching someone else's arm.

# CHAPTER ELEVEN

I hold this secret of Teaghan and the lab close. I am ashamed too. Did I behave the right way? Did I embarrass myself? I keep my thoughts hidden, but my body doesn't keep my secrets.

In the morning, I find a new growth on my wrist. A mulberry fungus, like fresh plums. Teaghan's growths, emerging from me. I tense with dread. Silas will notice. I suddenly wonder if shaving is something the men made up to make us look like their old wives, or something we did to cover our tracks. I go to the mirror with a butcher knife and shave myself. I cry and cry. I shiver and stop crying. Long before the last growths are nubs, I am sick with numbness. The fog is terrible.

At dinner, Silas asks, "What happened?"

"I . . . " I prepared for this. But my throat is dry, the fog too oppressive. I want to lie my head down. "I wanted to be more like Pamela."

"Oh," Silas says, his voice deepening. "Come here." He holds me. My skin is so dead that I barely register his weight, just the impulse to move away from him. "You're just like her, my love. Don't worry. I know you are. Deep down, you are the same. It doesn't matter what you look like."

Soon after, there's a storm. I don't like the electricity in the air. I don't like the numb tingle of my newly shaven body. It gives me headaches. My jaw is sore from clenching.

Silas worries at the window. He puts his hands in his pocket, tilts his head so he can peer up and see the dark clouds.

"That's a lot of lightning." While he stares through the begrimed glass, I stare at the back of his head. Prickles of cold, then heat, wash over my body. I don't know what he's going on about or why. I've stopped listening. He turns to face me. "Is . . . is something funny?"

"No."

"Oh." He clears his throat. "It's just that you're grinning."

"No I'm not," I say, grinning.

He blinks, taken aback. He opens his mouth, then closes it. His hand covers his eyes as he rubs his forehead. "I'm sorry. These storms bring out the worst in all of us." He shifts his eyes over to me, then back out the window. "If the lightning starts to make you feel strange, tell me. I think I should skip work today. I'd get soaked on the way over anyway."

I leave the room. The storm gets worse.

Silas stays home to keep an eye on me. The first day, he follows me around, asking intrusive questions.

"Do you feel extra awake? Is your tongue bigger than normal?"

The second day, he stands in the doorway of whatever room I'm in. Sometimes he whispers, too quietly for me to hear what he's saying. On the third day, he sits on the couch, watching the rain and the lake-lake stretch. For days he watches. Then one day he stops. He grabs a stark, wooden footstool meant for reaching high shelves in the pantry, and pulls it in front of the blank TV on the wall and watches the emptiness reflected on its surface until his face empties. After two days of this, his face hardens in anger. I think I should probably tell him to stop staring into the TV, that it isn't good for him, but I am afraid he will turn his hard anger on me.

Eventually, that's exactly what he does. As I put a bowl of fermented grain porridge in front of him, murmuring that he should eat, he grabs my wrist and jerks me toward him.

"Open your mouth. Wider, wider." He pulls me so my chin is against his beard. He repeats himself, too slow, too loud for how close he is to me, "Wider."

I am startled, and I do as he says. He grabs my jaw and sticks his fingers into my mouth. His face juts too close, breathing hard, his volcanic breath is caustic against my skin. The blood surges in his throat, bringing out the man he kept buried from me but was there all along. His fist is as tight as a vice against my teeth. My mouth has been tender, and it hurts more than it should. His fingers poke and probe and smash my lip. My eyes trail water. His fingers come away black.

"I know what this means. Do you think I don't know what this means?" Silas locks eyes with mine. I don't know how to answer, because I don't know what it means. My heartbeat is a bell tolling through me, rattling my insides. "What's her name, huh? Give me her name."

I squeeze my eyes shut. I can't control my mouth with him squeezing it like that, couldn't say a word even if I wanted to. All day her name lingers in my skull. His hand gets tighter, his nails dig into my gums. He wants me to complain, I'm sure of it, but he won't let me move my mouth. I try to pull away, gently, but something strange happens. An image erupts painfully inside my head. Inches deeper and deeper into the core of my brain, until I see it clearly. Swarming cicadas infected with Massospora. Their genitals and abdomens falling off, a white plug of spores bulging in place of their lost parts. The dismembered cicadas drag themselves toward each other. Half-eaten, barely functioning, brainwashed by psilocybin and amphetamines, on the brink of death, and all they want is to fuck.

Silas pushes me away. My neck snaps back under his force. As my mouth radiates pain, I try to regain my bearing.

"Ugh." He sniffs his hand and sneers, then wipes it on the back of the couch, leaving ashy streaks. "Disgusting. Leave the food."

His eyes are locked on me as I set the bowl on the floor. I stand there, not knowing what to do, panicking. I can feel his hate radiating off him like heat. I reach out and touch his knuckle and a thought shudders through my brain the way ivy burrows into the sides of crumbling brick houses. It is grit underneath my skull, sandpapering the soft folds and fleshy ducts there: her nature will make her leave me.

Silas slumps. He turns away from me and stares at the TV again. I know this pattern all too well. Violence simmers inside him. His feeling of sudden defeat will only make it worse. Next time, he won't let go. And if, one day, he finds Teaghan at the window, we will both die. He can't suspect me of betrayal. I have to stop this now.

All my life, I've had to learn about men so I could survive, so I could be something a man wants to keep around. I draw on that knowledge now. I close my eyes. I invoke a ghost, I invoke an angel. I invoke the dead wife. I think of the photos of Silas and Pamela. Their arms around each other, their teeth shining, their eyes shining. The pictures of Pamela in all the places they've been together. I feel her growing inside me like a light, a light the color of discolored photos, the color of Massachusetts and Nevada, of bridal veils and stolen birth stools. I think of what it's like to be ancient and immeasurably sad and dissatisfied. I shine her out of me and get on my knees and close my eyes and bow my head like someone chastened. When I lift my face and open my eyes, he's staring at me. He looks raw, startled. A little scared. It isn't beauty or fear that gives us power, it's nostalgia.

I soften my voice like I've heard done to a wounded child. "Silas?"

"Is it . . . what's wrong?" he asks.

"Silas, haven't you known me all your life?"

I blink slowly, wearing someone else's placid face. I don't

know what she was like, but I try to disembody myself and hope that it's enough for him to fill in the blanks with his own memory. He reaches out with shaky hands. He grips the edge of my shirt, grips it too tight, like he wants to touch me but is frightened. He leans his forehead against my throat, and another image worms into me, this time of a man. Tyler. The man's name is Tyler. He doesn't look good. He will die soon. His shirt's unbuttoned, showing his gaunt belly, his rib cage. His bare feet are muddy, as are his knees.

"Do you remember," Tyler asks, scratching his throat like speaking hurts, like the ghost of the rope is already around his neck, "when we first found Derek's wife in the barn? We were so horrified that something like her could exist, and that he kept her from us. We were so close to killing him. Now just about everybody has their own wife. Do you think when we burned her, her spores, I don't know, got into us? Brainwashed us?"

"Silas, Silas," I say gently, like Mom would console me when I got hurt. She couldn't soothe me with anything but her voice, but I smooth his hair and comb away his bad memories. "Silas, Silas."

When he drags me close to his face with a whimper and a drawling need, I can tell I have invoked Pamela. Or, if not her, I've invoked something that he remembers and likes. In several of the pictures, she and Silas were kissing. But he is disgusted by my mouth, so I tilt my face down, so he doesn't think about my mouth. So he doesn't think about the differences between she and I. He lifts me by my shirt until I'm standing. He holds my sides with his hands. He envelopes me in his arms, lays his head at my chest. He inhales me, then stops, because I don't smell like her. But my hair is like hers. So he takes it in his hands and presses it against his face and inhales again.

"Your mouth hymenium . . . " His voice is muffled against my shirt. "Are you changing because of me?" He says it with such tender hopefulness. I pat his head, grateful he's not looking at my face. It's my duty to do this for him. We are all unhappy. Who am I to think that I could have something I want. He lifts me and directs my legs so that they wrap around his torso. He starts to say, "Remember . . . " Then stops, because of course I don't.

I say, "I remember."

I am a theater. I am a shape-shifter. I am the girl whose father cut off her hands, I am the three sisters the devil married, I am the body beneath the Juniper tree, I am the devil's grandmother. I drag my nails against his scalp as he carries me to the couch. When he lays me down, the panic flares. I can't let it show on my face. He must see the romantic face he remembers. I conjure thoughts I would never think. I think them hard enough that they will become my own. *I am awkward and new at loss, but your sadness is incomprehensibly ancient.* If I say this in my head with enough conviction, it will surface on my skin.

He says, "Remember Venice? Los Angeles?"

"I remember."

*I will take on your nightmare burdens so they become my own.* This is what Pamela would say. This is what a good wife would say.

While he takes off my shirt and his own, he asks, "Getting drunk in the mountains in San Diego?"

"I remember." I fold myself into him. *I am enough to excise your sadness.*

While he strips himself down to the skin, he says, "Eating terrible egg salad on the bridge over the highway in Indiana."

"I remember." I see a flash of him in the darkness of the lab, surrounded by beds of prone women, deciding which face should be our daughter's. Digging inside her to get what he wants. I shiver. *Despite your sorrows, you are gentle and wise.*

"Touch my hair, my face." He kisses me, like he did the last time. The taste of him has changed. He tastes like iron now. Maybe it's me whose taste has changed. He kisses me with a look of gluttony, and I try not to think of the heave and slurp of his mouth until he pins my hips onto the couch cushions and says, "Stay just like that."

*Teaghan, help me. Teaghan, Teaghan.* But I can't think of her now. I shut my eyes. *I'd never be with you and think of someone else.* There is something swelling in him and closing in me. His breaths are ragged, like his lungs are too small and rusty for the amount of breath he needs to sustain himself. Like he is not used to needing so much.

When he lowers himself onto me, I have the feeling that he is burying me under himself, a permanent interring into the couch, where I will be stuck forever.

I put my hands on both sides of my face and stretch my skin to stop it, but the rushing blood is still there, around my mouth, as I stretch myself into a wild, silent scream. I lose control. Something inside me lashes out. Something in the center of me decides I do want to summon the ghost of violence that lives in his body, after all. I want a head-to-head. I want something to tear my teeth into, something to bear down on. I know it lives in there. I saw it, like the boiling shimmer radiating off the asphalt in August. I want to bite him, I want to gash him open. I want to meet his anger body with mine. My visceral rage comes out as an explosive sob, a loud, reflexive moan that I bite down on in the middle. Hearing myself sound like that frightens me, but Silas is encouraged by the sound, would've been encouraged by any sound, I think. He groans, and groans again.

I must keep myself safe. I close my eyes and hear the pounding of rain on the roof and the pounding of blood in my human parts, and I think of the stillness of water. There is nothing as still as still water, nothing with so much potential for so much movement that can sit in one place for so long. I think of myself sitting still and evaporating. Evaporating up and away, and, and, I don't know anything about evaporation except that it makes the water less. Where did I learn the word evaporation? It must have been from Silas, like Teaghan said. I know nothing else. It makes the water less. So I become still, and I become less. I breathe and become less, and the storm is quieting and I wrap my fingers into his hair and peel his face away from mine until he groans and groans one more alarming groan of hurt and sorrow and collapses. He leans off me so I no longer have to endure his entire bulk. Still, he is too much weight to bear.

He falls asleep like that, his arm dangling off the couch. He got even more out of it this time than last time. I don't understand that shuddering groan and don't want to. It is easier now that he has lost consciousness. To keep him asleep, I pray into his hair, *I promise that from now on, I will be good to you.*

On the couch, I watch the storm stop, then start, then stop again, then start again. The rain comes in unending waves, like the sky is breathing messily. I try to understand what happened. It was like touching Teaghan, but much worse. And why did I only see clearly those horrible things? When he was mustering up the good memories with Pamela, I could sense merely vague impressions, mostly saturated colors, or an unshaped brightness left on the eyelids like when I press my fingers into them too hard.

He doesn't know how to share like the women do, naturally and easily. My body must have reached into his and grabbed what warnings I needed. I still feel sick from it.

I've been awake and under him for a long time when he finally wakes. He does so with a ripping startle, as always. He looks at me. I'm afraid to look back. I'm crying. I've been crying. This will be what does it, what makes him know I was just pretending.

I'm afraid to look back, but I do. He smiles. He takes it as a good sign, that I'm crying. I don't understand why.

"It's okay," he says. It's not okay. "It's okay," he says as he pats my thigh. "From now on, it will be okay."

I smile hesitantly. He smiles back again, and is fine. Even my unconvincing smile has made it all fine. He is inducing this glamor just as much as I am. He gets up and looks for his clothes. He rubs his face, his hair, stretches his neck. He looks at me and chuckles. He pats my knee, gets up, and leaves.

# CHAPTER TWELVE

I have never been as alone as I am while trying to fit my life into Silas's. Never been so isolated as when I push myself away from my own skin so he will see someone else when he looks at me. Even minimal pretending is draining. I am so exhausted that I even begin to sleep at night, though the sleep is restless, and in my dreams I am trapped in a house of concrete and tile. My mouth is dry and stiff and clenched tight. In my dreams I trail after my mother down a long hallway, carpeted in red, its walls and ceiling red too. She wears a braid, like she never did in life. I reach out and grab the braid as it swings against my mother's back, but whenever I grab it, it severs from her scalp. I drop it and look up and my mother is still ahead of me, in the intestinally long hallway. I never catch up to her.

I wait for Silas to become disillusioned, but he seems happy, walking around with his eyes unfocused. And where is Teaghan? I had said that I wanted to see her again *soon*, but her soon is not my soon. Silas asks me if I mind if he calls me

Pamela. I say I don't. I really don't. I don't care what he calls me. Pamela is just as good as Nicole. He uses both names, as if they're interchangeable. He rubs my arm as he passes me. He pats my knee when we sit next to each other. The lake-lake becomes swollen from the storm, then shrinks in the heat. Any time Silas opens the window, a fertile, putrefying reek of the muck at the edge of the receding water drifts up from the bank. He doesn't go to the library to work. He stays by my side. His presence is cheery, pleading, and heavy.

Now, when he has me swallow spores, he strokes my head and asks me if I remember Kansas, Cincinnati, the burger place, the watermelon towel we kissed under, the van, the train, the only apartment we ever lived in, the motel where we got the flu. I give in to the inertia of the body. I say yes, I remember.

"It's okay," Silas sometimes says to me, out of nowhere. And I see that I've been crying. "It's okay. From now on, it will be okay."

I try to keep from swallowing the spores he spoons into my cheek, but it's getting more difficult to hide them when he won't leave my side. Sometimes it isn't until he falls asleep that I can sneak out of the room and secretly spit. I know that I am swallowing some. At night, when I'm lying on my back, the taste of it leaks into my mouth like bile.

One evening, I am thirsty. I become out of my mind with thirst. I drink all the water in the house. It becomes night, and

Silas is still not home. I'm going insane with thirst. There are rain barrels outside, with mycelial mat filters, but it's a lot to maneuver in the dark while holding a lantern. But the lake-lake is nearby, swollen with rainwater.

I run outside. The yard slopes down, and I struggle not to fall while I stumble across it. The hill is sleek as exposed organs, as wet as mushrooms growing in a mouth. As I trip down the slope, I see a plastic toy bucket, bright and neon even in the dark. Its side is caved in, but it's still managed to collect some rainwater. Once, when the people of earth, that is, the people of Greece, stopped praying, Zeus got angry and withheld the rain. Crops died. People starved. I bury my face in the bucket and guzzle. The water is sludgy and slimy with growth, must be riddled with toxins, and yet it feels cleansing. I gasp for breath when the water is gone. It's not enough. I wipe my chin. There's a chill all over my skin, and goose bumps on my stomach. My bones feel cold even though the weather is warm. I'm trembling, something is weakening inside me, something unraveling or liquifying. I am greedy for more. When the people, grieving their dead, began to pray again, Zeus gave the earth rain again. What punishment wouldn't a god inflict to get a little attention?

I'm about to run the rest of the way to the lake-lake, get on my hands and knees and lap up water like a wild animal, or maybe just plunge in so I can open my jaw and let the entire body of lightless water gush into the black hole of my mouth, when a hand squeezes my shoulder. I gasp and drop the bucket, and it rolls down the slope and catches again in the grass.

"Silas," I hiss.

Silas investigates my face, his mouth drawn into a white line of sympathy. "You're pregnant."

A great heaving rushes out of me, and my legs buckle. "I don't feel good."

Silas gently guides me by my shoulders. "Let's go lie down in the house."

I lean on him. It feels good to lean. I lean on him all the way up the hill, across the porch, and back into the house, then shakily, to the couch. I lie on the cushions and put an arm over my eyes. Moving is too strenuous, my body too heavy to lift.

"Silas?"

He grunts. He's not far away. I shake my head and regret the movement.

"I don't think I'm pregnant. I think I'm going to die."

"That's what it always feels like."

"Do women die?"

"Some women do," he says. I open my eyes to look at him. Something spasms inside me. A dread. A curling panic. His face is grim as he watches me. Death looms, heavy and bearded and white faced. I'm falling backward. I throw my arm over my eyes and squeeze them tight as tears erupt in their corners.

"Are you hungry?"

I'm about to say no, but actually, I am hungry. Very hungry. Starving. I nod, worried that if I open my mouth to answer, I'll vomit all the water sloshing around in my stomach. I want darkness, I want stillness, I want peace.

The Hyades sisters made the rain. When their brother died in a hunting accident, they wept from grief, then were turned into stars. Suspended in the glittering ether, their grief rained down on the world. What women have sacrificed themselves to make, a man has the power to give or withhold. When I asked my mom, she said the book didn't mention why the Hyades sisters were turned into constellations.

I crack open my eyes. Silas is holding a bowl of something in his hands. I'm so hungry, but also so nauseous I can't move. Gently, he crouches beside me. He picks up a tiny spoon resting against the bowl and brings it to my lips. I still don't want to budge. I'll be ripped apart if I do. I'm so grateful to him for moving the spoon for me. The food tastes too much. It's warm, though. With each spoonful, I feel calmer.

"My head hurts," I whimper, because I don't know how to find the words to tell him that I need help, that I'm tipping backward into a deep well.

"It's the light. It's too bright for you right now. Come on, let's put you to bed." He slides his hands under my body. He's so big, he picks me up effortlessly, and I fold into his chest.

When I was little, I thought someone changed the sisters into stars out of pity, so they wouldn't feel their grief. But are they not frozen in their suffering? Does grief change if the body that holds it does? It must not have been pity, then, that sent the sisters to their eternal places.

"Silas?" I whisper.

"Yes?"

I open my mouth, but I have nothing to say. I don't even think I meant to say his name.

The Hyades sisters were more useful frozen in the sky. And so there they remain, grieving.

Silas is close to me, touching me, breathing on me, and I don't even have the energy to mind.

# CHAPTER THIRTEEN

In bed, my heartbeat throbs in my earlobes. It labors throughout my body and convulses in my chest like a storm cracking above the house, then fading, then returning with a jolt so hard it shakes the roof. Something cold and hard germinates in the pit of my stomach. It spreads slowly, like the puddle under a small drip. It grows fingers that sharpen and needle into my flesh, branching out of my center and down into my thighs, up the ladder of my ribs. A malevolent cobweb unfolding inside me.

My insides rearrange themselves. Before tonight, it was hard to believe that a handful of dust could grow into a person, that I would know that person better than myself, love them more than anyone, would rearrange my life and love to fit around her. Now my body distends painfully, tumefies around this tiny, intrusive seed. I am not giving my body to my daughter, she is taking it from me. My abdomen is stiff and I can't move. I can't sleep. Silas does, beside me, though I barely notice him.

Once, he wakes up and says dreamily, "You're pregnant," and touches me gently on the stomach with awe. I can't tell if he's awake or if he knows who I am. He starts snoring again even before he lays his head back down on the pillow.

Then, in the middle of the night, I become otherworldly. I can feel the nerves in my retina stretching, loosening. There's no longer any difference between sleeping and waking. The dreams unfold from me and blacken the room with their flickering movement. Tiptoeing on swollen feet, they turn back and bleat, wagging their haunches. Wolves with bow ties, toads with boots. Trees with mouths. Men with axes and bears with brides. For hours, all I do is lie in my bed, waiting for the dreams to settle, to flatten themselves into the shadows. But as the hours pass, they crescendo and grow wilder, grow teeth and soft voices.

Spider-soft threads cover my face. At first I think they're insect legs, but when I strain with the effort to lift my arm to touch my face, I realize it's a veil, like the brides of old. Or a shroud, like the foremothers. I claw at my cheeks, my eyes, before I realize it's a dream. That I'm not even moving my hands, that's part of the dream too. Even then, the feeling of the cloth over my face doesn't disappear. I am being entombed in the bed, will stay here until Silas pushes me into the lab.

Night turns into day, and the halo of sunlight peeking around the curtain is blinding and burning and gives me a terrible headache. Even with my eyes closed it gouges into my skull. I moan until Silas rushes through the door. I hadn't even noticed him leaving the bedroom. Without a word from me, he knows what the problem is and uses duct tape, our precious duct tape, to seal the curtains to the wall. The darkness is better. I can't see anything in the room except for the dreams, which are unerringly bright. They tug at my blankets, touch my toes, reach for my hands. I hear noises outside the window. Conversations, gun shots, sometimes screaming.

A shadow stands over me again. It breathes heavily as it comes and goes. Sometimes it's Silas, but not always. In whichever form it takes, it tends to me in the same way that Silas does. A long rope of a braid, sloping down the figure's body, restricts its movements as it drags its feet across the room before disappearing back into the house. Silas whispers things to me, but the figure never speaks. The luciferin lantern Silas carries, trails in and out of the room, back and forth, as he enters and leaves. The figure's feet whisper against the floor as it comes in, also carrying a light in its bare hands, its light like a glowing heart.

"Do you feel numb?" Silas asks.

I didn't hear him enter the room, but I am aware of the weight of him standing over me, something solid in the darkness. He doesn't carry a lantern, and I wonder how many times he has come into the room and then left without me noticing at all.

I jerk my head in a single nod. My vision spins, swirling color in the blackness.

"That's the baby's mycelium." His voice is a pleasant tingle on the back of my neck. "Numbing you as it works its way through you, gathering nutrients. Eating you, really." He chuckles, then clears his throat to stop. "Luckily the threads are small, just one cell wide." My eyes strain to find him. He continues, "Once the mycelium works its way through you, after it has no more room to grow, it will fruit. And we get to see the baby. It will appear right here, at the center of you." He poises his finger over my stomach, where my belly button would be if I were a man. "It won't look like much, at first. But all the parts will be there, in completion. It just needs to soak up your moisture to get bigger. When it starts to move its fists and legs and opens its mouth and starts rooting for a nipple, we can remove it from the stipe—the stem—that attaches it to you. And then it'll be ours forever."

He moves his hand down, and there's a warmth above my thigh as his hand lingers over me. I can taste his desire as it floats around him, but I am grateful he is holding back.

"I am amazed at the intimate knowledge the mycelium has of your body. Each hyphal tip has an organelle that only fungi have, which guides the hyphae through your body like a little brain, releasing exometabolites as it sees fit. It changes and reroutes your processes, but it doesn't damage them, at least not permanently. At least, not much. It turns you into the perfect substrate to grow a baby." He stops. "I'm sorry. You're miserable. I brought you a wet washcloth. Is it okay if I wash you?"

A wet washcloth sounds like the best thing in the world. I don't want to move to say so, and luckily, he doesn't wait for an answer. He slides off the towel covering a luciferin lamp on the dresser next to the bed, and the room is cast in a pale green glow. My pupils shiver as they readjust to sight again. Silas's eyes are wide and dilated in the dark. He touches the washcloth lightly to the back of my hand. At first it's painful. Like the terrible prickle of sensation that returns to my arm after I've slept on it for so long that it's gone numb. A bolt of adrenaline shoots up the back of my spine. I want to jerk away from his touch, but I can't. Then, slowly, a relief. A kinder tingling approaching normality. My vision smears with grateful tears. Tears, though moisture is so precious to my body.

"I could tell you were pregnant a couple days ago." His pupils shift back and forth beneath the gash of his long lashes. He moves the washcloth to the side of my face. "Women's skin is hygrophanous. Which means, when it's normal and has enough moisture, it's a little transparent. We can see inside you. When you're submerged in water, it's even more see-through. Pregnant, your dry skin becomes opaque, like a man's. Like how a woman's used to be." His washcloth reaches my mouth, and I gasp. "You can speak, I think. Your circulatory system is more blood-based at your mouth. More animal than mushroom. But you don't have to say anything if you don't feel like it."

My bodily sensations have been so overwhelming, I hadn't thought of speaking. I press my lips together, and when I release them, they fill with blood. The thought of clearing my throat seems too monumental, too many systems to engage, so I don't do it. My voice is scratchy as I say, "I knew that."

He cocks his eyebrow up, bemused. "You did?"

"Yeah. Mosquitoes only bite me around the mouth, but they bite Reese all over."

I have always known about the blood in my mouth. I used to like the taste. The first time I tasted it was by accident. I fell and hit my lip when I was small. For a while, I used to gnaw on my fingernails. I'd slide my nails between my teeth and under my gum until I could taste the blood. My gums were slotted with callouses.

Men are filled to the brim with blood, are always under the explosive pressure of their own liquid. A man cuts himself just about anywhere and blood gushes out of him. Maybe this is why men act the way they do. Always stressed out. The constant heat and movement inside them, hunting for the smallest crack to spill out.

"Yeah, that's right."

"Is that why men like when women are pregnant? We look more like your first wives when our skin gets dry?"

"No, no. It's not about that." He laughs softly. He swipes the washcloth around my lower lip. I can feel a quivering. I think it must be my lip that trembles, not his hand, though I can't tell. Perhaps he's trying hard to be gentle, to touch me only lightly. He holds the washcloth to the side of my neck. My head tilts over his knuckles, involuntarily, like I have no more command of my body. My mass wants to cradle around his wet hand and absorb, absorb, absorb. My neck flesh is wet enough that I can tilt my head again to face him. He smiles with half his mouth. "I find your body fascinating."

He pauses his work with the washcloth, like he's

embarrassed, or said something he shouldn't have. He's like a child, exploring some new territory, not sure of what he can get away with, not sure of how guilty he should be about his curiosity. He resumes sweeping the washcloth over my wrist.

"Nobody can extract your fungal parts from your animal parts. You are your own thing, down to your very bones, which are a mixture of mushroom chitin and human collagen and calcium phosphate. You are a fully integrated being."

"Has someone tried to take us apart?"

He shakes his head. Not so much to answer, but to ward off the question. He dips the cloth in a bowl of water and wrings it out. Such a calming, sweet sound, the trickle of water.

"Even your flesh has fungal attributes." He rolls the cloth over my palm. "Your hands are rugose." He sweeps his hand up my arm and rests it on my shoulder. He squeezes the cloth languidly and moisture trickles down my bicep in dawdling rivulets. "Your armpits are squarrose." He pauses over my chest. "Your umbonate and silky, sericeous breasts." He tickles my chin with the tip of the washcloth. "The inside of your mouth is gilled." He lowers his washcloth to linger above my pubic mound, but doesn't touch it. "And here." I wish he would. This time, I might benefit. Like the rest of my body, my vagina feels parched and desperately needs the water. "Are teeth."

"Teeth?"

He grins. "A mycological term. Around your labia, there are a layer of teeth, a different texture of hymenium. They aren't like the teeth in your mouth. In fungus, teeth are pliant and supple." He hovers for another moment. If I could, I would lift my pelvis to meet the washcloth, offer it some relief. He lowers his hand and the washcloth pushes against my thighs and slides down my knees and shins. I sigh and close my eyes. My skin awakens, softens like a sponge. Pliant and supple. "I'm not supposed to tell you about your body."

"Why?"

"Because we—they—fear that you'll use it against us." Silas's eyes are shining, wondrous.

"Against you?"

"And anyway, maybe I'm boring you . . . "

"No. I want to know."

"You do? Maybe you shouldn't encourage me." He looks to the side, as if making sure we are alone. He's becoming drunk, I realize. On what, though, I don't know. It isn't Saturday. Or is it? I can't remember how long I've been lying here. "There used to be an old argument about lichens. Who enslaved who, the plant or the fungus? An archaic argument that seemed settled until you women came along. Who is more in control, the mushroom or the woman?"

"The woman, definitely."

"You're so confident." He laughs. "But I don't know if it needs to be hierarchical at all. What if both organisms coexist peacefully, in the same body, to mutual benefit?" There's a long pause. I concentrate on the washcloth as Silas swipes it up and down the length of me. He presses it against my ankles. "From what I can tell, the mycelium isn't all that different from the placenta that fed human fetuses. Completely human fetuses. I wish I could show you what placentas looked like. They're fascinating. Veins and rivers. The circulatory systems of animals, leaves, fungi, earth, they all look the same." He separates my toes and squeezes the washcloth between each of them. "The placenta did what the mycelium does now: gives the baby nutrition and oxygen and removes waste. It developed from the cells of the baby, not the mother. It's what manipulates the mother into loving her child. Hijacks her brain and body, floods her with hormones. Much like a parasite. I mean, the baby is a parasite. But one born of love."

Something has changed, something within the room. Silas is buoyed in the light. He moves in a more pronounced, deliberate way. I sink a little into the transition between wakefulness and dreams. But Silas seems to be transitioning with me, like the room is a river and we're both being carried along. I remember that I should be mad at him, that I hate him. I remember why, but it's not so important anymore. I don't feel angry anymore. I feel quiet and secure. He's making it up to me, the wrongs he did me in the past.

"You know, fungi have been manipulating organisms for so long," he says. "And in a lot of different ways."

I try to say something, but my tongue swells too big for my mouth, the scratchy skin of it is too tacky and sticks to the roof. Silas brings the washcloth to my lips again, and squeezes. A rush of water eases and relaxes my gums, my tongue, my tonsils, my throat. A grateful surge laps into my heart. I don't even have to ask before he responds to what I need.

"Fungi use growth hormones to engineer plant roots. The

roots branch out and find their way to the fungus within the soil, so the plant and fungus can form a symbiotic bond."

He reaches out and folds his hands in mine. He sighs, like the touch of my hand is as good to him as the sponge feels to me. He is warmth sliding under my skin. Comfortable, this time. I wonder if, to him, I am coldness sliding into his. Like we are submerging, one below the surface of the other.

"But it's not just the fungus that changes the plant. Both change each other. Their metabolisms change. They get sick less often." He closes his other hand over mine. Another wave of warmth floods into me. "It's called 'homing,' when hyphae move through the dirt and fuse together to become a network. Homing is the ability to find each other in the denseness between." He smiles down at me. "I haven't talked about this with anyone new in so long. Anyone who cared, or wanted to learn . . . It's nice. I forgot that people could find this interesting and not stressful."

"I like it too." My voice is slow and out of balance.

He lets go of my hand, reluctantly, and takes off his shirt. I look at him curiously. Hair grows across his back, his chest, trails down his stomach. His body is so strange. So different. I don't hate it. His smell isn't even that bad today. He lies down on the other side of the bed. The mattress groans, and I feel a slight tug of the sheets beneath me as they are pulled by his weight.

"I don't want to— I can't—"

"No, no, of course not!" He shakes his head. "You can't even move. I just want to lie down and sleep. I could sleep in another bed, but I sleep better next to you. Is that okay?"

"Oh." It comes out a whisper. "Okay."

"It's okay?" he asks. I nod. Because of the water he brought me, I'm not so dizzy when my head moves. "I know it hurts."

"It's okay," I say. "Thank you."

He blinks back at me, staring, his pupils bloated and inky. His hands are folded under his face. I can see his wrists, that tender part of him where his veins poke out. That blood-filled and blue labyrinth enmeshed inside him. I see scars too. On his knuckles, on his chest, his arms. His body, haunted by wars and famines I can't imagine. Since I've been born, the amount of food has waxed and waned throughout the seasons, but there's always been at least a little to eat. Mom told me that wasn't always the case, especially in the beginning, when the men were establishing themselves. Living as long as he has, Silas has experienced so much. I suddenly want more than anything to protect him. Us women, the only defenders ushering the men back from that abysmal pit. It is too much for one woman. It takes many wives to help bring them back to themselves. Each woman bringing her own wisdom to her man, who will feed and house our daughters.

There's something fragile in Silas's physical presence, something I've never noticed before in any man. His skin seems oddly tender. Easily ripped open. I can see the shape of his bones as they press against the inside of his meat, like some part inside him wants to be exposed, wants to come out and express itself. He's so vulnerable right now that I can even imagine him dying. This ancient man, this bulk and strength, even he will die someday.

If I just reach out and take his hand, he is so sweet and tolerant right now, he'd just watch me as I nibble a nail off his pinky finger, as I—

But I want all of him. I want to absorb him into my skin like I absorbed the water. If only I had enough mouths, I could lie on top of him and feast, all at once, with all my limbs and torso and hands, take him into the whole of me. His skin will break open, his organs dissolved, and his rot will be sweet as fruit. We would become one. I'd grow from him, out of him, with him, using his body and the nutrients in his flesh to grow in ways I couldn't possibly without him.

"I think the baby will come out soon."

His words bring me back to myself. My eyes focus on his.

"You think?" I ask dreamily. He is standing next to me, beside the bed. Something metal swivels in his hand. "What's that?"

"Uh, handcuffs. Restraints. I don't have to if you don't want me to."

"It's okay." My words waver. Maybe I'm falling asleep.

I watch his face, hovering over mine, beard tickling my wrist as he secures me to the carved headboard, locking the handcuffs around a wooden ivy shape. Parts of it have already broken off.

"Just for protection." Silas is radiant, angelic. My face stretches, slowly, smiling for real for the first time. He squeezes the fingers of my bound hand. "It's okay, you'll forget they're there."

And I do.

Eventually, he has to go.

But, like spring, he comes back again. Each time, his shining face and tiny light is like a choir breaking out around me. Tear-salt swells in my eyes, though there's no moisture to wash it away. He talks to me softly, but I don't know what he's saying anymore, so consumed am I with this new sublime hurting. He brings relief with him. Dips his fingers in cold water and trickles it down my sides. My skin guzzles hungrily from his hand like a rat left alone in the grain bin.

Without leaving, he returns again. He hovers over me, his knees at my ribs, holding a sliver of wood. A strange thing to bring someone. He pries open my mouth. I am languid and pliant, no resistance in me, and it doesn't take much to overpower me. At first, I hate his fingers in my mouth. An intrusion I can't possibly resist. But it lasts only a second. Then, I am consumed by the succor and wonder of it. The rich wood permeates my mouth, better than toasty bread or fresh fruit, better than anything. The sliver takes a long time to wane and finally disband. The fibers seep through my saliva, seasoning my mouth-flesh, percolating down my throat, like warmth. He comes back, mists me, and gives me a tender slice of bark. I am grateful, so grateful.

Silas sleeps well. He leaves the luciferin lamp on. For the

first time, I am happy to have him lie beside me. Though when I turn my head to look at him, by the time my eyes reach him, it must be morning, because he has already gotten up and left. I am as slow as the moon across the sky. Mice breach fearlessly into the open spaces of the room whenever Silas is gone. I am glad it isn't winter, so they don't search around my body, hoping for a man's heat. They keep to the outskirts of the room.

The figure I can't get rid of hovers over me intermittently. Once it places its hands on my chest. I open my mouth to scream, but my mouth stretches and the air that fills my passageways chokes me worse than a dirty rag. I can't cough or retch or move, but eventually, the sensation and the figure goes away. Its outline, a burn mark, hangs in the air. That, too, eventually evaporates. Silas returns. In the quiet, he pulls the clothes out from the drawers where I folded them. He brings me the yellow dress with white spots. He cannot move me, so he drapes the dress over my torso, straightens it at the shoulder and smooths it down my thighs. The material doesn't feel like anything, my skin is too strange to me, like a crust has grown over it made of someone else's skin. He puts silver rings on my fingers. I cannot see them, but I imagine they look like smaller versions of the handcuffs on my wrist. My body, full of echoes. Then he puts the heavy necklace around my neck. It doesn't stay at my sternum, but slides to the lowest point of my throat. It makes me feel my pulse too hard. I wait for him to tell me what to do, but he doesn't ask me to do anything. The pressure of the necklace gives a tinged hiss to my breathing. He lies next to me. He puts his arm around my waist, and the dress bunches beneath the crook of his elbow.

"You're beautiful," he says to the darkness, against the sensitive part of my earlobe.

I ache. I'm coming undone, my insides engorge. My veins are filled with stone and metal and glass. I am a bag of man-made things rather than living meat, and nature has come to swallow me. I don't panic. The idea of dying is fine.

It's daytime. I can't see it, but I can feel the sun behind the duct-taped curtain, behind the glass, behind the gilded distance of the world.

I am glad to be in my precious darkness. I am glad to be unmoving. My body splinters, disassembles, and I am dead around my baby. The baby is mewling, patting the muck of my body, an instinct to feed, driving her to plunge her fists into the messy pit of my corpse and bring the pulp to her mouth, but she is poisoning herself.

Silas comes in. He gazes over the landscape of my ruins.

"Don't worry." He isn't talking to the baby, or to me, but to someone unseen behind him. "They're just fruiting bodies. They can't feel anything. And they just grow back."

I'm lifted over and through the house like sleep carries a person over reality. Silas's face bobs like the moon above my feet, guiding me through the hall. He's a sad guide, a serious one.

We sail past the house's seemingly infinite rooms, all familiar to me now. Another figure is behind me, hovering over me. I can't lift my eyes to see her, but I know she's there. For a moment, her face bobs into view. Mom. When she leans over me, I think, oh, but she doesn't have Mom's hair. She has my hair. When we get to the stairs, the tilt of the bed becomes upsetting, nightmarish, but I can't move my hands to hold on. The bed bumps hard on one of the steps.

"Fuck!" says Mom, above me. I've never heard her say that word before. "You're going too fast."

Silas says, "It's okay. Hey, it's okay. He doesn't feel any pain."

Mom, I want to say, it's not true. I'm hurting so bad. The bed thumps against one of the stairs again and jostles me. I slide a little and I want to scream, my mouth is already open wide and splitting. I want to scream and scream, but I have no voice left. All my blood and energy is redirected into the surging body inside my hurting body.

"Fuck!" Mom half weeps. She always sounds like that now. Like she's barely come up for air.

"It's okay." Silas is frantic, like he's not sure if Mom was listening before. "He doesn't feel—"

Mom's voice whips back, like thunder cracking, "That's not as much a comfort to me as it is to you, Silas!"

Eventually, this dream slides away from me, slides out from under me like passing minnows, my dreams are sediment in the black room, pulsing and rising with an unseen tide caused by the moon and air and me. I don't feel the weight of emotions, don't feel the weight of the dreams. I'm doing just fine.

There is thunder outside. Real thunder. It cracks again. I can feel something happening. It feels like I have to pee. I haven't had to in a long time, all the moisture has been absorbed either by my body or the daughter at my core. The mycelium within me recycles the waste and fluid. Silas must have told me that. I don't know how else I'd know it, otherwise. My stomach softens like uncooked dough, and my center expands. Lipless and dark, a mouth opens on my abdomen. A funk rises. Sulfur and buried iron, old rain on hot asphalt. It isn't too painful. More like someone put an icicle on my stomach, and the cold is melting through me.

A wrinkled knob peeks out of my stomach-mouth. Just the hint of folded, wet flesh. Like a fat tongue, searching for teeth to rub against. A bulb that swells to a tumor pushes through. A stem extends beneath it, like a bony finger. The pustule rises unevenly. A small crack splinters, then ruptures. Chunks of skin peel back, each piece like a tentacle flexing, touching something hot and receding. My heart leaps excitedly. For there, curled and lumpy, about the size of my thumb, is the homunculus form of my baby-to-be. All her limbs, her toes, her tiny skull. She is still curled against the stem. She is a rich bruise color.

She begins to swell. Her tiny toes balloon, then her legs, her stomach, her arms. Wobbling slightly, her head fills out last. Her skull extends, then rounds. Large, fetal eyes, murky-black and shining through the translucent skin of her eyelids.

Not quite a human face, but almost, with the pulse of fontanelle on top. When I move to touch her, my wrists catch. The rattle of metal reminds me that I'm handcuffed. Good. As disorientated as I feel, I could accidentally hurt her. I don't know what I'm doing. I can't imagine how clumsy I am right now.

I stare. Only for hours, maybe, though it could be longer. I am content to just feel her. We are a closed circuit, sharing blood and nutrients. I can feel the liquid in me rush and flow into her. Some returns back to me, and in the same way I felt Teaghan, I feel her. A small, burgeoning pulse. A curious, bright bug. A sweet bud with so much potential. A new beginning. A new her, a new me. If I could, I'd give so much more of myself so she could grow.

"Hello, I am your mother," I say to the baby. And suddenly, hearing it said out loud, I become afraid. Not for myself, but for her. I am inadequate. How can I be a mother?

Finally, her face inflates. I tilt my head up. I am eager to see my mother's face again. But as the baby absorbs even more blood, I see that she does not have my mom's face.

It's been a long time. A long, long time. My mind expands and slows to protect itself from the ache of consciousness. I must eventually sleep, but my dreams are only of me lying on this bed, looking at the ceiling. Sometimes, in my dreams, there are other bodies around me, trapped in their own minds, softly expelling spores into the atmosphere. I smell the odor of cement and moisture and old chlorine.

A figure comes to my bed and stands at the peripheral of my vision like a splotch of inflammation about to give me a headache. The figure clears its throat. It's a man. A familiar one. A dad. The dad I had before.

Dad hovers above me. I see his beard. He breathes in my spores, though he doesn't seem bothered by them. He lifts his hand, like he's about to brush my hair away from my face. I think I remember him doing that before. I remember someone like him doing that before. His hand is close to my mouth, where the mushrooms are pushing themselves out. For just a moment, his eyes slide over the rest of my face. His first two fingers slip inside my mouth. He takes his knife out of his shirt pocket and opens it with the flick of his thumb.

"Don't worry," he says gently. "This won't hurt."

He grabs the back of my neck and lifts it. My neck is stiff, my body is stiff. I feel my hair get caught. It's gotten so long. He puts the knife to my mouth. At first, my innards resist. When he cuts out enough mushrooms, he picks up something else.

"Just a speculum. It won't hurt."

He shoves it in the hole he's made and opens my throat wider than it should go. I have the urge to gag but can't act on it. He pauses and looks up at me. He opens his mouth like he's going to say something comforting, but then he looks away. My throat expands as it gives way to the widening tool. Dad opens my mouth with his fingers. The bloodless incisions part at the corners of my lips. I can feel cold air in the meaty flaps as they expand. Now it's easier for Dad to push his knife and a few more fingers inside. He saws. The smaller mushrooms surrender easily to the blade, but there are tougher, woodier ones in the center of the bunch. A razor-hot hurt streaks through me, like a convulsion. I let out a cry, but I am old enough to know that no one will hear it. He arranges my mushrooms in a row on my pillow, where I can't see them, and continues to labor with a workman's efficiency. He pushes his fingers in deeper. The mushrooms' spongy bodies yield to his pressure. He doesn't look at my face. He doesn't expect a response. There is something dead inside him.

Dad whispers again, quieter, as if to himself, "It's not going to hurt." Dad pricks open the sore things in my throat with something long and sharp. He scrapes against the opened blister. I can feel pain, a relief of pressure, something coming out of me, and more shivery relief, followed by more pain. Every time he withdraws his tool, a spurt of black clumps stick to the end. He's not done, though. He punctures more, yanks my head around to get at better angles. He wants more. He fills up a purple pouch he takes out of his pocket. I recognize it. He drinks whiskey when he's celebrating.

Finally, he lets me go. I am relieved. There are squares of light above me. He wriggles the tool out of my mouth and carefully returns the mushrooms he carved away back inside me. Once, he fumbles and knocks them onto my chest.

"Fuck," he says, looks over his shoulder. No one is there. Just the bodies around me, tucked in their own beds, mouths open.

When he's gone, it's even more of a relief, despite the unending and painful boredom. At first, the mushrooms that Dad left inside my mouth still smell like me, but the longer they sit there, unconnected, the stronger they smell like something else. Like the soft smell after Thanksgiving, when all the leaves become a brown mush on the ground. The smell gets bad, then worse, then goes away altogether. New mushrooms muscle their way through my throat and push the dead ones out. The bodies all around me are exhaling, exhaling, exhaling. The dust swirling above us eventually settles and coats our skins. The light from the windows never reaches our faces.

I need water desperately. And more room. How long has it been? A week, at least. A month? I'm drying out. Is Silas punishing me? I feel the need to stretch out, though my limbs are as straight as they can get.

"Silas!" I yell, straining to hold my mouth open. "Silas!" I yell again, but my mouth is so dry that the words stick in my chest.

I try to yell again, but this time, my voice won't work at all. A cicada outside screams a throaty death rattle on my behalf, and more join in. A whole chorus, a whole swarm, screams. I hear the mice in the room, loping around the room in tormented circles. Their naked feet scramble across the floor, kicking up dust, and it's like lightning currents crackling through the air. A static of fur and bald skin and quivering eyes, a swirl of electricity in a place that hasn't known that sort of energy in a long time. My husband's reek mixes with the smell of rodent urine. Ghostly scratches make me think that they must be chasing each other, but then when they dart over my toes, I see their heads are wrenched to the side, and I realize they are running because of the cicadas, the shrill noise is making them crazy like it's making me crazy. They run to escape the sound, but the screams are closing in on the house, and there's nowhere to go.

An ache, a searing pain, drives straight through me, hot on my electric spine. My body tightens. It feels like nubile branches are crawling up and out of my throat, closing my breathing holes. I can't scream. I want to scream.

The figure I can't get rid of stands over me, lifts its leg like it plans to kneel on my chest.

"Silas," I choke.

I feel a tickle in my chest that burns, like I'm about to cough or dry heave. I can't relieve myself of the feeling. The shadow grins, and its teeth are white and bare and brilliant, a stark grin inside a shadow. I want to thrash, but my hands are restrained. The cicadas must be in the room now, a cloud of wings eclipsing the bed, their screaming amplified. I wrench myself up toward my hands. My mouth finds the bed's headboard. Wood, sweet wood. My teeth gnaw and the headboard dissolves in my mouth. The chips of paint catch in my throat, but I don't care. I mash with my mouth and swallow.

Suddenly, I can move. A piercing pain ricochets across my stiff shoulders as I lower my hands, free of the headboard. I want to get up, but I am still tethered down.

I yank the baby out myself.

The stem breaks easily. I meet no resistance, like her flesh is made of smoke or a fragile dream. A few ragged pieces of skin cling to the edge of the stem. Abruptly, the cicadas stop screaming. I remember, then, that this isn't the season for them. I gag, cough, and swallow hard. There's a wad of strings enmeshed in my mouth. I tear at them and stare at the mycelial threads like corn silk in my fingers. The handcuffs hang off my wrists, heavy and clunky. A few wet splinters are stuck in the chain links.

The baby is still in my hands. Her limbs are limp and loose. I touch her tiny hand, and as I caress her soft flesh, realize that she is not a she at all. The fault of my body torn from the fault in my body is a boy.

The boy is dead.

It isn't sadness that wells up in me. It's not relief, either. It's something else. Nausea. I don't want to look at the tiny body anymore. The ballooned eyes, the alien, baby bird shape. I drop the child beside me and pull up the covers.

"I'm sorry," I sob. To the broken bed, I guess. Or to Silas, who owns the bed I broke, though that makes even less sense because he isn't around to hear my apology.

I tug at the stem still inside me. It's loose, like a starved weed in fallow, dry ground. I feel it giving. I tug harder and feel a scrabbling inside me like mice feet, like my bowels are emptying themselves too quickly. For a second, I fear the mycelial roots will come out with my organs still attached. They don't. There are a few pieces of muscle and specks of blood stuck to them, and it hurts, but it's not as painful as it could be. I wonder how many hyphae are still threaded deep inside me. I drop the fungal stub behind the headboard.

I've got to go.

# CHAPTER FOURTEEN

I cling to the banisters as I stumble down the stairs, my heart in my throat. The rush of movement is dizzying, and I wobble back and forth on weak legs, steady as soaked cardboard. I've been floating outside my body for too long. Now that I've crashed back into it, my skin is unsuitable and ill-fitting, like a three-fingered glove.

I stand at the top of the stairs, listening. I must leave, but I don't know where I'll go. The baby's gone, and everything has gone wrong, and I have to leave. It isn't possible that Silas is in the house. He would have heard me scream, I think. He would have come. As I stumble down the hallway, I look over my shoulder. I think about going into the woods, letting the poisoned and cursed land overtake me. It doesn't matter. As long as I'm not in this house anymore. A chill runs up my spine so hard it makes me convulse. I've got to go.

I would run if I could, but each thud of my foot on the stairs knocks through my whole body. I haven't regained control over myself yet. I'm not sure if my bones are solid anymore.

There's a rustling in the fancy bedroom, what Silas calls the master bedroom, the one downstairs that no one sleeps in. I stiffen. I don't know what Silas could possibly be doing in there. The bedroom door is open, but I can't see in without getting closer, the hallway's too long. I sneak toward the door. I grit my teeth each time a floorboard creaks under me. Silas still shuffles in the bedroom, murmuring to himself. Relief floods my body when I reach the end of the stairs. I reach for the doorknob, but it jerks in my hand, turning by itself under my palm. I yank away from the friction of the brass against my skin.

The door swings open, and Silas barrels through the doorway, his head down. Right before he knocks into me, he jerks his head up to see me. A shadow flickers across his face but dies quickly. "Nicole? What are you doing up?"

I try to sidestep past him, but I'm even clumsier than I realize. He's faster than me, and my fuzzy mind can't keep up.

"I've got to . . . "

My words fail me. I throw my hands at his face as I fend for my life. He's so much bigger than me. He grabs my wrists easily and pins them to his chest.

"You have to what?"

"To go to . . . "

I collapse, because I can't move and talk at the same time. I'm crying, but that takes effort, too, and I clamp on my tongue with my teeth to stop, then let my neck roll back. I give up in his grasp. Silas eases us both down to the ground and places me gently in his lap. He strokes my head and shushes me.

"It's okay, it's okay."

Eventually, he stands up and carries me to the stairs. When he puts his foot down on the first step, I writhe in his arms. I won't return to that bed. He murmurs something soothing as he retreats to the other side of the house. When he passes the master bedroom door, I crane my neck to look inside. Just as I start to close my eyes, I see a long rope dragging across the floor and a flicker of light like a beating heart in someone's bare hands. A figure. She stands in the hallway, staring into the bedroom and shaking her head no, no, no.

Silas takes me to the couch where he reads, and where I first began the tilt backward. He sits at my feet and stares at the ground. His face is solemn, pockmarked with age and worry. He looks different. Old, worn down, haggard. Strengthless. Sleep comes abruptly, like a blanket thrown over my head.

The form comes back. Its blurry visage hovers over me. At first I think it's my mother, because she comes with the smell of ointment and the sound of maternal rustling, as if, in death, she still wears too many gloves, too many clothes. I think in horror she is going to tell me again that I will get used to it, the last clear words I heard from her. But as she nears, I see that it isn't my mother. It's me. No, it's almost me. A familiar stranger. She pulls a blanket over my shoulders and rubs my arm through the blankets.

"You're going to a better place," she says as she leans closer to me. "All the Godzillas you could ever want." Her warm breath next to my ear is like broth. “And soon, we’ll wake you up.” Her voice starts to tremble now. “And I’ll be with you again.”

And then she’s gone.

I hear my son crying.

He’s hungry. I sit up in alarm. I feel a stab in the ribs and a brace of nausea.

Then I remember. Guilt rises with my panic. I climb the stairs, arms out in case I fall. My head scrambles to find an explanation to give Silas for why I’d leave my baby’s corpse in his bed. Nothing comes to me. I’m too frantic, too tired.

In the bedroom, the curtains are pulled open, the duct tape is curled and sticking to itself in clumps on the ground. The moonlight filters in. Silas is still and facing the wall. I creep in quietly. Breathing as little as possible, I stick my hands under the covers and feel around, cringing, expecting at any moment to clasp my hand around a soft, spongy, half-formed body. I never do. Silas must have found him before me. I scan the room but see nothing. I don’t know what to do. I’ve never heard of a boy being born from another wife, but I can’t blame it on that. I was the one who pulled him out. I thought I was going to die, and I pulled him out.

When I look up, Silas is no longer facing the wall. He’s staring at me. “There you are. Come to bed.”

I want to go into the forest to die, but I’m so tired, so I lie in bed next to my husband where I’m supposed to be, though it’s the last place I ever want to be again. I don’t know what went wrong. I don't understand what happened. I stare at the ceiling, imagining my baby's lidless eyes watching my breathing form as I sleep. Me, the monstrous thing that mothered and murdered him, then went on with its life.

I'm awake when Silas sleeps, and I'm awake when he wakes. He faces the wall, like it's more respectful if he sleeps that way, but I can tell when he wakes because his mouth makes an abrupt ripping sound, like he can only get away from his dreams if he's torn from them. He turns to look at me, slowly, so he doesn't disturb me. When his eyes meet mine, he goes rigid.

"It's over," I say.

"I know." He nods. "It's okay. Really, it's okay." His voice is low and soft. Gingerly, he reaches out and touches my arm. I hate his touch. I don't move away, though. My eyes pierce into his, then harden. He takes his hand back. Stiffly, with his archaic bones popping noisily, he rolls off the edge of the mattress. He lingers at the doorway and says, "Don't worry about getting up or anything. Stay in bed as long as you like."

I don't want to stay in bed, but I suppose it's as good a punishment as any. He doesn't want to murder me. I should feel glad. Grateful. I turn to the wall. I am done feeling grateful. Grateful leaked out of me forever. Instead, I think of where the sharp things are in the house. Knives in the kitchen, metal scraps in the basement, garden tools in the shed. Glass to break, chairs to splinter. In my mind, all the edges get sharper and sharper as I move my thumb back and forth over them.

In my dreams, I find Silas with his body embedded in the wall. He reaches out for me, begging to be uprooted. His forehead flickers with a fontanelle pulse, ready to be punctured and split open.

# CHAPTER FIFTEEN

Something builds in my chest and spreads slowly, like rust. I plod along, doing my chores. My body does the things it needs to do without me. I maintain the rain barrels, cook in the tub I've designated as the cooking tub because I can't get used to Silas's fireplace, and sit quietly next to my husband when he comes home. I watch him eat. I watch him talk. I watch him sleep.

Whenever I think of the baby, a numb buzzing fills my head. When his memory flashes, unbidden, I go rigid. In the middle of the room, in the middle of whatever I'm doing, I stiffen and my mind blanks, blanks, blanks, until I can find myself again. It takes everything I have to staunch the torrent of embarrassment and shame and force myself to keep going. Meanwhile, shreds of mycelium keep working themselves out of my body. I rip them out when they surface. It's like tearing fraying threads from an old shirt. Throughout the day, I wonder how much of me is unstitching.

---

*Where were you?*

When Silas walks in the front door, when he paces in his library, when he eats, I think as I watch him, *Where were you, where were you?*

I can't ask him directly, but it's all I think about. He kept me here, alone. Always alone, even raised alone, and I thought it was so he could have me all to himself, but then after I did what he wanted, he left me alone again.

Worst of all, I can't share my grief with the other women like I did when my mother died. And I can't give the boy to the earth. I can't feed his decomposition. He should be with the other mothers. I don't know where Silas put him, but I know he is alone, like me.

Something is clogged in my stomach. A confused knot doomed to be a scar, a fibrous gnarl that will no longer nurture growths. It's shocking, how terrible the grief is. How confusing. How complicated. How linked to all the women who came before.

I go about my day. I keep my hands stiffly at my sides so they don't accidentally touch my tender stomach. I stare at Silas. *Where were you? Where were you when I needed you?*

Silas suddenly has a lot of work, and I'm glad. It means I don't have to run into him. From outside on the Juliet balcony, I can hear Silas pacing in the library, talking. I can't understand his words, but I listen to his tone. He speaks to himself without inhibition or embarrassment. He inquires, beseeches, and sometimes argues, an argument that climaxes to the same short grunt of a yell.

In the upstairs hallway, I walk again. Walking is the only way I know how to preoccupy myself anymore. I touch the walls as I pass by them. I linger my hands in the framework of shadows made by the art, vases, and tables. And above me, I hear someone else pacing, and pacing, and pausing when I pause. Someone laughs below me, someone laughs above.

# CHAPTER SIXTEEN

My life is shaped by Silas. Days are long and muted by the sun and by loneliness. Time is fluid and airy, until the sky ambers and Silas walks home from work. Then my moments pass in a more regimented way. Dinner, washing dishes, sitting on the couch, lying in the bed. He quiets me, keeps me in place. He explains life as it was and how he wished it had been. At night, he calls me in a strained voice without looking at me. Time is marked by my pounding rage, thudding larger than my heart inside me.

I wait for Teaghan to appear again, but she doesn't.

One day, the waiting—for Silas, for Teaghan, for anybody—builds in my chest. It scours me clean of anything else. I am trapped in the house. I can't leave; I don't want to feel the heaviness of the sky when the walls drop away. My hands won't stop shaking.

I open the photo album and find the face I saw attached to me. Joseph. When Silas said that he'd chosen a face from my past, he didn't mean my past, he meant Pamela's.

When Silas finally comes home, he calls for me. I have been waiting for him all day, but when he trails through the house, calling my name, I remain silent. He finds me in the room of stone flowers and doesn't reprimand me for not answering. He has his own dreary and formidable cloud making him miserable. I drag my finger through a layer of dust on a ripple of stone petals.

"I didn't know that boys could get the plague."

Silas's body relaxes. In some way, he's pleased I'm so upset. He wants me to be sad. Maybe we can't be equals until I am as deeply versed in loss as he is.

"They can."

"We could be having sons as well, all this time?"

"Hardly any of the sons got the plague."

"What happened to the ones that did?"

Silas is silent for a while. Then, he says, "We're not supposed to have them in our lives. The other men agreed to it. I didn't. But you can't tell anyone what you know. It would be very bad for the both of us."

I spread out my arms, as if to ask, who am I going to tell?

He continues, "I know, I *know*, I haven't been forthright. But I promise it's for a good reason."

"Well, then tell me."

"You don't know what's coming, Pamela. You can't know. It's not your fault."

The thing that's building in my chest widens, a nervous energy building inside me, deciphering how it's going to exit my body. "You could tell me."

"I will. I promise that I will." He looks at the floor and shakes his head. "Trust me. It won't be long now."

I turn to the wall, to the stone flowers climbing up the walls, swirling on the ceiling, framing the rose wallpaper, always in bloom.

Silas leaves the room.

The figure stays in the house. She comes with me when I walk. I see her on the staircase, stuck beneath the stairs. Behind a door, fumbling with the lock. I see her standing between rooms. She looks lost. She doesn't know where she is. Of course. She doesn't know or understand who brought her here. I apologize to her for bringing her here. I see her in the bathroom, her hair loose and getting sucked down the drains. I see her lying face down on the floor. I see her in the kitchen with a long, impossible braid that she twists and kneads, like it's bread. She puts it in a bowl and stirs, she saws at it with a steak knife, but it never breaks. It's Pamela. It's always been Pamela. I see her cupping her hands and holding them out, like she's asking for something or trying to catch drops of rain inside. I have dreams of ash erupting out of me. It keeps sliding out of my body, but I can't tell from where. My mouth? My stomach? My vagina? I can't remember which part does what anymore. I find her facing a wall, her hands over her eyes, and in all her postures of grief. What could she be crying for? Pamela, stuck in the many forms of her misery. I touch her face and hold her hand, but I can't feel her skin. What I do feel is a throbbing, a deep-rooted headache.

Once, I follow her into the nursery, where she starts to cry.

"What are you doing?" Silas pants, alarmed, from the doorway. I must have been making some sort of noise to have him run in like this.

Like a sleepwalker, I look down and say, "I don't know."

I feel like I can't move, even when I'm moving, I want to say. I start crying too. He looks at me, his face pathetic with concern, and nods in understanding.

"It's okay." He opens his arms to draw me to him. "It will get better, you'll see. When it's the three of us again, everything will be better."

I realize he has the pouch with him, tied around his neck. He doesn't bring it out at this moment, but I know he will soon.

My child didn't have a name. It wasn't my job to think of one. The men are meant to do the naming. If it were up to us, without the knowledge of the old world, we'd choose the names of familiar objects: Bucket, Remaining Shoe, Smile, Teacup. If Silas did pick one out, I'm glad he didn't tell me. It would ruin something, I think, if the baby had been marked by the old world, marked by Silas, with a name.

I dream of the dawn and her lover. Dawn's face is pink and swollen and rupturing and endless, while her lover, granted immortality but not eternal youth, grows old and older. The dawn keeps him in a stone castle that pulses with the milky sea. The dawn brings in waves of servants. They shuffle around the stone castle, slowing down as the decades pass, their pops and cracks of old bones muffled by sheaths of old flesh. The servants become slow and slower, become stone, until the dawn sets them to the side of the immense hallways. And then the next wave of servants comes in and rustles through the castle, bundled in their pale skirts, breathing hot and young, but becoming old again, faster this time, and faster. The pale shadows of their bodies slivering as the first wave of servants turn to dust. And meanwhile the dawn's lover becomes older, and older, at the same pace as that first wave of servants who were dust in the cold shadows. And the dawn's lover should be dust. Instead, he babbles endlessly in a room with too many heavy curtains, too many oppressive paintings. Dawn crouches next to her lover, grieving and apologizing. Her face is not a face, but a rose.

My time continues to be measured by Silas. Whether he wants it that way or not, whether I want it, and whether he deserves it, my day passes like this: Silas is home, Silas is not home, Silas is home, Silas is sleeping, awake, out the front door, Silas is walking back in.

I think about how difficult it is to find meaning in a life spent alone. Sometimes I imagine a phantom son around me. A boy to have, a boy to hold. A boy to fill the house with a new song. Even though I know what he looks like, I usually imagine him golden and full of light, a stark contrast to the dark house. Golden boy. Aren't the old stories always filled with these rewards? Gold and a boy.

He'd never leave me. Never be wed off. He'd stay someone I could love forever. It's almost enough to tempt me into swallowing more spores. But then the rage floods in when I think of Silas.

I wake up each morning in loss, like a puddle of light around me. But I also gain something of myself each day. My thoughts are clearer and come quicker and I can recognize myself in them. My growths are extending. The caps maturing, the gills flaring, the stems elongating. Once, Silas looked at the ones Teaghan gave me. I saw confusion pass over his face, but he didn't mention it. He probably thought they were from the baby. Let us all glamour ourselves into a different life than the one we're living.

I will never swallow those spores. I will never have Silas's son. I will never be tied to that bed again.

# CHAPTER SEVENTEEN

It's Monday, but the rain barrels have become clogged with small sticks. Silas tells me to come into town with him so I can see how to fix them. There is a slight condemnation in his patient ask. After all, it was my job to make sure the mycelium mats were well kept. I don't tell him I'm the one who's shoved the sticks in there out of petty boredom.

We roll two wheelbarrows, each holding a congested rain barrel, down the roads. We push past the bygone wreckage, frozen in time and darkened by rain. It is as if the houses we pass are strange pimples in the earth's crust, volcanic pores about to spill over with soil-black, fertilized pus. We keep quiet. The houses, with their masks of vine and leaf, get smaller and closer together.

Maybe I'll see Teagan.

I can see how that could be a disaster. If the true me is unveiled at the sight of her, I won't be able to stop it. As much as Silas is determined to keep to his life of illusions, even he'd be able to see the truth, that it was never him who made my mouth spew black.

"Woof, this heat," he says, wiping his sweaty neck. "Can you believe it's even worse in other places."

He waves to the houses. "You know, eventually we're going to return all this back to the land."

"Back to the land?"

"Yeah. All this plastic, paint, just general bullshit. We're feeding it to the lab mushrooms."

"Mushrooms can eat all this?"

He throws out his arms and shouts, "We're going to make this a good place to live! We really are. It's going to be clean again. It's going to be a good place to live again."

He doesn't seem to need someone to answer, so I don't. He patters on, like someone singing an old song, not listening to the lyrics and forgetting they ever meant something in the first place.

On the center road, the effects of the recent storm and current heat wave are easy to see. More houses have crumbled. Old repairs have degraded under the stress of rain and wind. The people, too, have taken on too much moisture, and are sunken under the strain of the current heat.

"The tools we need are in a shed this way," Silas explains, nodding down the road.

A few women are chattering, but most are lounging on porches, as still as possible, bedraggled in the oppressive humidity. Even the children stick to the little shade they can find away from the adults. The men have that murderous, blood-clotted look they wear when they're hungover, bodies too raw, skulls that have been opened with too much force the night before.

"Why aren't they in the lab?" Silas murmurs.

He's talking to himself, but I answer anyway. "Maybe it's a good sign. Maybe nothing needs to be done in the lab, and you can take a break."

"Maybe," he grumbles.

We walk by a group of women sloped on a lawn, leaning crookedly against broken mailboxes and rotted benches. When the women see us, they move their fingers slightly to me in greeting, wipe their brows sluggishly, then lie still again. Three men sit on the curb on the other side of the street. When they see us coming, they look away.

"Shit." Silas picks up speed. "Come on, we better move faster."

We pass Reese's house. Brown trim, sides dappled with chips of amber paint. My mom's prison and place of death. It's strange to see it from the front.

Reese is in the doorway, staring blankly at his new wife, not so new anymore. She's lying on the lawn by herself, staring up at the sky. He must miss my mom too. It's a connection I don't really want with him. Somehow, despite the way he treated her, Mom had changed Reese, forced him into a happiness he could not feel on his own. Lifted him out of the thousand layers of grief-fossils that had settled on his skin. Nausea rises within me and doesn't stop rising even after I look away.

Silas stops abruptly in front of a house with cracked pillars and a cloak of ivy disguising its right side. He blinks in surprise, then anger. I turn and stare at the house. A man stands at the end of its driveway. I recognize him. Mom went rigid and blinked sadly every time he passed by. Maggie's husband, Aaron. I almost don't notice Eloise sitting crouched beside the hedgerow. She looks even older than when I last saw her. At her age, a couple of weeks makes a big difference. But she's a sensitive child, and her fear has always made her look older than she is.

Aaron shouts toward one of the open windows above the garage, "Hurry up!"

Maggie is on the porch. She's sitting in a wheelchair, something I haven't seen in a while, ever since one of the men who used one died. Perhaps this is his. She doesn't look the same. Besides the blank expression on her face, all traces of growth cluster have left her face, arms, and hands, and her brown, human skin has radiated uncannily to all the peripherals of her body. I stare at her as Silas huffs angrily next to me. Maggie, another Maggie, comes out of the house, slamming the door behind her.

Aaron yells again, "There you are, for the love of Christ."

Maggie ignores him and bends down to the Maggie in the wheelchair. She pats her vigorously on the shoulder and pitches her voice up loud and high like she's talking to a baby, though I've never noticed her talking to Eloise like that. "It's good for you to get some fresh air, isn't it? You were enjoying it very much, weren't you?"

Silas grabs my arm, too hard. He turns me and says, "Go

back to the house. I'll be there in a minute." His face is full of rage when he turns away, leaving me and the wheelbarrows to stride toward Aaron.

Maggie pats at her bouncy hair, then groans as she wrangles the wheelchair over a dirt ramp that has been piled up and patted down on the side of the porch, two wooden boards shifting uneasily under the wheelchair's pressure. Silas told me to leave, but I can't. I won't.

A gunshot goes off behind me, followed by the squeak of an animal hit and a woman cheering, "Got it!"

I turn and see Amaya with a gun tucked under her armpit, her fist raised in the air, her sodden curls plastered to the growth on the side of her face, oozing more in the moist air.

Silas is halfway to Aaron when he calls out to him, "What the fuck is this?"

A shadow passes over Aaron's face, but he erases it with a smirk. "How do you like the new addition to my family?"

Silas swipes his hand over his beard. "I mean, seriously? She shouldn't be out yet. She should still be soaking."

"You think she's going to start worrying about her skin?" Aaron glowers. The pair are standing close together now. Aaron is shorter, but bulkier and more compact. Next to Aaron, Silas is tall like a starved tree.

Maggie swings wide to avoid them as she pushes the wheelchair down the driveway with a stylish flounce. Eloise watches her pass by sullenly, but doesn't make a move to follow.

Silas points a finger in Aaron's face. "You should be worrying about her comfort."

Aaron knocks his finger away. "Maybe she doesn't want to spend her first conscious days in a fucking lab."

Maggie rolls up to me, smiling primly. "My foremother, Selma," she purrs. "Isn't she beautiful?"

She pats the woman on the shoulder again, like this woman is an infant, not the ancient predecessor of Maggie's entire legacy. The foremother stares at nothing. She's still caught in the liminal space before death. The only signs of her life are the gentle pulse of her throat and her chest sluggishly filling with and releasing air.

"She drools a little." Maggie dabs a cloth around the woman's neck and chin, her cracked and sliced-open lips. "But I made this bib out of my own shirt."

I'm astonished. I don't know what to say in front of this venerable being. Her body has clearly gone through an intense process. She's a thing melted, then hastily reshaped by clumsy hands. Someone sewed her cheek incisions. It looks like her jagged mouth extends too far into her jaw, her scowl now stretching to creaturely, froggy proportions. She gives off a masculine heat and the smell of something stale and chemical—an underground unkemptness. Her growths, at least the visible ones, are gone. Most of her internal ones must have also been removed, as her flesh is no longer distended. I can see the shape of her bones too well in some places. In others, her skin is loose and hanging, sagging in folded layers, like a half-buttoned blouse that doesn't fit.

Silas's voice is angry, but reasoning, reasonable. "It wasn't her. It was just the cathinone and the psilocybin. You know that, right? She probably doesn't even remember . . . "

Aaron's mean and challenging grin falls from his face. He steps closer. "You think you know her better than me? Because you—"

Silas steps back. "Aaron—"

"Fucked her a handful of times? I fucked her at least a hundred more times, okay? A thousand more times. She's my *wife*."

"Aaron, I wasn't talking about that." Silas glances at me. Our eyes connect, but he looks away quickly, lowers his voice, and I don't hear what he says next.

Aaron lurches forward and puts his hands on Silas's chest. "Don't say my name." He pushes Silas with a grunt.

"Out of her shirt." The words come out of my mouth so automatically that I don't remember thinking them.

Maggie looks up sharply. "What?"

I cough, pushing a mycelial thread into the pocket of my cheek to spit out later. "You made the bib out of *her* shirt. It was hers to begin with, right?"

Maggie growls. She yanks the wheelchair away from me, keeping her eyes locked on mine. "Come on, let's go for a walk."

She says it so pleasantly, I assume she's talking to Selma. But then she turns and beckons me impatiently. I can't help but follow. I want to get away from Silas and Aaron. Besides, I want to be near Selma. As Maggie walks down the street, the women perk up. They unpeel themselves from the ground and patter into the street to gather around Maggie. When almost a dozen surround us, Maggie decides that she has drawn a big enough audience, and stops to fan Selma and talk.

"She started blinking today!" she announces.

Everyone has wind headaches after the storm, and it takes a moment for the women to gather their equilibrium. In this heat, it's hard to stand upright. They pinch the bridges of their noses and itch their irritated growth stubble. Dust in the air aggravates their bloodshot, gluey eyes. They put fingers against their piercing temples and try to calm the nasty thudding inside. Even so, everyone has a smile for the foremother. They're looking at me too. Trying to see how I'll react.

Tyra says, "Can you believe it? Our own foremother."

"A foremother of our own," says Alice.

Maggie turns from side to side, obliging the crowd with a tidy smile. Somehow, her eyes always seem to avoid mine. Her hand never leaves the wheelchair, and she jiggles it back and forth, back and forth, as if soothing a baby who will start to scream if it goes still.

"The men gave her to us," says Clara.

"They had her all along," says Tyra.

"And we never even knew."

Where's Teaghan? She knew. We knew. Though we didn't know they could wake up. The foremother stares ahead.

Maggie crows, "I made her a little bib out of *my* own shirt." She wipes the woman's chin with the bib, though this time I don't see any saliva on it. She wipes a little too hard, I think.

The women look down at the foremother. Someone smooths her hair tenderly with their hand. Someone pats her knee. They talk to her in the way that men pray, in hushed voices heavy with reverence. Maggie steps back and itches her shoulder. A thin patina of clear, dried skin scrapes off. It glistens as it twirls down. Other fungus patches have dried against her body and become flaky. Her stubble is overgrown. Did Maggie not shave this morning? It seems impossible.

Gradually, I can hear the men's voices behind me, rising all at once, their argument floating our way. I look down the street toward them. A few more have gathered and are adding their voices, holding either Silas or Aaron away from the other or standing between the pair. Everyone seems cowed by Silas.

Eloise has wandered from her spot. She crouches alone on the sidewalk. Forlornly, she picks up a stick and draws against the cement, the scraping sound loud and grating.

"Don't worry, she's going to move out soon," Maggie says without looking at me or her daughter.

"Move out? She's so young."

"It's better for her," she says shortly. Maggie scratches at her shoulder again. The sap exuded is shiny and new and weeping. She mops a rope of the gooey discharge with her forefinger, then wipes it on her skirt. After shaving for so long, I wonder if it's a relief when everything starts to grow back in or if it's overwhelming and confusing. If the growths eventually feel unnecessary, more trouble than they're worth. "I have my hands full now. First wife is the favorite wife, you know? Eloise will be better off with Lottie."

My heart aches, looking at Eloise. I remember her small body in my arms, the jeans between us. "I could take her."

Maggie scoffs. "Like I'd punish her by sending her out in the middle of nowhere with you. Don't be selfish. She's already been through enough." She jiggles the wheelchair, and her foremother's neck starts to wobble. Maggie doesn't seem to notice. "Besides, she barely knows you."

I am so concentrated on Maggie, on Selma, that when a hand clenches my shoulder, I yelp. It's Silas. "Come on," he says gruffly. "Let's go."

We've forgotten the wheelbarrows and broken rain barrels at Maggie's house, but I'm not about to ask after them.

As we walk away, Maggie throws after us, "Remember to stay away from that Teaghan girl. She's bad news!" She laughs.

My heart tightens as I cast a quick glance at Silas. His hand grips my shoulder. One of my growths twists under his palm. I twinge at the pain, but will myself not to jerk away.

We walk together in guarded silence. When the houses start to space out again, and we can no longer hear voices on the wind, Silas asks, "Are you okay?"

"Yes," I say. He seems to have forgotten that I ignored his orders, which is a relief.

He clears his throat nervously. "I know seeing a human wife out of the blue, awake like that, must be unnerving." I look straight ahead. "Completely human wife, I mean," he amends.

"I didn't know they were here."

"Yes . . . " Silas draws out the word. "It's how we get the dust for babies."

"I see."

"If we did not have them, we wouldn't have you."

"But, if you can wake them up, why don't you?"

"Well, we can't wake them. Not really." He pauses. "The problem is they never go back to normal. They eventually become coherent, but it takes a little while. And even then, it's only for a few hours. Soon after that they die of something like ergotism. It's pretty ugly. Aaron has condemned his wife to a lot of unnecessary suffering, is what he's done."

"Oh." I think of her lying in the cellar, forever hurting in the pristine dark instead.

"It means that Aaron has given up," Silas says. "That's going to happen a lot more now. We're all getting older." He says, quieter, "We're all getting old."

We walk in silence after that. I don't know or care what he's thinking. I have my own thoughts. First and foremost, I want Teaghan. I want to talk to her about the awake foremother. I want to touch her. I want to learn what she knows, but also, to recenter myself. To recover what I've lost since we last met.

# CHAPTER EIGHTEEN

After something inside me breaks, everything is better. I am no longer erratic. I reach the crest and the sharp, glass edges of me are smooth again. My anger becomes soft, strange, and moonlit. The air in the hallway becomes as luxurious as timeworn silk, as the seafoam a goddess is born in. I become lost in its decadence. I find a rhythm. I feel a flush of desire, embodiment, like I am with Teaghan again. One that no longer thinks about futures or survival or whether I am pleasing someone else enough to keep myself alive. Something giddy. Not desperate, not grasping. Something willing to tear, something unafraid of the hidden core of myself.

While I am in this state, the house becomes malleable. The hallways change, the rooms, the shadows and walls. I glide through entryways, touching doorframes. I don't recognize anything. The house is a new house, just as my body is new. I think of knives, and become a knife, slicing through the darkness. Metal nudging for blood.

Once, a new door, a newly opened hole, transports me

into the library, where Silas has cordoned himself off. He startles at my entrance. His expression exposes him. I don't know what he's been doing, but it's a betrayal. I can see it on his face. I laugh. I laugh so hard I have to keel over and look at the ground, heaving. How bizarre, the situations we find ourselves in, in this house. Silas laughs too. At first it is a strangulated, strained laugh, absurd and cautious. Then, when I am on the ground, laughing, the madness of relief washes over him, and his laugh becomes wild and hideous, and we both laugh with our whole, grotesque selves.

The room deflates. I stop laughing. I am on my back looking at the ceiling. I turn over, still on the floor, crouching. Silas is hunched over his desk, grinning, wild-eyed. Something has changed between us. Two solitary beasts on the edge of their respective territories catching sight of each other between the blades of tall grass. I could go to him. I could show him my bones. We could be husband and wife, truly, ruthlessly, finally, for the first time. Instead I walk out the door, slamming it. I forgo dinner. Upstairs, I walk through the hallways, touching the peripheries. I am coming back to myself. There is no room for Silas. No room for a baby in my body, and no room for Pamela. There was never any room for them. There is only room for me.

The next day, I go beneath the house, down the uneven steps into the partially subterranean cellar. The air cools my body and the fragrance of concealed things grows stronger. The float of dust obscures my view, but my eyes adjust until I see the rows of rough-hewn wood shelves with glass jars lined on top.

There's something about this place, the cellar. The rest of the house is made with care, with artists' signatures, made with materials to last. Not this place. I run my hand over the coarse wood of the shelf, feeling the splinters dig into my skin. This place was made in a hurry, without any art or craft at all. Like it was dug out of the earth by desperate hands.

I pick up a jar of preserves and brush old spiderwebs off the side. When I turn to leave, I hesitate. I don't want to abandon the underground so quickly. It's cool and nice, while the day is hot and the light overbearing. I take a step and my ankle folds under me. The sole of my shoe has been loosening, flapping, but now it's come undone entirely. I catch myself but drop the jam jar, and the viscera explodes over the ground, strawberry giblets slapping across the whole stretch of the cellar, over the floor, up the side of the wall, licking the bottom of the shelves. I groan with annoyance, get on my knees, and gather the glass shards in my cupped palm, meticulous not to slice myself.

I don't know why, but something about the smell of the naked dirt, the bone-chill on my knees, the snarl of exposed roots coming up through the ground, the guts, the explosion of too-sweet fruit, the glitter of sharp glass between the sticky smear makes something swivel in my pelvis. I can't tell if I like it or hate it, but I think of her. Her grin grows and grows until her teeth slide away from each other, the gaps in her gums spread, and her face slides to the sides in quickening expansion. *Do you ever wonder what we could make on our own?* I gasp out loud in the darkness.

# CHAPTER NINETEEN

In bed, I lean over Silas. He's sleeping.

The most dangerous year for a woman is her newlywed year. The women occasionally discuss how it would be better for women to wait another year, at least until they turn three, to get married. At two, a woman makes too many bad decisions, too many poor choices that get her killed. Perhaps, if a woman waited until she was three, she'd have a better chance. But can we really fault the men for wanting wives when it is us who keeps them sane? They're eager to have us by their side, even if we are still shaped a bit youthfully, our minds not quite sharpened with the experience.

When I was young, I knew two was a difficult age, but I swore I would stay smart. The terrible twos, it's called. I think about that promise to myself and to my mother on the way out the front door, looking up into the blackness of the hallway at the top of the staircase. I search for the gleam of a pair of eyes, but it's so dark that anyone could be standing there, staring at me, and I'd have no way of knowing.

I don't know which house Teaghan moved into once she got married, but I have a feeling I'll know the place when I see it.

It ends up not mattering. I spot her standing in the yard of a blue house, waiting for me like she knows I'm coming.

I walk up to her, but the closer I get, the shyer I feel. I can't tell if she's smiling. The moon highlights the top of her head and the tip of her nose and leaves the rest in shadow. The mushrooms on her face have grown so long, they crest past her scalp, like a crown or a nest of coiled snakes. There is a heaviness lying between us that wasn't there before. I wonder if something happened to her in the storm too.

"Were you . . . " I stop. I want to ask if she really was waiting for me, but I'm too nervous. "Do you come outside a lot?"

She laughs a loud bark, like she's not at all afraid that her husband will hear her or notice she's gone. It cracks against the house behind us, then the houses beyond answer in echo. She reaches out and touches my hand. I can feel her enter me, and this time, feel a contented pleasure. We stand there, staring at each other, her gleaming eyes, pupilless in the night.

"I hate it in the house," she says.

I look at our entwined hands, then back at her. Her top lip is curling, shining now in a way it hadn't when her face was resting. She tugs my hand. "Come on, then."

Everything is so different in the dark. Each insect sound, each of our steps on the broken asphalt is brilliant and sharp. The leaves rustle in that way that heralds an impending rain. The fireflies beyond us, like faraway lanterns, swim away as we move through them and open up pockets of darkness.

She points to a house. "This used to be a big chicken coop before we were born. There's still chicken shit in it."

"What happened to the chickens?"

"They didn't work out." She shows me the fenced-in, barred-up house that used to be the goat shed. "Goats didn't work out, either."

I listen to our footsteps and her breathing as we walk for a while, until we get to the last house at the end of a line of houses. Its yard backs up into the wall that protects our compound.

She stops me at the edge of the yard. "This is the farthest I can get away from the center road."

"Do you ever go farther?"

She looks at the wall, where I'm staring. "Like, in the woods?" I nod. She snorts. "Of course not. None of the other women even come this close."

"Why?"

I think of what waits on the other side of the wall. Something ready to grab us and pull us into the mad chaos of the toxins.

"My mom used to tell me stories to scare me from leaving. She said if the things that live in the woods got hold of me, they'd kill me, or worse."

"Or worse?"

"I don't really know what she meant by that." She shakes her head. "But . . . when I stand here and look out there . . . "

We stare at the woods.

"Anything could live beyond there," I agree.

She lets go of my hand and starts to head around the back of the house, but I linger. Has anyone gone into the woods and come back alive? What if she didn't tell anyone and lives among the rest of us with her secret? What if she became a wife, and in her marriage bed, her skin leisurely poisons her husband whenever he dares touch her.

Eventually I follow Teaghan. I see that the whole rear of the house has collapsed. It has become a house-mask hiding a man-made cave. As we step over the debris scattered around the yard, I can smell rust and rotting clutter, the undefended core of the house wafting outside. We duck as far into the house's pit as we can and find a few rearranged dressers and old toys and empty bookcases. Teaghan uncovers a lantern, then lies on an old mattress that's been pulled off the frame. I lie next to her and sink into the wet, spongey bed. We look up at the ceiling and the partially exposed sky.

Teaghan says, "Sometimes I think about the building falling on top of me and no one can find me and I can't move ever again. It's dark and wet and cold, and the wood around me gets wet and mushy."

"How awful," I mutter absentmindedly as we stare at the smear of stars.

"What do you mean?" Her head snaps up. I glance at her and see her surprised face. My nostrils flush, I blush around the chin. "No. I want it to happen." She shakes her head, then lies back down so I can't see her. "I dream of the other women sneaking in, away from their husbands, and seeing the good thing I have. And they drape and weave themselves through the mushy wood around me and find their own places. And we all rest together and dream and speak beautiful songs. The men hate the way everything is crumbling. But not me. I like it wet. I like it old too." I see a star arch toward the earth. Not for the first time, I wonder how the stars replenish themselves.

"I like feeling old things and moving my hands around them and feeling the changes that have happened inside them. I like eating old things. I feel even more when I eat them."

A strap hangs on the mattress. I reach out and touch it. It's attached to a gas mask, child-size. I hold it up to my face, but it's too small. It smells funky, a smell I can't quite place. I put it down. "Aren't you afraid of mold?"

"I'm careful," she shrugs. She says it so carelessly, I have a feeling she isn't careful at all.

She walks her fingers up my leg like her hand is a little animal. Pale scabs bunching over her knuckles make it look hunchbacked and grumpy. She performs this so casually. I look at her askance, but she's still staring at the ceiling. Her touch is aimless. I haven't felt comfortable in my body lately, maybe never have, and her touch is giving me a prickling, discomforting sensation. Her fingers reach my knee, touching the downy buttons that grow there. Her turquoise fingers flutter over my burgundy skin. She purses her lips and her head falls to the side so she can look up at me through her lashes.

"Why do you think your mom never left the house?"

"We weren't allowed to."

"Plenty of women aren't allowed to. Why don't you think she never left even when her husband was off working?"

“I guess . . . ” I shift, but not too much, not enough to make her think I might be trying to move away from her. “Reese said that if he ever found out my mom took me outside, or went out herself, I’d be taken away from her. He was really strict about it. Or, I thought it was Reese. But I guess it was Silas.”

Teaghan sighs. “What we won’t do for our daughters, right?”

“Yeah.”

“Doesn’t that feel like a trap?”

“You mean, does love feel like a trap?”

She puts her hand over her face. “Ugh, never mind. Don’t word it like that.”

“Like what?”

“Shh!” Teaghan suddenly stiffens and makes a fist so that her nail scratches me. “What’s that?”

I go still, too, and try to quiet my heart, jerking in my chest. Something is shuffling nearby, right outside the house. I swallow hard. We are so close to the wall. Our eyes lock. Then she’s up in a bound, scrambling over the broken furniture, making so much noise I want to scream at her to stop. I follow after her, ungainly and dreamlike and slow.

I haven’t even cleared the furniture, let alone the shell of the house when Teaghan calls excitedly to me, “Nicole, come quick!”

She bends over the grass, too close to the wall. I don’t move closer; I don’t want to get so near the woods.

“What is it?”

She lifts her head. Her fungal extensions bisect her face,

one half of shadow, one of moonlit flesh. She beckons me, and I can't help but obey. I stand alongside Teaghan and we both stare. She's bending over a mound of fur. A rabbit, trembling as it tries to walk. Patches of bald spots cover its pelt, exposing its wretched, shuddering meat, shiny like glass or shifting water in the night. It makes a motion toward us, like it doesn't know we're its enemies. Like it's so far gone, it has this infantile desire for warmth, so desperate for comfort that it will beg for it from anything moving. I feel the urge to press it down against the ground. Pin it under my hands.

"Don't touch it," Teaghan stops my hand midair. "A wounded thing protects itself. Its teeth are sharper than they look."

Its eye shivers, its mouth shivers. It becomes a tense bundle of blood and muscle. A strange, pent-up movement, then its body releases. A thrill of unease and fear wrinkles into me.

"I think it's dead," Teaghan whispers in awe. She reaches out and grabs it. I give a little cry as she turns to me. "What?"

"The toxins. You're going to get it on your hands."

She grins at me and lowers herself to her knees. I watch with horror as she pinches its belly. Hooks her finger and uses it to tear into its stomach with her nail. A hard pinch opens up a gash in its fur. It ripples with the movement, the golden-brown outer fur, the almost black inner fur, the downy white beneath. She exposes the dark, silken guts inside. I stay quiet and watch her work. She rips the fur down its legs. Off the small bones, thin as kindling. The pelt comes away easily, as if it's been hanging loosely on the flesh like a robe ready to be torn off. She reaches into the meat and pinches off a piece of its innards. The wad between her fingers clings to its place. Even in death, the body is unwilling to let go. But Teaghan rips, greedily, and places the wet knob in her mouth. Her lips snap, her eyes close. She savors and groans.

"The toxins," I say again helplessly.

She opens her eyes and looks at me. They gleam with some sort of joy I can't fathom, a joke I don't get. I can see the red between her lips, her tongue pushing the meat to the side of her mouth and squeezing the blood from it. I have to look away from her.

"I do this all the time."

"You do?"

She nods.

Bared to the air, the ripe meat immediately begins to turn, to sweeten. I can smell it. Something writhes in me, a twisting, sleek greed. As it rises, it decimates my caution and fear. I bare my teeth and hungrily suck in the rusty smell oozing out of the slit Teaghan made, an opening that's humidifying and corroding the air around us. I can't believe how hungry I am. Hungrier than I've ever been in my life. I drop to my knees beside Teaghan and press into the fleshy pit inside the soft belly, pinching off a piece of pulp. No one has ever seen inside this rabbit before. No one except us. My hand hesitates next to Teaghan's. The side of my pinky finger touches the side of her palm.

"You do this all the time?"

"Whenever I get the chance."

I pull and rip. The organs are stuck together, more interconnected than I thought. Teaghan gently helps me. I suppose I am still nervous to use all the force required to tear a creature apart. The hot, slick blood eases over my tongue. A flood of saliva meets the blood and coats my mouth. I swallow and begin the process of the rabbit becoming me.

Together, Teaghan and I open the rest of the rabbit's skin. Pulling up the fur so that it folds into its fragile neck, like a shirt that hasn't been taken all the way off. Pulling again so that it's a hood over the delicate skull. The rabbit suspended between us, we lick the bloody inside. The sound of bones, dainty as matchsticks, snapping in our hands, the pop-feel of femurs snapping in our mouths, the vertebrae jangling in our hands. Tumors, caused by the curse on the land, nestle inside the meat, explode over the bones, and ripen in the brains and muscle. We eat those too. I watch Teaghan as the blood smears farther and farther across her face and up her arms, as the ravenous look on her face recedes into pleasure and then satisfaction.

The meat is solid and hot and bloody inside me, like a new heart. And I can feel the rush of sensation pooling around my core. A heat answering heat, answering blood. Teaghan leans against me, and now I feel a nervous, young, unfamiliar coolness. Every time she shifts, something shifts in me, though I am very still, impossibly still, like she is a creature just coming out from the forest, and I can't scare her with sudden movement. She is dangerous, like one of those creatures. But despite the danger, or maybe because of it, I don't want her to stop touching me. She is as unselfconscious as a chick with its nestlings, a kitten with its littermates. I know because I used to watch them in the backyard before my mom had to collect them in a sack and smash them with her heel, giving the wet sack to Reese to dispose of away from the house.

"You know all those tumors in the rabbit? Jacinta said the men don't have any of those."

"How does she know?"

"She looked inside her husband and saw."

"She looked *inside* him?"

"Yeah. She's old. She has to be wise. She knows how to do things not all of us do. Otherwise she'd be dead. But me, I know how to do something even she doesn't."

"What's that?"

Teaghan talks slowly as her hand meanders to her stomach. Her fingers circle her belly, lazily, tenderly. "I'm pregnant."

"Pregnant?"

"And not from my husband."

"Who's it from?"

"Me. All the women. No one."

"I didn't know women could make a baby without men."

"You didn't know? Like, deep down? You couldn't feel that?" she asks.

I shake my head.

"I could. All my life. You believe me, don't you? About being pregnant?"

I frown. "Of course I believe you. Why wouldn't I?"

"Nobody does," she sighs. "Sometimes I lie for attention."

She reaches out and touches a lock of my hair. She doesn't try to put it behind my ear or anything, she just touches it. When the rind of her skin chafes my face, dizziness washes over me. When Silas touches me, it's strenuous. Something to endure, something to armor myself against. But under Teaghan's touch, I flood. My veins pour out into my mycelium, a steady deluge of blood and fluid until each successive layer of skin and flesh gushes and expands. I feel as if I'm about to encounter a great mystery and recognize it as myself. The veil of her hair slips over the side of her face and tickles my own. I can smell her bedraggled shirt, worn for too long on her continuously seeping body. Her cool breath is a dark, trailing mist, swampy with the mineral tang of metal and seedy earth.

"I can show you, if you want."

She smiles slyly. Flecks in her breath float out of her lips, like tiny bits of dandelion fluff swirling against me as they escape her chasm. All the gilled places in my body swell. I expand, and it feels like there's no more room for me left in my flesh. My mass is heavy, too heavy to bear. I need someone else to share the burden. Now, when the thing rises in my throat, I'm not surprised. It doesn't hurt or scare me.

A gasp rustles in her mouth as I touch her. I don't know why I know where to touch, I just know. Her skin sweats, glistens, becomes transparent. Her shudders lengthen her body. Her spine stretches, unfolds, her muscles rippling beneath, cartilage popping out of place. It's beautiful, sensuous, like a snake moving along the glass surface of calm water. Her slippery, membranous skin is fully sheer, and I can see the meat at her core, the tendrils of veins amid the dark flesh and muscle and tendon. And the soft flesh of her outermost limbs, mycelium flesh.

She leans back, her hips twist, and she resupinates. She opens her knees, her thighs clenching, softening, then clenching again. She unfurls her legs, spiderlike. She pulls up her skirt and exposes herself. There are mucousy smears on the grass beneath her. The rich smell gives off the impression that it has fermented in a secret place for a long time, multifaceted and complex, fruity and earthy and tinged with blood and moisture.

Teaghan's vaginal fissures and the teeth around the rim of her labia fill with blood. They may be soft, but engorged as they are, they don't look it. Distended and jagged as stalactites, they look like they could do some damage. I touch my fingers to them. The gill walls of the flesh cling together, but swell wider, then come apart all at once, revealing her red velvet interior. Like the rabbit's, the gamey meat inside is marbled with skeins of pale cream. She opens wide, even her teeth stretching apart now, making room. I reach out and touch the side of her face. Her hair is sticking to her skin, as if she is sweating. I bring my face closer to hers. I want my mouth on her lips, either of her lips, and my breath in her throat.

Something uncomfortable and restless is building inside me. I need to change shape. I want to climb into her. Hooking my legs around her hips, our cores press together. Her turquoise skin, her yellow and orange and violet skin, a euphoria against my blue fingers and my burgundy legs. We become a patchwork of moving color, a rainbow of earth flesh. I sprout into her, and she sprouts into me. I relish the slippery press of her as she surges and flowers and opens beneath me in fleshy ripples. Her moistness, her darkness, her hair and folded flesh and layers of skin and woody nodules, I want to cling to her and absorb her into myself. She finds room for herself in my empty spaces, and I nudge back at her, greedily, hungrily, finding the places in her where I can expand.

I scan her skin with the palms of my hands. Bits of conversation, of memory, of light, flickering visions explode against the pads of my fingertips. I see eyes and faces and hands and furniture and shadows shoot past, like the flickers while running face tilted up under the lattice roof awning in the backyard as a kid, the riot switch of shade and blinding sun. I close my eyes, and the phantasms are even more intense against the darkness. I experience not just Teaghan's body and memories, but all she has absorbed herself. I'm experiencing a million things at once and cannot contain it all. I can't contain any of it, everything flashes by at a speed I can't comprehend. What dawns on me, though, is that we're sharing an ancient language of understanding. As the rest of the world decays around us, we rise, autumnal and nut brown, mouth-soft and shit-moist, we rise.

The flecks coming out of her mouth hit my lips as they spew, a hot mist that stings my skin. And then our mouths are tangling together, our legs, our labia. All of our drenched teeth enmeshed. We tangle, untangle, tangle again.

It begins to rain. We shouldn't be out here, in the rain, but the shock of the drops is refreshing. I need it. I'm tired and deliciously pulsing. Teaghan's skin is still glossy. I can still see deeply inside her, a corporeal no-man's-land with bundles of unconnected veins circling around themselves, going nowhere. Little confused mazes, nestled in her flesh, disconnected to the rest of her blood-vascular system. There's something unbearably sad about it, and something beautiful about it too.

"What's wrong?" Teaghan asks.

"Nothing."

"Hmm." She settles back down. "Want to see something awesome?"

She doesn't wait for an answer and slips out from under me, running back into the collapsed house.

"I think I already have," I say to her as she retreats. I lean back with a smile, feeling clever. I hope she heard me.

She returns with a luciferin lantern, sets it on the ground, then stands in front of it. Her flesh turns green and glows, her meshwork of veins are dark rivers inside the light of her body. Inside her, I can see a form. The ghost of something, a beginning, floating in fluid. Kicking and moving its limbs. An in-between, pulsing, minnow thing. Out of context, it might be an ugly thing. Horrific, even. But within Teaghan, it's miraculous. I can see how beautiful and wild and wholly original she is in this act of rebellion, this new and strange body she has created with her body.

"I haven't shown anybody yet. I wanted it to be you, since you believe me."

"I see it," I say excitedly. "The baby."

"I told you." Her voice is low, halfway between a song and something spoken.

I laugh, delighted, and stand up, putting my hand on her side. I can't feel the baby move, but between my fingers, spread wide, I can see the flicker of its limbs as it moves in Teaghan's chambers of organs. I run my hand over her skin, close my eyes, and surround Teaghan and the baby with as much love as I can. I fully believe she will be able to accomplish what I didn't. There's a sadness inside me, remembering my own baby, but also a brilliant happiness that I will be able to witness hers.

The world melts away, leaving only the two of us, the three of us. But the world still waits, ready to grab us. Eventually, our responsibilities pull us back into the soft edge of dawn, and we wade sleepily into our husbands' houses.

# CHAPTER TWENTY

I dream of a house with amber walls and floral curtains, where the couches are plaid and worn. In my dreams, it is familiar and safe, before the stairs collapsed and the house started to implode from the middle and it wasn't so good anymore. Full of places to hide. It's one of Teaghan's dreams, I realize when I start to wake. Transferred to me when we touched. I hold the dream as close as I can, warm and muggy in my chest, and ride out her delicious hangover, small aftershocks of the night before.

Other dreams unfold in toasty pulses. By the color of her legs, and a feeling I can't describe, I can tell I'm seeing a memory from Teaghan's mom. I watch her sitting on a red cushion, coral-red legs swinging as she looks under the table, where her best friend crouches, laughing. And then, another woman's dreams appear, of a garden she grows in secret, tomatoes and peppers and other vegetables she hasn't been given the names for, so she names them herself.

I blink, fully awake now in the burrow-stink of Silas's

bedroom. I'm groggy from lack of sleep. The taste of blood is still in my mouth, private and mellowed. I roll over. The sun glows bright around the curtains, and I realize how late it is. I itch my neck and see that my hands are covered in blood. I sit up with a jerk. In my Teaghan-filled stupor, I'd forgotten to wash. I wipe them shakily, then scratch at the skin with my nails. Did Silas see? Were my hands hidden under the covers when he woke? Except for our first, exhausted night together, I usually wake before him. Maybe he left for work early.

When I turn toward the doorway, I jump. A figure stands there, blocking it. It's Pamela. She mouths something, but I don't know what she's saying. But then, like thunder after lightning, after she stops moving her mouth the words hit me: *Cure him first.* She passes her hand over her face, and like the surface of water, it distorts, then rights itself again. She mouths, *Don't wake me up unless he's already back. I don't want to be alive without him.*

Later in the day, Teaghan shows up. I'm surprised to see her so soon, and rush to meet her at the window of the room with the marble floor, heavy green curtains, and walls the pattern of red leaves and gold pears. At the sight of her, a foamy taste rises in my esophagus. I swallow hard and seal my lips liquid-tight, though the burbling fills my mouth with suds.

She touches me, an easy welcoming of her elegant moon fragments into my body. She smiles and I smile. I run one of my hands up and down her arm, where her fleshy growths are like shriveled mouths. I palpate them gently with my fingers. They open more as I get closer toward the center of her. I stare at a fungus ulcer, crocus-yellow and perfect, nestled beneath the lobe of her ear and hidden inside her pink growths. Her eyes look past me, into the house.

"Now, come on!" She tugs at my arm. "Let's get there before the crowd does."

"Crowd?"

She raises an eyebrow. "Your sister, Maggie?"

She looks at me meaningfully, trying to beam a thought directly into my head, one I'm too dense to understand.

I crawl out the window. "What about Maggie?"

Instead of answering, she starts laughing. "I forgot to tell you. Yesterday, Maggie brought her foremother to our graveyard. You should have seen what happened when we started singing. Selma freaked out! She looked like we lit a fire under her ass. She was trying to get out of her wheelchair and run away from us and everything." She flings her arm out, bulges out her eyes in pantomime, screeches high and animal-like.

"I didn't know she could move."

"She couldn't until we started singing. Then she freaked!" She throws her head back and laughs again.

She is bubbly and buoyant as we make our way to the center road, and her happiness saturates me like a contagion of light. We find Maggie's house, and Teaghan jumps up the porch, clearing the dirt ramp in a single bound. In a cloud of gnats swarming in the shade of the porch awning, she pulls me close. I glance at the street nervously, but no one is around. She grabs my hand. "You know, you have some real anger issues."

"What do you mean?"

"Ever since we, you know, I keep having these dreams."

"I'm having them too." I smile.

She smirks. "I think I already got myself into too much trouble. Like, this morning, I was in the cupboard when my husband called out for me, and I thought, wow, he's like a little worm, wriggling in the soil. And I just kinda wanted to jump out and . . . " She presses her nose hard into mine. I try to focus on her eyes but can't, she's too close. She presses harder. "Do you feel those things when you're around me too?"

I have no idea what to say. Instead of letting me answer, she pulls away and bursts into the front door without knocking. Inside, she doesn't even announce herself.

"Teaghan!" I hiss. "Aaron's probably home."

In answer, she throws me a wink.

The entranceway was painted a peach color, though now the outer layer is peeling. The tint beneath is blanched and grimy and looks oddly like pale skin, with a crooked drawing of a faded sailboat, marking it like a tattoo. I peek into a side room. It's empty. Teaghan pulls me into the hallway. A breeze hurls through it, like we're inside a tunnel, and I wonder if a window's open, or if part of the house is missing. The wind is laced with a warm smell.

"What are they cooking? It smells so good." My stomach rumbles. I never had breakfast.

She shoots me a look, a little too wide-eyed. I can't interpret what it means. Finally, she calls down the hall, "Hello?"

Silence. A line of luciferin lamps draws us farther down the hall. I peek into the bathroom as we go by and am surprised the bathtub doesn't show signs of recent use. The smell gets warmer, breadier, stronger. More delicious.

"Hello?" She sings out again.

A spill of dust pours from the ceiling, followed by scritching and scratching in the room above us.

My eyes lift. "Someone's up there."

She shakes her head. "Just rats."

In the kitchen, there's a table with four place settings. Though the plates and cups are all empty, the silverware relatively clean. One of the place settings has no chair. The sun leaks in, bright and cheery. It is a nice place to have breakfast and look over the wild garden.

In the room next to the kitchen, we find them. Aaron is hanging from the chandelier by a rope. The glittering glass beads take what little light there is and splatter it all over the room. Maggie is on the couch. I can only see the silhouette of her head, but even from behind, I can see that not all of it is there.

"Maggie," I gasp softly.

I wonder how is it possible that the chandelier, twisted and lopsided as it is, can hold all of Aaron's bulk.

"That's what I thought," Teaghan says, like she's settled an argument with someone in the room.

Stupidly, I think, at least Maggie will be buried with her hair. Some of her hair, anyway.

I look at Aaron's purple face. It's misshapen, not quite right. Too veiny and bulgy. Like he's a tube of ointment in the midst of having his paste squeezed out between someone's fingers. The mouthwatering smell is so strong here, and my stomach gurgles. This time, I can't tell if it's hunger or sickness. It's too noisy with so many flies.

"Eloise," I gasp. My head whips behind me.

Teaghan leaves my side and walks around the couch. "Relax, she's with Lottie."

She looks at Maggie for a minute, then her eyes trace along the length of the couch. She looks up at Aaron, lifts her arms, and for a second, I think she's going to hug him or try to pull him down. She pushes him instead. He swings wildly. The hinges on the chandelier creak, the strings of glass beads wiggle and tinkle, the sound oddly aqueous and beautiful, as the ceiling groans with the effort of not collapsing.

"Don't!" I hold out my hand as if I could stop her at my distance. When she swivels her head to look at me, her eyes are wide with surprise. "The chandelier could fall on you."

Teaghan laughs, gives the corpse another push, and looks at me with one eyebrow raised to test me. Aaron twirls in a dizzying pirouette, the chandelier wobbles, the glass beads shiver, and a white light splashes across Teaghan.

When I stiffen and don't react, she nods toward the couch. "Look."

I don't really want to, but I do. I move closer. Selma is stretched out on the cushions, her head in Maggie's lap.

"There's no blood on Selma," I say.

"Aaron must have arranged them like that, after they both died, before he hung himself."

I blink, try to focus. "Why?"

She rolls her eyes and emphasizes each word with a twirl of her wrists, like she's stirring the air. "Who. the. fuck. knows?" She looks sideways at me. My stomach gurgles again, unsettled. Teaghan looks very unbalanced with her eyes rolling around like that. "Maybe he wanted to look at them while he hung himself. I heard them, last night."

"What did you hear?"

"Mostly screaming." She points to Selma with her chin. "She was trying to kill him."

"Did Maggie try to stop her? Or . . . help her?"

She shook her head. "Neither. She was in the backyard the whole time. I was the last one she talked to."

I frown. Teaghan would only know that if she stuck around long enough to see her get shot in the head. "What did she say?"

Teaghan shrugs. "Nothing much. She just wanted to look at the stars." Without looking at Aaron, she pushes his body again, more gently this time. "For hours, Selma screamed and screamed and clawed the walls. And then, there was no more screaming."

"Why did no one try to stop it?"

"Apparently this isn't the first time they've woken up a

foremother. They've just never brought one out of the lab before. The men were expecting"—she waves her hand to the bodies around her—"this. When their wife, their favorite wife, goes crazy, there's no turning back. That's why the men were so mad when Aaron woke her up. It was the beginning of the end of his life. That's what Jess said, anyway."

Died of ergotism, Silas had said. I should have expected such a violent backlash.

I ask, "What does that even mean?"

She shrugs. "Who knows? I don't really listen to old women." She hums the tune of the wedding song, but it's a little off, a little staccato. "My husband heard them screaming too. I opened the window so he could hear. 'St. Anthony's Fire!' he kept saying. 'St. Anthony's fire!'"

"Did he explain what that meant?"

"No. He doesn't always make sense. He's about to die. Sometimes he forgets who I am."

I look at Aaron. At Maggie and Selma. "Your husband's going to die soon?"

"Yeah. He rarely gets up from his bed. Sometimes men come to visit, and they talk to him, and I listen. The men say it's a miracle he's held on this long. That they shouldn't have let me be born. Every single one of them promised that, if he can't kill me before he dies, they will. They offered to do it now, but he said no. He likes to hear someone moving around in the house."

A fear runs through me and numbs my spine.

Teaghan prowls languidly along the couch, her finger

tracing the lumps and wrinkles and curves of Selma's body, like she did mine in the collapsed house. "The old wives were their real emotional support. We're only weak versions of them." Her nails drag up Selma's dress. Up her leg, her stomach, the fabric pools and wrinkles around her neck. I think of the rabbit we ate, the skin bunching beneath its skull. When she gets to the foremother's chin, she rests her hand over her open mouth, like she's covering up a scream.

Teaghan hums the tune again, and in the end, sings cheerfully, "When men fall down, when men fall down, they reach out and grab you, and your sister too, and your mother too, and your daughter too. Men don't like to be lonely, no, men don't like to be alone, no, when men die, they don't die alone."

"I don't remember that verse."

Teaghan moves the woman's jaw up and down with her hand. She drops her voice and says, "That's because little girls only whisper it."

I look up at Aaron. "But, why Maggie? Why kill her too?"

"Maybe he wanted someone to rot next to." Teaghan bats her eyes romantically.

"But he could have just let her live in the house by herself. He didn't have to kill her."

"Why let her live? Her legacy ends when her husband does. The other men wouldn't have let her live. Better he kill her. She belongs to him."

"But they could have scooped out all of Selma's spores and saved them." My eyes go wide. "Maybe they did. Maybe they're in the lab."

"Even if they saved them, who needs someone to look like that"—she points at Maggie and Selma—"ever again?"

"But—"

Teaghan watches me struggle, like a mom watching her child learn to tie her shoe for the first time. "The men own our lineage, Nicole. What does it matter if they kill one of us? Once the foremothers are awoken, we might as well all be dead."

We hear the door creak open and voices spill into the hall. A woman's voice rises above the rest. "Hello?"

Teaghan answers with a happy-go-lucky lilt, "In here."

More voices float in from the entryway.

"So, what's everyone's bet?"

"Lead pipe."

"I guessed wrench!"

"Hey, you said candlestick! Too late to change your answer now."

Sweat breaks out on my forehead. I press my lips together, then start to move away. Teaghan eyes me.

"I have to go." It comes out as a squeak. With all the new noise entering the room, I don't know if she's heard me, but I turn and rush through the kitchen.

The other women are surging in from the hallway, so eager and frenzied it's like they aren't even worried about knocking over a lantern. I press myself against the counter. When the swell of women pass by me, I scan their faces to make sure Eloise isn't with them. She's not. Neither is Lottie.

As I flee the house, unnoticed, I hear someone coo, "Poor Maggie."

Someone else answers, "At least she knew it was coming."

The next few days, I am dusty and deadened during the day.

I come alive at night. I come alive after Silas falls asleep. He leaves the windows open, and the urgent cries of insects leak inside, as well as the eerie screeching of owls and the liquid babbling of ghosts. When the wind hits right, it brings in the odor of the lake-lake. The humidity of the storms is gone, the full force of heat returned. The lake is drying again. The smell of long-submerged rot, now exposed to the open sun, keeps me awake and restless through the night.

I dream deliciously of Teaghan. Her splendor, her swelling.

I wake up one night with my mouth on Silas. I am suckling on his naked bicep. Horrified, I let go. He moans slightly, from somewhere deep in his dreams. There's a red mark on his arm. It's purpling. Bruising. I marvel at it, and his sleeping boulder form. He's so vulnerable, I could get a knife right now, slide it over him, open his skin, and carve little pockets in his nakedness, see the red inside of him. Silas stirs. I pull up the covers. My skin is gooey and damp. The blanket sticks to it miserably. I lay still, even though my legs are tingling. I want desperately to kick.

Where will Teaghan go once the baby is born? I blink into the dark.

I knew, of course, that there was no reason for Maggie to live if her husband died, just as I know there will be no place for me here if Silas dies. That Teaghan will die when her husband dies.

Maybe Teaghan could live in this house, away from everyone else. I'll give her half my food. Most of her noises could be dismissed as rodents, or what Silas calls "the house settling." Everyone will think she ran away for good. She said she's a good hider. The only problem is Silas. I toss and turn. Silas would find her eventually. No matter how big the house, no matter how good at hiding she is. No matter how predictably he sticks to his few, lantern-lit rooms, Teaghan will wander from wherever I tell her to stay.

Deep down, I know it's not so easy to hide Teaghan. No matter where I try to keep her, she will wander away carelessly, and nonchalantly get herself killed.

# CHAPTER TWENTY-ONE

The next day, Silas says it's time to go.

"Where are we going?"

He hands me a black dress. "The funeral."

We walk through the center road, which is eerily empty until we get to the end of our clean water stream, rather pathetic this time of year, even with the recent unseasonal storms. People are milling around a small, mottled house, plain except for a stained glass window in the shape of a dove. Inside, I am stunned by the heat. The smell of the men is only somewhat diluted by the complex odors rising from the women. The smell of ripening. I don't understand why they have to do the funeral inside this miserable building, when outside in the shade by the filtered stream would be much better.

The men are in the front benches, the women in the back. While I am in the center aisle, Reese flings his gaze to me. I stop breathing. I take a step back. He looks at me with a stranger's eyes, like he's never seen me before. I go through a disorientating moment where I think, maybe we haven't met, maybe this is just someone who looks like Reese and is not Reese at all. He has always been one of those broad, plain-faced men whose emotions are easily readable. One of those big, direct men who has never had a reason to hide his emotions, because no one challenges him. So when he looks away, his face unmoved and unchanged, I see that I'm not even a passing thought in his head.

I sit next to Esha. Silas opens his mouth, as if about to say something. Then he looks up at the front and seems to change his mind. He whispers, "See you after?"

I nod. He nods back, then finds a place among the men.

Teaghan is with Eloise and Lottie, none of whom are looking at me. When I turn, though, I see Esha is smiling wide. I smile back. I open my mouth, but a man wearing gray walks to the front and Esha puts a warning finger to her lips. The gray man talks about Aaron for a while, how good and strong he was. How loyal and faithful and smart. How beloved. A humble son, a loyal friend, a hard worker. The men nod their heads in agreement and wipe away tears. His tone is so grave, I barely even notice when he transitions into Bible verses. The room gets hotter. The doors are left open, but there's no breeze. The gray man's voice rises, then falls. The lilt and tilt of his sentences sobers me and leaves me adrift. The sun pierces through the windows. The dove window catches the light and shines over us. The men are hunched forward; the women are draped on the backs of the benches. The shimmer and quiver of flies move around us, seeking shade and stink. The flies nestle in our growths, getting sticky until they're swatted away.

The pests leave the men alone, making only the back of the church whine and buzz.

The women start falling asleep. They stop swatting away the flies. The men seem haggard and wary, stooped under a familiar weight. The funeral is too long. It's hard to breathe through the smell and the claustrophobia of all the households crammed into the smallest building on the center road. I think of the cool underground kingdom of beds and streams that never dry up. I close my eyes and start to dream, the slanting cant of the man's voice pulling me along passageways filled with foul-smelling children and flowers of ash. Glass women, stone women, women made of leaves and brick and eyes of beady red berries.

In the end, the women cry too. We're crying about Maggie, and the foremother we gained only to lose so soon, and we're crying about all the daughters who will no longer be born because this man isn't there to keep them in his house. Ursula sobs. Her daughter looks like Selma, like Maggie. The daughter hunches down, bewildered. Once the men remember she exists, I don't want to think about what will happen.

The funeral is too long, but then it's over. The women are apparently not allowed to get up before the men, which is its own form of torture. Men have no sense of urgency. Their lives stretch on and on, so a day means nothing to them. They stoop under the mundanity of their dreary weeks, brush aside their many wives as they cycle through them. Maybe this is why, when the funeral is over, the men stand up so slowly, exhausted, hungover, bumbling and dragging their feet, feeling around for their dropped hats or searching for something else unnamed they might have lost. As soon as the last man steps into the aisle, the women spring forward, sidestepping their husbands who block the pews with their barely moving bulk, like a river rushing around boulders.

The men shuffle through the door and squint against the sun. They huddle in groups of three or four. A few are bruised and heavy with grief. Others look tired and muted. The women bound outside and start running as soon as they hit the street. They jump over the stream that runs in front of the church and stand in the shade of the house across the way.

I almost bump into Reese again, which throws me into a panic. I dodge him and hide behind a clot of men. When I look up, the women are all staring at me. No one speaks. They're standing as a wall, a splatter of vibrant mushroom color. I imagine them linking hands and growing, growing taller than the houses, taller than the wall surrounding the compound, taller than the trees beyond, walking the earth as the tallest creatures to ever walk, everything else meek and small. A panicky sweat erupts in patches over my body, and I try to remember exactly why I wanted to come here and be with these women. Instead, the memory of my wedding arrives in staggered flashes. The women spinning and pushing me, hissing in my ears, the sound of them cackling.

The stream cleaves the field in half. The noise of the trickling grows stronger as I walk into the road. I walk slower than I need to, since I don't know what to do once I cross. The mycelium mats are spaced apart from one another, catching leaves and clutter as they filter our water supply of toxins. I look up.

Teaghan is the first to shout, "What's taking you so long?"

Esha says, "We're waiting for you."

I clear my throat. "Waiting?"

Lottie says, "The men had their funeral, now we'll have ours."

I say, "We still have to bury Maggie?"

"No." Esha laughs. "Yesterday was her burial. Today is her funeral."

I look behind me at the men, then back at her.

"It's going to be a good funeral." Teaghan approaches the river, her hand held out, gloveless, as she reaches for mine. "The men will be too busy with their booze and their sorrow to check up on us."

I nod. It's time to take my place among the women. I reach for her hand, but before I can step closer, a hand darts out and grabs me.

Silas.

He's staring at me, hard. "I told you to meet me after, remember?"

"I remember," I say.

"I have something special to show you."

I want to argue. He got to go to his funeral, why can't I go to mine? Whether Maggie and I got along or not, she was my sister. But the deeper truth is that I feel overwhelming relief when I turn my back on the women and put distance between myself and their wall of waiting eyes and beckoning, crow-like grins. As Silas pulls me away, I take one last look behind my shoulder. The women are flooding down the road, the delicious hum of them retreating to the graveyard.

# CHAPTER TWENTY-TWO

Silas and I walk side by side until he puts his hand out to stop me. We're standing in front of a ruined house. The only parts that remain steadfast are a few pillars, the rest of the house rotting around them. He takes me to a metal bench, tilted in the mud, and after we sit, pulls out a few brown things from his pocket and gives them to me.

"What are these?" I poke one, and it gently gives in to my finger, like buttons of wrinkled flesh. There are tinges of blues, about the size of a fingerprint on its surface. When I flip it over and see its shriveled gills, my mouth flushes, and I tilt my chin down so Silas doesn't notice.

"Mushrooms," he says. "To eat."

"Eat?" I pull back with horror.

He chuckles. "I know it seems like a strange thing." He pauses. His face stills into a look of patience, but the way he repeats himself, I know he's irritated. "I know it seems strange, but it's really not. Before we lived on the compound, we ate meat all the time. And men are made of meat, aren't we? It's not cannibalistic to eat other species."

I frown. I don't like the idea. I don't like to think of him stealing my experiences with Teaghan, claiming them for his own as well. I squint at the caps in my hand. One of them still has a long, thin stem attached. It's wispy, like the ends of shredded cloth. I may be part mushroom, but the rest of me is meat, and I wasn't repulsed while eating the rabbit.

I ask, "Are you going to have some too?"

"Yup." He pulls out a few more caps from his pockets.

"Jacinta has growths that turn blue like these when they bruise. Her husband says they're particularly dangerous, so she gives them to him to dispose of when she's done shaving."

"Uh, don't worry, these aren't dangerous." Silas clears his throat. "They're just . . . intense."

I jostle the mushroom caps in my palm. "Intense?"

"Yes. Eating them is an experience. Like learning an ancient language." He moves his hand across his eyes theatrically. "Or seeing God." A mischievous smile builds on his face. "Ready?"

I'm not. "Sure."

He pops two caps into his mouth and grins toothily. He's using his lower teeth to push the mushrooms against his incisors, as if he has mushroom fangs.

Deadpan, I say, "That's funny."

He laughs, tilts his head, and gulps them down. The protrusion in his throat slides down, then up, then down again, as he does. I'm watching his throat so intently that I barely notice when he leans over and takes the caps out of my palm. He pushes one gently against my lips. I open my mouth, though I wish he wouldn't do it this way, and he carefully slides the cap into my mouth. It's chewy and dry. Unpleasant. I wish I had water. I swallow as best I can.

"So, what's seeing God like?"

"Like you already know what it's like, but you forgot. And this will make you remember." He taps his mouth. "Some people believe that when humans started to consume psychedelic mushrooms, that's what made us intelligent. That our relationship with mushrooms is what makes us human." He reaches out and buries his hand in my hair. "Don't be afraid."

"I'm not afraid." My hair tickles and snags on the prongs of my ear, and I hear a rushing sound almost like water. "Should I be?"

"No, not at all. Not when you're with me." He smiles. "And anyway, you'll see soon enough. It happens unusually fast for me. My mind has adapted to the trick of it. But for you, it'll happen even faster." He runs his thumb over my lips, staring. When he draws it away, I see specks of black on his skin, but he doesn't seem to notice or care. "You know what's beautiful?"

"What?"

"Here, in the great outdoors, I'm swallowing at least ten spores with each breath. All different types of species. But when I come home, I'm breathing in a hundred of your spores alone." He tilts his head. "A long time ago, some people believed that kissing was sacred because we share our beloved's breath, this holy thing that gives us life. With you, we don't even have to be in the same room. I just breathe you in, and you live inside me."

I don't like sitting. "Can we go somewhere else?"

"Where?"

"Anywhere."

"Sure." His eyes widen. Bulge abnormally, monstrously, out of his head. Like something is behind his eyeballs trying to pop them out so that it can escape from his freshly emptied eye socket. He grins. "Want to go into the woods?"

My eyes are filmy. Dream resin floats like pond silt in my eyes. It's difficult to focus when the landscape begins melting into itself, folding and refolding. We walk through the streets, this land of death. Shadows creep over the splintered houses, and it looks like dusk is escalating into night, though I know it's barely noon. But the elongated shadows come anyway, with blunt wooden teeth and red gums nestled in the darkness of their centers. They skitter over the houses and eat the human leftovers, all the wood and plastic, all the birds and flowers, all the life and the death, and they leave emptiness.

"Do you see them?" My voice doesn't sound like my own.

"See what?" Silas asks cheerily.

"The shadow creatures."

"No!" He laughs. I watch them as they take down what has been built, as they slowly level everything to the ground. They ignore us, so I'm not afraid. "You'll see, Nicole!" Silas is so far ahead, he has to shout for me to hear him. "Hallucinating is great! Wonderful! Nothing like you heard."

I haven't heard anything, and I don't know what he's talking about, but that never stops Silas.

Over his shoulder, he yells, "Hallucinating is a way for the mind to heal itself. When we cut ourselves, we immediately try to stop the bleeding, as if blood is the problem. But the blood is the body's defense system. The cut is the problem, and it needs the blood to heal."

I see a worm on the ground and stop to observe it. It's wobbly, upset over the hot asphalt. I can feel its suffering throb inside me, in my nerves, and I want it to stop. I glance at Silas. He's not looking. I pick up the worm and eat it. It tastes good; it tastes like the end of suffering.

Silas says, "And, if the body has figured out a way to heal wounds, wouldn't the mind have found a way to heal trauma? Hallucinating isn't just a by-product of the mind trying to heal, it's the healing system itself. It's the blood sealing the wound. Can you believe that in the old world, doctors got rid of hallucinations by forcing people to take pills that flattened them out, locked them away until they stopped seeing things others couldn't?"

I imagine flattened people, little puddles of skin, organs, and eyeballs smeared to the side. I can still taste the fidgety, gelatinous echo of the worm on my tongue.

Silas shouts, "All the other men still have the same mindset. But not me! Not you and me!"

I catch up to Silas when we reach the wall. I didn't even

notice us approaching it. I crane my neck. The wall has been here since before our men came. I wonder what the people who built it were afraid of. In the old world, who were they trying to keep out? Silas climbs the wall on all fours. Amazement balloons inside me. He's climbing a ladder leaning against the wall. A ladder, for anyone to climb, whenever they wanted. After he gets to the top, it will be my turn. My feet become cold. Numb, even. What are we doing? Why are we doing this? The woods is an alive, cursed thing. A place that can change anything with just its touch. I hear a crow call out, a throaty warning, dark and ominous. I remind myself to breathe. Then I panic. If I stop reminding myself, will I stop remembering to breathe? I look down at my feet, feeling a tightening sensation in my throat. The baby's mycelium is finally outgrowing me. It corkscrews out of my heels and embeds into the earth. I will have to stay here forever. I lift one foot but see that there's no mycelium beneath it at all. I can barely believe it. In fact, all I can see is my burgundy skin. My foot is bare. Where is my shoe? I laugh. I lift my other foot and see that I still have one of my shoes on. Where did the other go? At the bottom of the sole, there's a hole. I can see my skin showing through, but no loose mycelium. Everything's okay. I squint at the wall to get a closer look.

"What's all this black?" I had always thought the wall itself was black, but now I can see there's vegetation covering its surface.

"Black mold. We use it to help keep out the radiation. They use it in rockets, too, to keep out space radiation. Or used to, anyway." I don't realize I'm holding my finger out, a hair's breadth away, until I hear Silas yell in a panic, "Don't touch it!"

"Right, right." I can't touch it. The plague, the disintegrating, the boneless heaps of walking flesh.

Then I think about how I touched Teaghan, and all the fungus on her body, and that didn't do anything bad to me. How Silas just had me eat a mushroom. How I walked into the lab, like it was just another building.

"Silas?" He's already made his way to the top of the wall. He stops and looks back at me. I raise my voice so that it will reach him. "Is the woods dangerous?" I'm not sure if I'll believe his answer, but I want to ask anyway.

He laughs. It sounds like the twisted, mechanical laugh of a doll in his house. Like he's swallowed one and is now using her voice as his own. "Don't worry. Just be careful not to touch the mold."

I take a deep breath and steady myself.

Silas disappears.

"Silas?" I call. I sound too small. Like there's no way my voice could reach him.

But still he answers, his voice far away. "Just use the ladder."

The ladder is rickety and embedded with a growing crust of leafy brambles. But it held Silas, so it must be able to hold me. Luckily, I am better with my hands than I think. Better with my body. My feet propel me up faster than my mind can understand. I don't have to think at all. I'm swimming fluidly through the air like a bird who's been flying her whole life. I want to go farther and farther into the sky, but I hear a rustle next to me. Someone is next to me. A body. Slowly, wide-eyed, I turn my head. It's a wad of branches. A tree. I know they lean over the edge and extend their jointed sticks and shake and throw off their leaves into the compound. Still, it surprises me to be next to one, so near I could reach out and touch it. A hush falls over me as I watch the branches shape-shift and shimmy, becoming one animal then another, mouths opening and closing, paws extending into human-shaped fingers, then curling back into blunted hooves. When I climb back down the wall, it isn't as easy. My downward movement makes the wall look like a black river, rushing up, up, up. Even when I close my eyes, I see the black movement rush into the heavens. I'm surprised by the ground. I fall to the earth with a thump.

Silas has his hands on his hips and a loose grin. His face is smeared and pulsing. "You okay?"

"Yeah."

He steps forward stiffly to help, but I don't need him. I shake myself off and stand. The forest flows around me. I breathe in the rich colors, its odor of sifting and shifting. Branches shuffle the unfolding mosaic of leaves. Slivers of jade. Clots of moss in every crevice, in every wet fold and corner. Curls of ferns pleat through the underbrush and hang from the shoulders of the trees. I hear a bird erupt in song somewhere near, then another even nearer. A brittle, shrill sound that eases into a graceful and melancholy melody. I breathe in and remind myself to breathe out, then breathe in again. The forest breathes with me, weightless as a dream.

The trees tower over us like rustling, creaking giants, as a never-ending army. Not an army, I think to myself. I have been thinking of the forest as an enemy combatant all my life. But here, at last inside of it, I realize that's not right. Just like the first time I looked out over the graveyard hill, I am again confronted with the enormity of the world. This time, though, I'm not overwhelmed. I don't want to lie down and give up. I am exhilarated. I am in awe. The forest is awake and alive and exalted.

"I can't believe we're here," I marvel.

"It's not such a big deal." He quirks a smile. It's eerie in the speckled half-light under the trees. "I've had to climb over higher."

He keeps talking, but I turn away. It's hard to concentrate on him while the forest changes around me, a whole theater of shimmering. A buzzing overwhelms the skies, trembles the earth, floods my chest cavity, and seizes my heart. I duck and cover my face. Then I realize it's an insect buzzing near my ear. Silas doesn't seem to notice my panic. He looks radiant and gleeful.

"I've been wanting to share these mushrooms with you for a long time."

The trees emit a rustle, big and animal-like.

"You've been eating them by yourself, haven't you? All those times you came home. I wasn't certain if you were drunk, or sad, or what."

He nods. "I've always suspected and feared, growing up, that I'm just"—he thrusts his hands out for emphasis, then hits his chest—"garbage." He levels his hands out and they float in the air. "Refuse drifting in the solar system."

I turn back to the trees and listen to the continuous exhale through the leaves instead of Silas's voice.

"When I eat the mushrooms, when I commune with them, I realize that I'm not trash. I'm just . . . nothing."

The woods are whispering, *shhh shhh shhh*. Like a mother putting her baby to sleep.

"I want to be king of the universe, right? Not *nothing*." He puts his fists in the air and yells, "King of the universe!"

I hear my mother saying something. My name, then something else. I can't quite catch it. *Shhh shhh shhh*. My mother is shushing me. Her mother is doing the same. And her mother. I shake my head in confusion. I can't think back that far. I sigh, contently, deeply. Of course I have memories of my mother's mother. Of course I have my mother's, buried somewhere. When I was very young, my mother carried me in her arms to breastfeed me. Not even the men try to stop that.

Silas's voice intrudes again. "Which is where the idea of trash comes in. It's my ego and self-importance. Assigning a negative value when really there isn't any value at all. And when I take the mushrooms . . . I understand it so fully, and the fear is gone. I'm okay with being part of something so big and immense and wonderful as the universe, even if I'm such a tiny germ within it. The smallness doesn't matter. And that's why it's addicting." He laughs. "I mean, the endogenous amphetamines don't hurt, either."

I feel a comfort radiating through me, humming. It's coming

from my foot. My naked one. I kneel down and put my hands on the earth. I sense a flowing. I can feel it with something other than my hands, my ears, my eyes. It's a reaching, circumfluous sense. The trees are just the surface. The mushrooms, too, are just the surface. I feel the mushrooms carpeting the earth, their roots and mycelium beneath. So many species talking at once, a chorus, helping each other survive. I wriggle my fingers into the soil and feel the mushroom thrill within it. The dry wriggle and insect squirm. It is an immensity, a slow stretching that isn't only physical, but like the amplitude of time. I gasp in delight. I close my eyes.

So much fungi. An upheaval of fungi, seething, surging. Like rivers, like veins. Conducting the honorable feat of weathering rocks to make soil, of directing nutrients to the trees and making the forest grow, of breaking down death and organic tissue into soil and food. The sacred act of turning the past into the present, into the future, into the world I walk on and breathe in. Something stretches inside my skull. My mind eases. I think, and it's no longer difficult. I breathe, and that, too, isn't difficult. The branches of myself untangle. It would be so beautiful to join the lull of the earth.

I whisper to myself, "This forest is so old."

My legs are wobbly and restless. I want to cool them off. Plunge them into the earth as an act of devotion and let the pressure of soil soothe my irritated meat. If I could shed so much peripheral movement and busy wandering and scrambling over surfaces, I could just focus on the underneath. Turn inward and become part of the movement of the earth, the movement of the whole. I dig farther into the dirt with my hands and kick off my shoe. I could plant my legs in the dirt. Close my eyes and cover my face. Sleep and dream and conduct and nourish and be nourished in turn.

Silas's voice irritates my ear. "Actually, the forest isn't that old. These trees were pretty small when we moved in. Like, my size. The forest burned down plenty, even before the wars. But you know what brought it back?" He beams.

My skin prickles with goose bumps. "Men?" I tilt my head. "You?"

"No." He looks proud. "Pyrophilic mushrooms. They're the first organisms to come back after a devastating fire."

He's studied fungi all his life, but he's missed the point entirely. I close my eyes and try to block out his voice. The hum of energy in the soil is much like the hum of the women together. The men ruined the land for themselves and the animals, but where does that leave someone like me? Someone like Teaghan and her baby? Could we live in the forest, even if the men cannot?

Silas is still talking. "The spores lie in wait in lichens. Then when the lichens' bodies get burned up in the fire, the spores are released. The mushrooms grow, then the plants, then the insects, the birds, all the rest. Nature starts again. You start it up again."

No wonder the old people believed in a god, an outside creator. They couldn't believe that something like a forest exists of its own accord, is the proprietor of its own reshaping. But here it is, so obviously alive, so obviously re-forming itself to fit its own needs. The forest is the god of its own body. Silas had said his body had figured out how to heal itself. That his mind had too. Why not believe earth was capable of that?

I sink into the earth and feel the mushrooms in the dirt. It feels like coming home. Of finding relatives I knew existed, but upon meeting them, realize they are exactly like me, living a life I've always wanted to live. My hands are in the dirt and I'm laughing. Silas is standing over me. He's enjoying my laughter. I find it patronizing, but also funny. I want to stand up and smack his face.

He sweeps his hand to the side. "Look at this sycamore!"

I look up. "That tree has a name?"

His face radiates, delighted. "Yes! All the trees have names. Oak, maple . . . " He has a self-assured, self-satisfied face on. "Another maple. Uh . . . an ash, maybe?" He turns to me. "You know, the mushrooms on your body have names too." He touches my forehead. "Weeping toothcrust." He brushes the side of my face. "Bearded fieldcap." His hand trails down to my neck. "Destroying angel."

I pull back. "Don't call them that."

"Call them what?"

"I don't like those names."

He laughs, more bemused than anything, which annoys me even more. "You shouldn't be ashamed of your own body."

"I'm not ashamed."

He turns his gaze to me, languid and full of trust. "I want to ask you something. Something big."

It takes me a moment to register the sound in my eardrums as my own heartbeat.

"I've always felt trapped here. No real way out. That's not a surprise. I think we all feel that, from time to time."

I can't tell who he means by "we." Does he know how ridiculous he sounds, to say he is the one who is trapped?

"But lately, my wandering spirit has come back to me. I've been feeling like there's another way. I feel like something, something big, is calling me." He nods to the woods. "I never wanted to stay in one place. I want to leave, and I want you to come with me."

"Leave?" I blink hard, trying to focus.

I feel a twinge, something viny twirling through me. My vision is a little blurry. I rub my eyes.

He says, "I want to go back to the person I was."

"You're just going to leave everything? Everyone?"

"No, not you."

"But everyone else?"

He sighs. "Most of the men still alive aren't even mycologists. They came here to work the farm. I'm one of the last who has any mycological knowledge at all."

"So it's all up to you?"

"So it's all up to me. And, this is the thing. Most of the men left don't have any real connection to their wives. They're giving up."

"What does that mean?"

"Well . . . I told you I'd tell you. And now I'm going to tell you."

"Okay."

"There is no plague."

"What?"

"We developed a way to filter microplastics out of our bodies," he admits. "Mycoremediate ourselves like we do with the earth. We expected it would help with radiation too. But we couldn't control it. The other men want to just get rid of this place. See what's left of the world and destroy the evidence of what we've done here. Kill you and the other wives."

"Kill us?"

"But I refuse. I want you to come with me when I leave."

I repeat, "They're planning to kill all the women?"

"Yes. And after they finish mourning Aaron, they're going to pull the trigger." He clears his throat. "So to speak." My heart thuds. Silas catches my hand in his. "Come on, the earth is dying. Let's be someone else besides who we are here, you know? I want to be on the road again. I want to be with you. I'm sorry for everything. The lying. I had to get some things in order, but now I'm done. Now we can be free."

"And what do you think is out there?"

"Well. I think people are dying of radiation out there. A lot of them. Maybe not all of them. But that's not going to hurt us. The fungus inside us protects us from it. It, at least, still does that." He grabs my hand. "Come on! I don't want to be in a tragedy anymore. This is a love story. This is *our* love story."

I close my eyes so I can't see the ugly hope on his face, but through his hand, I can feel the bitter chemicals that writhe in him. I can feel the fright in his body, his want for something in return. For a second, I think of putting his pinky fingernail, the tiniest thing of his entire body, into my mouth. I think of biting down until my teeth clip the slender bone. But I don't. Pity crests in my chest. I lean into him. My chin against his sternum, my forehead on his neck.

"You were the ones to give your families the fungus."

He swallows, and I can feel the pressure of the swallow against my skin. I feel his sigh of ancient sadness. "Yes."

We are all so unreachable. So alone. And him, to have lived so long without being able to reach across the expanse around him to find a hand. It's pitiable. I want to ease his vulnerable parts. I want to smooth down the sharp, glass edges of him so he can find the center of himself. So he can learn, finally, to stop thrashing against the world, against what he can't control. Though this has always been my duty as wife, I never felt like I wanted to until now.

"Silas, why did you do it?"

"We were trying to save everyone."

"No, I mean, why did you give me Joseph's spores. Would we have had to hide him from the other men?"

"Yes," he admits.

I sidle a few crabwalk steps, tilt my head, and look at him from a different angle. I look at his neck, at the vein there, pulsing hard. The shape of his jaw clenched against his cheek. The roundness of his skull on top. "Did you make Reese keep me alone all this time, so I'd be willing to hide in your house, alone with the baby?"

Silas blanches. "That's not what I—" He sputters and takes a big breath. "Your soul is connected to his."

"Pamela's soul, you mean." I want to see the way his jaw moves inside his head.

"I—" He looks away. "We wouldn't have had to hide in the house for long. The plan was always to leave."

I say, "Killing us has always been the plan. You wanted to wake up your wives, and then you were going to kill us."

"*Their* plan. That's why I didn't want a wife. I didn't want to lose another wife. I only agreed to your birth after I gave up on finding a cure for Pamela. I know it's hard for you to understand," Silas begs. "But this is our chance."

His eyes are so big and wet, like a baby's. There are things he doesn't understand, and can't understand. Places that he can't possibly reach with the shape of his body. But I can. I entwine my fingers with his. I feel inside him, like I could feel inside the earth. The reverberations of his heartbeat, the whoosh of his blood. His lungs, his skin, his teeth, his skull, his eyeballs and nerves and wiring. I tilt my head to look at him again. Yes, he is very big. A towering giant. But the whole contraption of his body is so simple, so easy to undo the seams of him. As easy as tearing apart the worn threads of his shirt. As easy as hooking a finger into his belly, just like we did with the rabbit.

I could get the answers I want. I see that now. They're just sitting in his brain, like fruit waiting to be picked. I don't have to figure out if he's lying about Pamela, about me, about anything. I could just know. I could just reach in and take what I wanted. He pulls away, quickly, like I shocked him. He suffers so much from loneliness. He considers his species the only steward of the earth, never mind that there are so many beings guiding the world. His species's destruction of the earth weighs heavily on him. I could relieve him of this guilt. Make him part of the earth again. I could be something that saves him. He backs away.

"I'm sorry. I'm sorry." He crouches down, his hands between his knees, and breathes out, slowly this time. "I'm not going to hurt you." He gets up, steps back, and puts his hands up defensively. "I'd never do that. I'm not like that. I never meant to hurt you."

Reflexively, I say, "I know."

Silas says, "We've all had a lot of trauma . . . but I'd never hurt you." He adds gingerly, "And I know you'd never hurt me."

I can't answer. Something spills out of my skin.

"What . . . what are you doing? You're . . . you're . . . " He looks at me with bald terror. But this is not the instinct I had while I was pregnant, to devour. It feels like knowledge. Like a language I knew and just remembered. It feels like a decision. I could do this to a plant, I could do this to an animal. I can do this to Silas. As I curl around him, his eyebrows cross in apprehension. "Is it safe?"

I don't think I can find words to answer him. His face collapses. He's sad? Resigned? But, whatever he's feeling, he reaches out for me, just as I reach out for him. I tangle my fingers in the snarls of his beard and cradle his chin with my palm. I stretch over him, my bones loosening, ligaments stretching, and I enwrap him in my flesh.

"Homing is the ability to find each other in the denseness between," I say.

In answer, a thousand clefts erupt in Silas's skin.

*It's a miracle.*

My skin tents at the pores like fingers poking against the tarp of my hide. Then another finger, then more.

*This is what plants and fungus do. Create a symbiotic relationship with each other.*

A hundred fingers, a thousand fingers. A sharp pain like a hoard pinpricks through my skin as the fingers needle their way out.

*They mesh bodies. The plant skin invaginates in response to the fungus.*

I think of when I saw Silas for the first time, standing in the darkness of the door. His face the face of Death. Ancient and sad.

*This is how evolution works. This is how the face of the world changes. How eras shift into different eras.*

And now, his face is amazed and innocent. His eyes are so wide, his whole face dilating, not just his pupils, swelling with pleasure, with ecstasy. He doesn't bleed. The pressure of his blood has turned low. He is a slab of meat that has already sat for a long time. Like the holes were already there, waiting for me to open them, knowing I'd come eventually.

*It was fungi's partnership with plants that brought plants into land. Without fungi, there would be no life on land. For eons, fungi have shaped the earth and all its life-forms. They shift how the world works. Many species of plants have evolved so they can't live without a mycorrhizal partner. Is this how humanity must evolve?*

Bits of my body sink into him. Silas, always so full of explanation, is speechless. His jaw is rigid, the pattern of his teeth strains against his taut skin. There is greed and hunger in his eyes, like wet and rolling marbles. He wants more, so I ease in further. He makes little sounds, like he's bewildered by his own pleasure. His skin clefts puss around where I enter him. Tiny white, oozy mounds rupture around my urging strands. He is a constellation of stars now, a celestial pattern, burning bright.

*It could go bad, though. Even the purest of symbiotic relationships can turn parasitic, if it turns out a partner is not worthy, or becomes too sick or unhealthy. In lichen, who is in charge? Fungus or plant? Fungus or human? If there are two consciousnesses, which one guides the combined body?*

I feel the strain leave him. The boundary where he ends and I begin, blurs. Such intimacy, such closeness I've never dreamed of having with a man. The pulsing of him, like the sea, quietly into me. Rush and sound, then a pause, another rush and sound. A melding, a sliding of one into the other.

*And now, a new era begins with her, with me. With us.*

His thoughts don't feel painful in my skull this time. As the exchange of fluids happens, so does the exchange of thoughts. His moisture, his heat. Our nutrients circulate within each other. His mouth opens slowly, as if by opening this mouth, he can stretch the other fissures to guide me in deeper, closer to the center of him. I probe further, encouraged. His body submits to me like a flower opens in the morning to the sun.

From inside his body, I can sense all his mycocomponents. In his mouth, his teeth. His skin. His gut. Spores in his lungs as he breathes. So much of his body is not human cells, this thing that inhabits him, that responds to me so readily, that connects us, like biological imperative, or symbiosis, or love.

I think of my mother, telling me the Greek story of how the world came to be, pointing to the pictures in our book. How age-old beings come together and age-old beings fall apart.

At the same time, when I curl into Silas's brain, touch very lightly his gray matter, very lightly the white matter, too, I see only flashes of his memories. A brother. Agar plates and petri dishes. Parents. Spawning bags and syringes. Pamela. Inoculation plungers and glass jars. Two dogs. Pamela. Filter discs and scalpels. Joseph. The news, bombs in other places, the falling apart. Pamela. Pressure sterilizers and pH Indicator Strips and graduated cylinders. Back pain, headaches, stomach cramps. A new house. Joseph stumbling, Joseph laughing. Pamela laughing, leaning back, walking backward through a doorway. Sobbing. Sobbing, Pamela sobbing.

His current thoughts are lighter and airy, merely passing through his brain. I filter past that and find deeper, well-worn tracts. Certain memories of his that are swollen and warped from him having gone over them again and again. A beginning and end of the earth, a beginning and an end of everything.

*Gaia was birthed alone in the empty darkness.*

*And then Gaia found another being in the universe, the sky. Uranus, handsome and blue, filled with stars and darkness. And they did what two beings do when they are the only two beings in existence: they fell in love. And from that love, Gaia grew all the things on her body: all the plants and mountains and air and thriving greenery, and she gave birth to her first children: the Titans. All her children loved her, and her warm body, her good nature. And they feared their father, who hung above them, terrifying and vast.*

Pamela doesn't want to do it. Silas does not tell her the specifics of the trial, he mostly calls it an opportunity. He purposefully withholds some pieces of information and accidentally withholds others. When she learns what will happen, too late, they're already at the compound. She does not want to do it. She says, we haven't been here for that long. We can just take the hazmat suits and go. Silas says, you don't know how much exposure we've had already. Pam, we don't want to die of radiation. Pamela says, but what happened to Roseanne? I don't understand what happened to Roseanne. Silas wraps his arms around her and says, that's not going to happen to us. It's an adverse event. It's such a small percentage of that happening. Think about it, Pamela, we could be the forefront of saving the world!

*Uranus hated Gaia's sons. His sons. He was disgusted by them.*

Pamela is still not convinced, so Silas goes into Joseph's room. No, no, no. Silas goes into his son's new room where he has set up his old Godzilla posters, whose every movie he's watched a hundred thousand times, and his Xenomorph posters, whose movies he's not allowed to watch yet. Silas sits on his bed. No, no, no. Silas deepens his voice, like he's not talking to his son but to another man. No, please, no. Pamela isn't there. No, no, don't think about the things we said. They're so awful, so awful, I'll die if I keep thinking about it, I've got to stop thinking about it. I'd have killed myself already if—

*Uranus flung Gaia's sons, his sons, into the deep and dark and terrible pit of Tartarus.*

Joseph, Joseph, Joseph. He takes his medicine like a good son, he takes it like a man. Pamela, hysterical, tries not to let Joseph see how gripped with fear she is. She doesn't want to scare her son. Pamela, hysterical in the dark. Pamela, wide eyed, screaming and ripping out her hair in the dark. It doesn't matter how well or badly Pamela hides her fear, Joseph's fear soon rises of its own accord. The fear is so strong and terrible it warps his personality. It makes him recede. Joseph cries as much as a toddler, as a baby, he pleads and wails in pain. Silas remembers when Joseph was an infant and he dropped him, and the wailing was his fault, all his fault. It was hard to tell, it's hard to see what goes on inside the body, all he had was Joseph's wail of pain. Joseph, Joseph, Joseph, his mouth swollen open. Joseph, his stomach swelling. All the empty cavities of him swelled and filling: the spinal, the cranial, the abdominal, the pelvic, the thoracic. His lungs, his bladder, his ureters, his intestinal tract, and his ear canals. Joseph, terrified. Silas, terrified. Pamela comforts Joseph, is stronger than Silas, Pamela holds Joseph through it all. Pamela, Pamela, Pamela, standing on the staircase sobbing. Pamela in the doorway, Pamela in the corner, Pamela in the empty bathtub. Pamela beneath the blankets. Pamela lying on the kitchen table, her hands crossed over her chest, eyes open like a corpse's. Joseph, slowing down, Joseph, Joesph, who can't move anymore, can't talk. Pamela holds Joseph long after it's obvious Joseph is gone, holds him and cries over him, cries in a horrible choking way. It's not healthy but what can Silas say at this point. During Joseph's turning, she would not look at Silas. But now that he is gone, all she does is stare at him. Her eyes follow him wherever he lugs his grieving, murderous self. Pamela, Pamela so forgiving, Pamela so full of hate. Both of the people Silas loves are deathly silent.

*Gaia, Mother Earth, loved her children deeply and could not forgive her husband for his betrayal.*

Silas takes Pamela to the edge of the woods where no one else will see. Pamela lets herself be led and stares as if she doesn't know where she is. Silas says, let's run away. Pamela looks at him, and her eyes are empty.

*With her shaken, sun-hardened hand Gaia scavenged from her gut the hardest metal she could find.*

She asks, you want me to leave my son behind? Silas says, I'm sorry. But if I inject you, you'll fruit. We didn't know. The first trials were small, done on only a handful of men.

*Gaia crafted a sickle with the metal from her body.*

Pamela says, I already took it, Silas. Silas says, you did it without me? Pamela nods, I did it without you.

*She went to the Titans, her beloved sons, and told them: Take this weapon and kill your father and set the world free of his cruelty.*

She says, everything that Joseph is, and everything he was, and everything he is supposed to be is lying on that gurney with him.

*My beloved sons.*

Everything I ever loved lies with him.

*My beloved.*

You have to fix him, Silas. You made it your job to fix him. I'm going now, so it's all up to you. Whether my son lives or dies is all up to you. Just like you wanted, everything is up to you.

*Take this weapon, my beloved sons.*

That night, Pamela starts turning. It takes days.

*Mother Earth took on a second husband.*

It takes days, but she does not plead or cry and scream like Joseph did.

*She took, as her new husband, the cold and enormous seas.*

She will not speak, she will not move, even when she is capable of doing both. She swells, she fills the bed with musk and fills the room with spores and the smell of deep caves and raw fluid and rotten birth.

*She sank willingly into his watery depths.*

When the fungus fills her, it is like filling an empty and lifeless chamber.

*She lost the color red first. Then she lost orange, yellow, green, violet, until the world was only blue.*

She presses herself against the wall so that Silas can't see her glorious fruiting bodies, her blackened mouth, her belly swollen with new life for the final time.

*Then she sank past the point of light and color.*

He comes into her room and says her name and she doesn't respond. He leaves her bread, he leaves her water, he leaves her wine. He leaves her the last of the candy.

*Past the point of music and words. Past the point of knowing, past the point of understanding.*

He touches her, he calls her name. She does not respond. He cannot pry her from the wall, her new growths have stuck to it, embedded themselves into it.

*And she sank blissfully past the memory of the husband she hated.*

Because Pamela faces the wall, Silas does not see the moment when she is dragged to the other side and he loses everything.

Silas reaches out for me. Slowly, since he doesn't have as much control over his body as he's used to. Why does he reach out? To stop me? To strangle me? To bring me closer to his mouth in an eternal kiss of surrender? I don't know. With both hands, he reaches out.

I open wide, wide. All my openings are wide. My teeth are not soft, and they are not pliant. They are longer and more jagged than ever before, engorged and growing in response to my own need, just as the rest of me has been. It is so easy to find the valves of his body, the vessels, and constrict them and direct their flow to me. He is like a labyrinth of secret rooms, each opening in front of me as I go through. The hot blood fountain of him sprays into my mouth, and I'm siphoning the heat from him, the plasma, salt, protein parts of him. A flood that, like a tide, rises and falls with his quickening pulse, as if he, too, has responded to my needs, his heart banging away to pump it all the harder into my chasm.

My skin parts imbibe his human parts, dissolving his bestial oils and glands and blood. He thrashes and writhes against me, and there is a scream inside him trying to get out, but his large mouth is smothered, and all his other mouths are useless without voice. I can hear it, though, a vibration that fills me. An all-too-ugly scream, an all-too-human scream. I don't mind. While he thrashes, I work at him from the top, work my way to his bottom, work away at his wet insides. I snap his bones and snap, snap, snap, it sounds like a baby doll coming apart at the joints. It sounds like wood snapping, like the pieces of a headboard coming off, over and over. The mushrooms beneath work on his toes. Their mycelium laps up his blood. A certain joy to share a meal, as we absorb, absorb, absorb.

My task done now, I lie on the ground, reeling, dizzier than I was after spinning at my wedding, dizzier than I thought possible. I am filled with so much blood. The mushrooms around me hum. I am silent inside. There has been too much, all at once, and now there is only blood and blankness. The heat is stifling, pushing me down with hands that seek to keep me here forever. It wants me to sleep, it wants me to join, it wants me to forget my humanity and become softness and growth.

But I don't. When I hear my own voice again, when my

thoughts start to form fragments cohesive enough that I can understand, I rise. I climb the ladder. I am in full control of my body, which is strong and satiated. At the top of the ladder, I look back at the trees and wave. They wave back. I go over the wall.

# CHAPTER TWENTY-THREE

Walking through the streets, tinted by the fading sun, I don't know why I am not more panicked. But I am a new creature, tunneling through my underground world. I am filled with purpose as I cross through the compound's elongated shadows; I flicker in and out of the expanding darkness, the dissipating light. I hear a whooshing that's probably my own heartbeat in my ear, my excessive blood flowing to places it's not used to.

When I reach the graveyard, I see the women. A great rush fills me, and for a moment all I can do is watch them. They're busy building something out of collected wreckage. No men are around. I'm glad. I sink into their languorous puddle and join their hum. The air is thick with our floating debris. I look up at the mound of trash. They've reshaped it into a woman.

"Who is she?"

"She's a gift," says Amy, beside me. The roots of the bone-deep growths on her forehead push her face down and smash her features into her cheeks and chin. The men don't like to look at any of us, but they especially grimace at her. My mom put a three-month deadline on her life once she got married. So far, I'm happy she's outlived it.

Beside me, Tyra says, "She's Mary."

Mary is mountainous, almost as tall as a house, made of building scraps and car pieces and broken furniture, left-over trash from a bygone era remade anew. Her legs are criss-crossed, her hands in her lap, her head tilted down, smiling benevolently at us. Her eyes are made from the smashed bits of plastic from the back of a car.

"She's beautiful," I say. Her sudden appearance is an apparition, a miracle. I turn to Tyra. "Silas says the men plan to kill you."

"We know," she says.

"You do?"

"Yeah. That's why we're giving them a parting gift."

I frown. "You're giving them a gift, even though they plan on killing you?"

"Everyone gets killed eventually," Victoria says. She's grinning, something I've never seen her do, unabashedly expose her mouth of black mold in joy.

"And, for the finishing touches!" Allison labors behind me, using both arms to heft a full bucket.

Clara claps her hands. "Blood!"

I look behind me and search for Teaghan. I can feel the thrum of her, somewhere. "Blood?"

"Yeah," drawls Tyra. "The most important thing Mary did was give birth, of course."

"Of course."

"Emma saw pictures of her foremother giving birth. She said there was a bunch of blood."

"So after Aaron's funeral, we went through the entire compound. Purged every little critter we could find," says Clara.

"We want to make it historically accurate," says Eleanor.

Allison calls out to Emma, "Where was the blood in the pictures?"

Heads swivel toward Emma. She rolls her eyes back and her arms swing over her head as she shouts, "Fucking everywhere!"

Allison totters to the statue. A few women help to heave the bucket up to Tyra, who sits on Sara's shoulders. Tyra splashes the blood against Mary's head, so that it streaks down her face and spills down her chin and puddles on her chest. More women pour more buckets of blood all over Mary's lap. It stains her belly and splashes up her arms.

"It's like we're giving her a bath."

"A blood bath," trills Tyra.

"They're going to love this."

"A good gift."

Jacinta says, "Makes sense why they're so obsessed with blood, doesn't it?" She sweeps her hands over Mary. "Their birth cycles are filled with it. They're born in blood and usually die in it. Most of the time when they feel pain, they look down and see blood. That's got to do something to their brains. It's pathological."

"Unless they hang themselves. No blood then," Anna says, licking her thumb to clean Navya's pouting face.

"Maybe that's why a bunch of them do it that way," says Clara.

Tyra draws her finger down her cheek, like a tear. "How sad."

"And romantic." Navya giggles.

Anna rolls her eyes. "She's always throwing that word around. She doesn't know what it means."

Jacinta sighs and folds her hands in front of her as she admires Mary. "But us women, we could go our whole lives without seeing our own blood."

Jacinta looks so stately and solemn today, her hair in long curls down her back and a black shawl draped around her shoulders. Last year, Mom said she was nearing a decade, and perhaps by now she's surpassed it. She certainly looks that old. Pendulous caps grow at her jowls, dragging her face down, giving her a heavy, regal air. I've never seen her with such large growths. I look around and notice other wives haven't shaved today. Some of their growths have already matured.

Teaghan finds me. Looking at her is like coming out of amnesia. Remembering myself and everything I've ever loved. She's wearing Maggie's apron, pinched tight around her middle. She's trying to hide her expanding stomach, but it's not working. She's much too big. Some part of me already knew, even before Silas told me, that the end was near. Something inside me has always been waiting for the end. I see now what Silas meant when he was talking about the babies he lost. The end is a relief because the dread of waiting is over. Now it will just be pain, which we are all so used to.

She looks into my eyes and smiles. "I'm glad you came back."

"You knew I left?"

"I knew Silas took you."

Jacinta, close enough to overhear, fishes in her large front pocket and shakes a glass bottle in front of my nose. "Guess what my husband brought home from the lab last night?" She grins, pummeling forward in her excitement. "Never mind, you don't have to guess. It's booze!" She holds it up, looks at me and cheers, "To returning after a man takes you away!"

The women cheer. She passes it to Anna beside her.

Someone behind me asks, "How do we get the men to see their gift?"

"What if we made a fire?"

"The men don't like fire."

"If you make a fire, the men will come and stamp it out."

"Let's summon them with a fire. Let's make them stamp it out."

There's still a lot of trash leftover. Enough to burn. Six women build a fire, not too far, but not too close, to Mary. The stench of burning garbage rises in the graveyard like a fog. It stings my eyes as it rises and billows out. We wrap around the fire as it grows.

"What shall we do while we wait?"

"Let's play pass the nut," says Teaghan.

"Yeah, let's pass the nut."

"You start, Betsy," says Anna. She throws the glass bottle at Betsy, who fumbles with it, but catches it at the last minute.

Betsy upends the bottle into her mouth and chugs. The men are precious with their booze, but this is clearly not the first time the women have gotten ahold of it. The women lick their lips in anticipation, though Betsy already drained it dry.

"She didn't share," I complain to Teaghan.

"Don't worry. You'll see. Besides, we're too young to be the drinkers."

"Drinkers?"

"You'll see," she insists impatiently.

"Here's the nut!" Anna shouts.

It's not a nut, but some sort of seed pod or maybe a chrysalis. No one uses their hands. They press it between their elbows, their knees. Women drop it and use their mouths to pick it up again. Everyone wears a feral look beside the fire. It looks like a stupid game, and I don't get why everyone is so happy to play it, but I get caught up in it anyway, laughing.

When it's my turn, I understand. I'm next to Teaghan. We are forced to touch each other, and the daunting task of passing the seed pod without our hands makes us press against each other all the more. It's not just the sensation that comes through her skin, I feel the press of all the links in the chain of women. A devilishness rushes through me. A stupid, wild grin spreads across my face. And as we push our knees together, I grab her hands for stability. I feel the soft velvet of her fingers, the hard, cracked crusts of her cuticles, the hard moon-slices of her nails. The reflection of fire shines in her lacquered eyes.

A flush of *her*, metallic and warm, gushes through me. A flush of *her*, quiet and strong and wooden and spiral-shaped. A flush of *her*, a tumult of waves, leaving an aching chaos in its wake that always yearns for more. I also feel another flush of warmth I don't recognize, which must be the booze.

I pass the nut to Clara, and I can feel the rush of her sizzling into me. When the nut is gone, passed down the circle, I am still holding Teaghan's hand, feeling heady pulses as they throb through my bones, echo into my hips, and curl my toes. I stare at the women around the bonfire, which is gathering power. I am filled with love. Everyone is stretching into a new shape. Today, no one looks like a wife. Their human frameworks are less relevant, buried within the vibrant, colorful flesh exploding over them in crusts and rusts and warts.

Sara passes it to Eleanor, who has clusters of ear shapes all up the tawny fleece of her arm. She passes it to Lottie, who has plump, concentric rings around her bicep. Anna grabs the nut with her toes, and as she stretches out her leg, I see sappy strips of purple flesh dangling from her knee like wind chimes. When Emma accepts it between her clenched knees, the yellow, delicate cups growing out of her shin catch the sun. The blue splatters, like drops of dew along Amanda's scapula, glint in the fire. Stacy has a red, corpulent lump that emerges beneath her bottom lip and extends past her chin. An extra, exposed tongue that can't fold into her mouth. When she smiles, the top of it stretches and widens with her lip. It jiggles as she moves. And when she tilts her head back to laugh, it hangs in the air, gulping along with her, wagging and beckoning. We are an ecosystem submerging into another ecosystem as we share with one another. One being seeping into another, into another, into another. One being becoming many, and many becoming one.

I hear behind me a little girl's voice, "Ring around the rozella, cunt full of spores, ashes ashes . . . we all fall down."

The world is buoyant. I'm a leaf riding a glassy stream, ripples of happiness radiating out from me, touching the rest of the world. I do hear someone crying, but when I look around, no one seems sad. I only see smiles, the big mouths broadened by growths, eyes widened with joy. The globe of sun disappears, eaten by the horizon. The last of the light drains from the sky. But we make a light of our own, our bonfire, with its poisonous smoke.

The men never come to stamp out our fire or to receive their gift. I'm glad.

Mary's eyes, made of bits of red glinting, twinkle down on us.

Esha and I sit cross-legged in the dirt, facing each other. Her lovely pupils are dilated. She sways back and forth, oscillating sluggishly, like a weed at the bottom of the lake-lake. Voices rise around us. Women's voices, but they are duskier, richer than usual. I drift in and out of the liminal shadow that cushions waking life. Esha's face is lax. When she smiles, it spreads across her face like tea seeping through paper. Her gums are shiny, her teeth slimy, her mouth reeking of sweetened meat, sparkling with globules of crystallized salt.

"I'm really drunk." She tilts her head. "Are you?"

I admire the white, fleecy swellings, like the heads of cauliflower, fanning over her sternum and up the swirl of her neck. So lucky she isn't married yet.

"I ate mushrooms earlier today. I think I still feel them."

"Sometimes I eat mushrooms, too, when I find them in the buildings."

A laugh bubbles up inside me, and I can feel my own body jostling sweetly in the laugh's vibrations, my muscles spasming, then relaxing. "You do?"

Sugar spreads across her lips, stretching white across her skin when she smiles. "Yeah."

"Aren't you scared?"

"Why would I be scared of mushrooms? They're on my body."

I breathe. It feels so calming to breathe. My body relaxes around the bellows of my lungs. The sonorous sound of wind in my cavities. I'm smiling up at the sky. Clouds drift closer. I wonder if it will rain. When I look back down, there's a man across the way, behind the chain-link fence that surrounds the graveyard. I watch him watching us. I stare at him, then blink slowly as recognition dawns on me. It's Aaron.

"There's Maggie's husband," I say. "But isn't he dead?"

His outline disappears first. Then his peripheral boundaries. Like a slow-burning log, a red-glowing rim eats at his edges, cutting him down to his core until only his head is left. Only his crooked smile, full of teeth. At last, that too disappears.

I stand up with a jerk. "Where's Teaghan?"

"I don't know. She was just here." Esha's skin is scaly, flaking off in twisting sheets like layers of birch bark.

"I have to go find her."

"Okay." She starts to get up, but stumbles. "I don't think I can get up."

"It's okay, you can stay here."

I walk through the graveyard. The sun has faded from the earth, but not from the sky. Women are on their knees, digging in the graveyard dirt.

I'm too woozy to feel her. "Teaghan!" I call.

"We're playing Find the Mother," someone says behind me.

As I pass another woman, she says, "We're finding the Mother."

"Okay," I answer without stopping.

The next woman says, "They sweep this land clean."

The next has dug a hole so large that I can only see half of her, the other half hidden in the earth. "They're so old."

"Thousands of years old."

The women keep coming, then going, as I pass through them.

"The men are tiny in comparison."

"Blips."

"Compared to the mother."

I wipe my face. It's wet. I don't know how.

I almost run into another woman. "Have you seen Teaghan?"

She says, "All the mothers have become one mother."

"They've joined the Mother, beneath our feet."

Someone reaches up and grabs my wrist. It jolts me to a stop. Her eyes are wide and quivering. "Don't you know her? They're under your feet."

Up ahead, the next woman echoes, "The men have been pouring chemicals here so they don't grow."

Another echo, "But she's still here, far down."

And another, "Under your feet."

I loosen the woman's grip on my wrist, finger by finger. "I can't right now. I have to find Teaghan."

"Teaghan always leaves."

"It's what she does."

"She always comes back, though."

"The Mother knows so much."

"They're hungry all the time."

"Thousands of years of hunger."

I stumble. The slender, ribbonlike growths at my throat swell, squeezing my breathing passageways.

"Find the Mother, find the Mother."

"The first to find her wins."

Their digging kicks up the chalky, sour earth, and I start coughing. I'm the only one. The other women's faces are shrouded in clouds of dirt, but they don't cough. Almost as if they aren't breathing with their lungs anymore.

"The men pour their ugly chemicals, but their liquid only goes so deep."

"So deep!"

"When the men come out, they plan to poison us."

"But we won't let them."

"We will find the mother."

"She told us we would find them."

"They said we'd find her today."

"She said it would be okay."

"Teaghan!" Her name comes out half-cooked, a childish squawk.

"Shhh shhh."

"Shhhhhhhhhhhhhh."

"Shhhhhhhhhhhhhhe says it will be okay."

My legs pound against the cracked earth.

"Teaghan," I whisper hoarsely.

A few shouts go up. "We found her!"

I halt, panting, my throat growths are so swollen and choked with dust I have to stop running or I won't be able to breathe. A knot of women, clustered to the side, have dug deep into the earth. I see their backs moving up and down, the backs of their heads as they dig farther.

"She found the Mother!"

"She wins."

"We all win!"

Then I hear a scream. I don't know who it is. The beginning is like any human scream, but then it strains and whistles and pitches high. Like a knife into my skull. The women converge. They swarm the hole, they jump in the hole, though it is not big enough for all of them. I am too close. I fight against the sea of them, pushing out with my hands up as they bump against me, fighting to get to the hole. Wet eyes and red, open mouths surround me. I hear another scream, and then another. Each holds a high, desperate note, then splinters into the sky. Their wails pull at strings inside me, plucking them until they break.

One of the women in front of me, Clara, drops to the ground and screams. And as she does, I can see why they've sounded so odd. Mycelium comes up from the ground. It slithers into Clara, climbing through her feet, through her legs and torso. As it moves through her, it changes her shape. In order to make room for the mycelium, her body must change. It warps, expands in some places and narrows in others. When the mycelium reaches the top of her head, it tugs her toward the ground, pulling down her flesh. It opens holes in her body, especially at the throat and eyelids, where the skin is thin and more fluid than flesh. Her throat is as porous as a cheesecloth. I see her muscles and quivering cartilage, newly exposed and spasming, the lubricating mucous and the blood sluicing out, absorbed by the fungus before the red stream hits the ground. She does not lose any blood. The sound that comes out of her is like a flute left in the wind.

The women scrabble against me, trying to get to the hole. I don't understand their need, why they want what I just witnessed, but their discordant energy sinks its claws into me. I throw out my elbows and hands and run. Miraculously, I find Teaghan. She's curled on the ground, weak as a mouse pup. The scent of her is strange. Loamy, coppery, polluted with a sour spice I don't recognize.

I hear someone to the side of me say, "Maybe we will keep her for ourself."

"Yes. Why give her to the men? It's us who made her."

"Drag her here."

"Keep her for ourself."

"We never liked Mary, she was a woman of antiquity made for a man of antiquity."

"But we'll keep this one, we like this one."

"Our Mary!"

"Drag her over here, she's not far."

"We'll keep her."

"The Mother said it will be okay."

I clutch Teaghan as another scream sounds out. The women form a chain. As it lengthens, woman by woman, the chain circles the graveyard.

"Don't die, please don't die," I plead.

She looks up at me. She doesn't look like she's in pain, she just looks sleepy. "We're not dying. We're changing. You could change too. Come. Be a part of us." Her voice is disembodied, her eyes are saturated.

"No," I say, horrified.

"It's up to you. You've always been kept apart. Why keep yourself apart now?"

"I can't. Don't ask me to."

"The Mother told us it's going to be okay," she says sadly. While I'm mourning her, she's mourning me. She pulls something out of the apron and holds it in her hand.

"What's this?"

"The key to the lab." She pushes it between my fingers.

I'm holding her when the threads come for her, and she screams. Her expression balloons, her eyes bulge in excitement, like she's being lifted and swung to great heights by large hands. She shivers until her jaw and throat are gone, sucked into herself along with their thick, blue veins. As she's tugged toward the earth, the core of her rearranges.

"Teaghan!"

There's no longer a closure to the vast chasm inside her, and I can see the palpitating muscle, the nests of ruptured blood vessels where her tongue used to be. I make a movement to help her, but she shakes her head. Because I don't want to make her do something she doesn't want to do, I let her be. All the other women have entered the chain, which circles toward itself, almost closed. They have draped themselves around each other and become one mass. Jacinta, Sara, Lottie, Jess. I can barely tell who anyone is anymore. They've lost their shape. I reach out and grab Teaghan's face, which is crusting over. Her eyes are bits of jelly that wobble and spill. I try to hold her in, keep her inside herself, keep her as she is. But it's useless. I cannot keep Teaghan if she doesn't want to be kept. The mycelium already has taken hold of her. For the last time, I let her go. The chain comes to meet her, and she becomes one of the links.

She looks like a clay statue left out in the rain to liquify. They all do. I wonder about the baby. I grieve for the baby.

They're a complete circle now. A ring of women, dissolving into gluey, vague lumps that could be feet, or hands, or skulls. I look into the hole. The mycelium is an exposed tangle of mesh. Some hyphae are as thick as bootstraps, some as delicate and gossamer as spiderwebs.

I stand outside the ring of women, as I always have.

# CHAPTER TWENTY-FOUR

The night is beautiful. The stars assert themselves in the purple and deepening sky. I smell dry grass, still cooking in the heat. My ankles are heated by it, like I'm walking on a body.

I go to the lab to find the men.

The men aren't there.

I enter the large room with all the foremothers, and Joseph, and the other sons. They are beautiful, but all I feel is a throbbing, a hard throbbing I recognize as anger. It's mine, it's theirs. Theirs, grown old, ancestral, fermented into something stronger. I stand beside them, still and quiet and throbbing, with an ocean expanse of people and mushrooms surrounding me, suspended in their darksome language. Something inside me begins to move. A worm, a wave, a toe of growth rising.

A lantern is resting next to the hand of a foremother next to me. I agree with Maggie. The men have been using the lanterns on purpose. To mark women they want to die for death, just as Reese did to my mother. Just as they all do, to keep us in fear of touching each other. I pick up the lantern and crush the glass in my hands. In my rage, I become incandescent.

The sky is dark. The moon's teeth slice downward, making monsters and corpses out of wood and brick and stone. The men have trapped themselves in their houses. They must have heard the screaming and become afraid. They have all the guns, but I have all the fire. With all the furniture piled up at the windows and doors, they've made the perfect fodder.

I revive the last of the smoldering bonfire and carry it from house to house, like a beating heart in my careful hands. I sit with the women while I watch the smoke spew from afar. I feel the scatter of the men's bones, once nestled in the men's bodies, when they are released from the threshold of skin. I lie down, next to the women, and can feel our pulse quicken while we listen to the houses burn, and the husbands wail and weep.

Some of the men escape from their burning houses. I chase after them, and when they fall, their eyes are white with terror. It turns out, they've always been afraid of me. They've always been afraid of us.

# EPILOGUE

Teaghan gives birth in the heat of the night, under two sisters, the two sentinels that guard the graveyard. Mary, and the other.

I turned the men into art. I made my own woman. Her grin, made of many teeth from many mouths and a few rib bones, is not as placid as Mary's. Everyone is together, the women I watched from my window as a child and all our foremothers.

The day after the fire, I carried the foremothers out of the lab before burning it down. When I leaned each foremother against the ring of women, I could feel them converge. I could feel the small vibrations, like whispering. In the coming days, the tangle of mycelium traveled out of the hole and through the chain of bodies and threaded their way into the foremothers as well. When the mycelium eased into the ancient women, their strain and pain seemed to leave them. Their stiffness gone, their muscles relaxed. Perhaps I'm projecting. Perhaps the mycelium is just doing what it does, eating. But now, when

I sit near the foremothers, I no longer feel their anger. I choose to take this as a good sign.

That same day, I went to find the body of my son. I had seen Silas's memories and learned where he buried his body by the lake. I thought perhaps I would exhume the child and bring him to the tangle of fungus that is the Mother, but I quickly realized how pointless that would be. It only took a moment of digging into the earth to see the white threads and black shoelace ropes. The Mother is already there with him, beneath the pile of stones, around the lake, extending far beyond the compound's borders.

I've returned to him many times since. I scatter seeds and nuts from the woods around him, to feed his growths. I water his stones when it is hot, though water is hard to keep on earth these days. It usually hangs in the skies. I talk out loud to him, sometimes, like he is alive. I tried to find serious words, but nothing I said ever felt good enough, so I speak to him in baby language instead. Are you warm enough, are you wet enough, sleep little baby sleep, here is a lullaby I remembered, and here is a lullaby I made up. A lullaby of nonsense, of things I've learned from the world. During the wet season, a patch of growths pokes up through the ground. Red and slender, like the ones that grow over my chest. I am glad he is taken in by something wilder and larger than me.

These days, I feel so alone. I do everything by dreaming. I wake with a pulse at my temple, an urge to *come closer, come closer*. And now, here I am, surrounded by the ribbon of women. I have no idea how much they witness. I can't even tell if Teaghan is aware. There's movement in her stomach. An animal-limb shifting. It's not like my son when he was alive and rooted to me. Slowly, like a soft exhale, Teaghan's stomach splits, emitting the loosening smell of velvety wood and trapped rain. The mushroom flesh cracks and gives way. In the days leading up to today, I had been apprehensive and uncertain. Another prick of uncertainty squirms inside me now. And yet, acting on some buried instinct, I kneel under Teaghan and put my hands out to catch her baby.

"Come out, little one, come out."

The first thing I see is a leg, then its companion, and then a fist. Then, all the tiny, blossoming mouths. I bring the wailing bundle of squirming growths to my chest. I break the veil, that transient, ethereal membrane that cocoons the newborn's body, and close my eyes to breathe in the heady scent of cap and stipe and flesh. I feel myself catapulted into the past. I feel Teaghan inside the baby. But I feel more than just her, more than all the women beneath the ground. The baby is many things. When Teaghan was above ground, she ate feathers and paint chips, squirrel and brick, metal and grass. Below ground, the women have been busy. Teaghan has eaten soil and worm and beetle, river and blood and wing and fossil. All of these things have been integrated into her child. Our future holds so much.

I touch Teaghan, one more time, on her split stomach, the wound where her child left her, a mark of separation. Melancholy washes over me. I wonder if it will heal, if anything can grow from it again. But her body doesn't work that way anymore.

The baby gets restless, so I put my hand on the tiny butterfly of her twin shoulder blades. I feel her mouths closing over my hands, soft and urging. My touch calms the baby, and it calms me. The soft mist of the baby's breath slows to a damp rhythm on my shoulder. I don't have food for the baby, not yet, but I find myself telling her that I will find what she needs, humming an old song, barely remembered. I hug the baby to my chest as we move toward the edge of the graveyard. I pat her back. I reassure her and myself that it doesn't matter that I don't remember the song. We will find new notes to replace the forgotten ones.

My circadian rhythms get broken. My bodily processes get broken. In order to take care of her, I break myself. Sleeping, eating, smiling, crying, a pattern dictated by a small and beautiful tyrant.

I end up not naming Teaghan's baby. My baby. Everyone's baby. In the beginning, I call her Puffball or Button. I chew up worms and spit them into her mouth and call her Chickadee. I give her water; I give her wood. There is nothing she won't eat.

Teaghan and I find each other in our dreams. I see her and the other women standing behind her, as obscure as fog. When Teaghan lifts her hand, they all do. When she bends toward me, they all do. I am weak with relief.

I cry out, *You left me.* I can tell even in sleep that my face is wet.

*You didn't come with me*, she accuses back. *I wanted you to come with us.*

She doesn't mention the baby, who I am raising on my own. For this I am bitter. I am angry at Teaghan for not only leaving me, but leaving me to be a parent alone. No one should ever be forced to be a parent on their own. There are times when I am pacing, pacing, trying to get the baby to stop crying, and I think, I could just sink into the oblivion of the ground, and feed the earth. But what would become of the baby? I would do anything for the baby. Even this misery, I would endure for her.

The weather never much changes the graveyard sister made of metal and glass, and yet the weather very much changes the woman made of men. In those first days, the flesh of the second sister grew a fuzz. As the year tilts toward autumn, she begins the process of lovely devouring. Her flesh becomes a beautiful black melting. Green growth twists through her now, finding pockets of sunlight through the bones and teeth. The graveyard is catching life again, now that the men aren't around to stop it.

I am not always a good parent. I am not always a good person. But I love the child. I put more of myself into the child, and the child puts more of herself into me. I do not shape her much, she shapes herself. I just make sure she doesn't die. Sometimes, that feels like enough. Often, it doesn't. The child confuses and angers me, she's the thing I love more fiercely than anything I ever knew or could ever know. Is it all worth it? Being alone, like this, to know her? I don't know. How can you measure something so big?

I call the child Kitten, I call the child Grouse. She needs less comfort from me now, or at least, less comforting touch. I call her Root when she learns to find her own food. She mostly needs knowledge from me. I keep nothing hidden; I tell her everything I know. What I know is not enough for her.

She is neither daughter nor son, she doesn't have to worry about having a husband or a wife. She must find her own place in the world. I wonder often if Teaghan knew this, and that is why she made her out of so many things, so she would be at home wherever she is, whoever she is.

The child finds knowledge elsewhere too. She finds it in trees and mushrooms. She finds it in birds and animals and stones and wind. I'm surprised by how innately wise she is. I am never enough for her. At times, she is not enough for me. At other times, she is more than enough, she is everything, and I want nothing else. I call her Salmon, Dragonfly, Mourning Dove, all migratory animals who cannot help but wander, until the day she tells me to stop calling her anything.

She says she'll return home, and by that she means to me, wherever I am, when she's ready. And then, Teaghan tells me in my dreams, *You don't have to be there. The child has everything inside her. Be with us. You can still choose to be with us. We are shaping the world from below.*

When I wake, when my body loses the paralysis of sleep, I shake my muscles awake by crying. I want to be with my child. It hurts me to think the child never needed me. I close my eyes. What does Teaghan know? She knows a lot. She knows the languagesome dark, she knows how to redirect the world from below. But she doesn't know about the child and our relationship. She doesn't know what the child needs. She doesn't know what I need. I am shaping the world, and myself, from above. I forgive Teaghan. She knows a lot. She doesn't know everything.

I stay near the location where the child leaves me, though I have a feeling she will find me wherever I am. I cannot help but stay nearby, just in case. I find new and small ways of existence in the forest. I find peace, sometimes, and get to know myself better while I am waiting for her to return.

It takes her longer and longer to return. And one day, it dawns on me what is coming. She rises from her bed in the early morning, as the fog is lifting like steam from the ground. She is quiet as she prepares.

I say, "Wait." She blinks at me. She didn't know I was awake. "How far have you gone?"

She looks me in the eye. Her eyes are hard. She isn't sure if I am going to try to put a stop to it. "Far."

"Have you gone to the sea?"

She lifts her chin proudly. "Yes."

"This time, take me with you."

She's hesitant, but in the end, she does. We walk a long time. I look at her. Is she the same age that I was when I left for my wedding? It's hard to tell. She ages differently than I did, but it's been many years since she was born. She looks at me with impatience, she's much quicker in the forest than I am, but she's still wise enough to understand that this trip together is necessary. That though she wants to go, she will eventually miss me. I've always been around, waiting for her.

I smell the ocean before I see it. It smells as I imagine. I think of my mother and wish I could tell her I made it here with her unknowable and wise granddaughter. We stand at the edge of the water. I look at her. She's so full of plans.

She says, "I'm going to see how far I can swim out."

She's part river, so I say, "I bet it's pretty far."

"It is far."

I look at the child, smelling of salt, standing in the sun. I look her over, at her eyes, her ears. Her mouth, her laugh, her growths, her hands her lips her sprouting face her bared teeth her smile her toes that have elongated from the nubs they once were, her fingers, her odor which has sharpened since we slept in the same bed, her head on my chest, when I worried and cried and dreamed as I inhaled her breath her hair her stories her song her—

I let her go. I watch as she swims with determination. She is so strong. I don't know how. She shaped herself that way. The ocean's froth washes over my feet, cleaning them, making my cuts sting.

I am empty. Bereft. A mother who's had her child taken: an ocean at high tide, unable to contain herself. I am just glad it is the child who has taken herself away from me, and no one else. That is the natural order, I decide, for people like us. I walk home. It takes forever. I am so tired. I am aching.

I ask myself, "Do you want to see what's out there?" I ask it out loud, so I don't feel so lonely, but hearing my own voice with no one left to answer me makes me lonelier.

I don't. I don't at all want to see what's been done to the

world. I just want to be with Eloise, Jacinta, Esha, Jess. I want to be with Teaghan. I want love and closeness. I want my child to come back, but I know that's not up to me.

In the graveyard, under the sisters, the grounds are covered in a new kind of flower. I have been afraid to touch any of the women, though there are times, especially when the child was gone, that I've ached for touching. I was scared that if I felt them again, I'd want to join them. Now, I am ready for this. I take a breath, lean forward, and touch my hand over Teaghan's split belly. Through her skin, I feel the soft pulses of the women, beating in the long dark. I can feel how they are a circulatory system. My heart joins their rhythm, my growths thrum.

I can feel the change of the earth. The women are changing it from the inside, like fungi has always done. Things won't be the same after this, but they never are. I am proud of them.

The threads come up through the ground and take me. I begin the process of unraveling. I can feel the child's vibrations as she travels, as she fails and learns and thrives and sorrows. I am with the child, I am with Teaghan, I am with the trees and the rain, I am with Eloise and Esha, I am with the worms and my mother and my son and all the ancestors. I grow and grow. Together, we grow larger than ourselves.

# ACKNOWLEDGMENTS

This novel wouldn't exist without the many hands who shaped it. Thanks to my amazing agent, Kurestin Armada, who knew what I was trying to do before I did. To the Portland writing community who welcomed me, including the Willamette Writers critique group who read early snippets. To my Viable Paradise cohort and teachers who gave me the confidence I needed. To readers of an early draft who encouraged me: Stacy Johns and Scott Bigger. And to B. Zelkovich, who read an early draft, some of a later draft, and who is the AD to my HD. To Portland Preschool for All whose care and support gave me the space to edit.

Thanks to my editor, Sareena Kamath, who astonishes me with her wise understanding. Thanks to the whole Saga team who brought this novel into being: Jéla Lewter, Stacey Sakal, Savannah Breckenridge, Camryn Johnson, Christine Calella, Karintha Parker, Ella Laytham, Kimberly Goldstein, Emily Arzeno, Kayley Hoffman, Joe Monti, and Tim O'Connell.

Thanks to Kior Ko, who created such a spectacular, dreamy

piece of art for the cover. To the kind and intimidatingly talented writers who gave me blurbs.

To all the books I read for research, with special thanks to: *Radical Mycology* by Peter McCoy; *Let's Become Fungal! Mycelium Teachings and the Arts: Based on Conversations With Indigenous Wisdom Keepers, Artists, Curators, Feminists, and Mycologists* by Yasmine Ostendorf-Rodríguez; *The Mushroom at the End of the World* by Anna Lowenhaupt Tsing; *Mushrooms of the World* by Giuseppe Pace; *Mycelium Running* and *Fantastic Fungi* by Paul Stamets; *Entangled Life* by Merlin Sheldrake; *Organic Mushroom Farming and Mycoremediation* by Tradd Cotter; and the work of Terence McKenna.

Thanks to my kids: Rowan, Finn, and Bo; it's been my favorite thing in life to witness you grow.

Lastly, thank you to Gabe. For all the writing help and all the love. For reading multiple drafts and always getting it and always liking my work more than I do. For everything.

# ABOUT THE AUTHOR

Laura Cranehill is an amalgamation of horrific faceless things who lives in the Pacific Northwest with her spouse and three children. She is a writer and poet whose work has been published in *Strange Horizons*, *Vastarien*, *ergot.*, *PANK*, and multiple award-winning anthologies. *Wife Shaped Bodies* is her debut novel.